Burnt Water

BOOKS BY CARLOS FUENTES

Where the Air Is Clear
The Good Conscience
Aura
The Death of Artemio Cruz
A Change of Skin
Terra Nostra
The Hydra Head
Burnt Water
Distant Relations
The Old Gringo

Burnt Water

Stories by

Carlos Fuentes

TRANSLATED FROM THE SPANISH BY
MARGARET SAYERS PEDEN

FARRAR, STRAUS AND GIROUX
NEW YORK

Translation copyright © 1969, 1974, 1978, 1979,
1980 by Farrar, Straus and Giroux, Inc.
Author's Note © 1980 by Carlos Fuentes
All rights reserved
Some of these stories were originally published in Spanish in *Cantar de
ciegos,* copyright © 1964 by Editorial Joaquín Mortiz, S.A.; and in *Chac
Mool y otros cuentos,* copyright © 1973 by Carlos Fuentes and Salvat
Editores, S.A.—Alianza Editorial, S.A.
First published in hardcover by Farrar, Straus and Giroux, Inc., 1980
First published in paperback, 1986
Printed in the United States of America
Designed by Bruce Campbell
"These Were Palaces" and "The Mandarin" first appeared in English in
Antaeus, "The Doll Queen" in *TriQuarterly,* and "The Old Morality" in
Playboy

Library of Congress Cataloging-in-Publication Data
Fuentes, Carlos.
Burnt water.
Contents: Chac-Mool.—In a Flemish garden.—Mother's
Day.—[etc.]
I. Title.
PZ4.F952Bu   [PQ7297.F793]   863   80-19148

To my dear friends
Dorothea and Roger Straus

Author's Note

I own an imaginary apartment house in the center of
Mexico City. The penthouse is occupied by an old revolutionary turned profiteer, Artemio Cruz. In the base-
ment lives a ghostly sorceress, Aura. On the eleven inter-
mediary floors you will find the characters of the stories
that are now collected here. True, some have fled to the
countryside, others are living abroad, some have even
been evicted and now wander in the internal exile of the
"belt of misery" surrounding this great, cancerous stain of
a smog-ridden, traffic-snarled metropolis of seventeen
million people. By the end of the century it will, fatally, be
the largest city in the world: the capital of underdevelop-
ment.

My imaginary building is sinking into the uneasy mud
where the humid god, the Chac-Mool, lives. There, a
birth is recalled, that of the oldest city in the Americas,
Tenochtitlán, founded in 1325 by the wandering Aztecs
on a high lagoon guarded by sparkling volcanoes, and
conquered in 1521 by the Spanish, who there erected the

viceregal city of Mexico on the burnt water of the ancient Indian lake. Burnt water, *atl tlachinolli:* the paradox of the creation is also the paradox of the destruction. The Mexican character never separates life from death, and this too is the sign of the burnt water that has presided over the city's destiny in birth and rebirth.

CARLOS FUENTES
Princeton, June 1980

Contents

Burnt Water

Chac-Mool

It was only recently that Filiberto drowned in Acapulco. It happened during Easter Week. Even though he'd been fired from his government job, Filiberto couldn't resist the bureaucratic temptation to make his annual pilgrimage to the small German hotel, to eat sauerkraut sweetened by the sweat of the tropical cuisine, dance away Holy Saturday on La Quebrada, and feel he was one of the "beautiful people" in the dim anonymity of dusk on Hornos Beach. Of course we all knew he'd been a good swimmer when he was young, but now, at forty, and the shape he was in, to try to swim that distance, at midnight! Frau Müller wouldn't allow a wake in her hotel—steady client or not; just the opposite, she held a dance on her stifling little terrace while Filiberto, very pale in his coffin, awaited the departure of the first morning bus from the terminal, spending the first night of his new life surrounded by crates and parcels. When I arrived, early in the morning, to supervise the loading of the casket, I found Filiberto buried beneath a mound of coconuts; the driver wanted to get him in the luggage compartment as quickly as possible, covered with canvas in order not to upset the passengers and to avoid bad luck on the trip. When we left Acapulco there was still a good breeze. Near Tierra Colorada it began it get hot and bright. As I was eating my breakfast eggs and sausage, I had opened Filiberto's satchel, collected the day before along with his other personal belongings from the Müllers' hotel. Two hundred pesos. An old newspaper; expired lottery tickets; a one-way ticket to Acapulco—one way?—and a cheap notebook with graph-paper pages and marbleized-paper binding.

On the bus I ventured to read it, in spite of the sharp curves, the stench of vomit, and a certain natural feeling of respect for the private life of a deceased friend. It should be a record—yes, it began that way—of our daily office routine; maybe I'd find out what caused him to neglect his duties, why he'd written memoranda without rhyme or reason or any authorization. The reasons, in short, for his being fired, his seniority ignored and his pension lost.

"Today I went to see about my pension. Lawyer extremely pleasant. I was so happy when I left that I decided to blow five pesos at a café. The same café we used to go to when we were young and where I never go now because it reminds me that I lived better at twenty than I do at forty. We were all equals then, energetically discouraging any unfavorable remarks about our classmates. In fact, we'd open fire on anyone in the house who so much as mentioned inferior background or lack of elegance. I knew that many of us (perhaps those of most humble origin) would go far, and that here in school we were forging lasting friendships; together we would brave the stormy seas of life. But it didn't work out that way. Someone didn't follow the rules. Many of the lowly were left behind, though some climbed higher even than we could have predicted in those high-spirited, affable get-togethers. Some who seemed to have the most promise got stuck somewhere along the way, cut down in some extracurricular activity, isolated by an invisible chasm from those who'd triumphed and those who'd gone nowhere at all. Today, after all this time, I again sat in the chairs—remodeled, as well as the soda fountain, a kind of barricade against invasion—and pretended to read some business papers. I saw many of the old faces, amnesiac, changed in the neon light, prosperous. Like the café, which I barely recognized, along with the city itself, they'd been chipping away at a pace different from my own. No, they didn't recognize me now, or didn't want to. At most, one or two clapped a quick, fat hand on my shoulder. So long, old friend, how's it been going? Between us stretched the eighteen holes of the Country Club. I buried myself in my papers. The years of my dreams, the optimistic predictions, filed before my eyes, along with the obstacles that had kept me from achieving them. I felt frustrated that I couldn't dig my fingers into the past and put together the pieces of some long-forgotten puzzle. But one's toy chest is a part of the past, and when all's said and done, who knows where his lead soldiers went, his helmets and wooden swords. The make-believe we loved so much was only that, make-believe. Still, I'd been diligent, disciplined, devoted to duty. Wasn't that enough? Was it too much? Often, I was assaulted by the recollection of Rilke: the great reward for the adventure of youth is death; we should die young, taking all our secrets with us. Today I wouldn't be looking back at a city of salt. Five pesos? Two pesos tip."

"In addition to his passion for corporation law, Pepe likes to theorize. He saw me coming out of the Cathedral, and we walked together toward the National Palace. He's not a believer, but he's not content to stop at that: within half a block he had to propose a theory. If I weren't a Mexican, I wouldn't worship Christ, and . . . No, look, it's obvious. The Spanish arrive and say, Adore this God who died a bloody death nailed to a cross with a bleeding wound in his side. Sacrificed. Made an offering. What could be more natural than to accept something so close to your own ritual, your own life . . . ? Imagine, on the other hand, if Mexico had been conquered by Buddhists or Moslems. It's not conceivable that our Indians would have worshipped some person who died of indigestion. But a God that's not only sacrificed for you but has his heart torn out, God Almighty, checkmate to Huitzilopochtli! Christianity, with its emotion, its bloody sacrifice and ritual, becomes a natural and novel extension of the native religion. The qualities of charity, love, and turn-the-other-cheek, however, are rejected. And that's what Mexico is all about: you have to kill a man in order to believe in him.

"Pepe knew that ever since I was young I've been mad for certain pieces of Mexican Indian art. I collect small statues, idols, pots. I spend my weekends in Tlaxcala, or in Teotihuacán. That may be why he likes to relate to indigenous themes all the theories he concocts for me. Pepe knows that I've been looking for a reasonable replica of the Chac-Mool for a long time, and today he told me about a little shop in the flea market of La Lagunilla where they're selling one, apparently at a good price. I'll go Sunday.

"A joker put red coloring in the office water cooler, naturally interrupting our duties. I had to report him to the director, who simply thought it was funny. So all day the bastard's been going around making fun of me, with cracks about water. Motherfu . . ."

"Today, Sunday, I had time to go out to La Lagunilla. I found the Chac-Mool in the cheap little shop Pepe had told me about. It's a marvelous piece, life-size, and though the dealer assures me it's an original, I question it. The stone is nothing out of the ordinary, but that doesn't diminish the elegance of the composition, or its massiveness. The rascal has smeared tomato ketchup on the belly to convince the tourists of its bloody authenticity.

"Moving the piece to my house cost more than the purchase price. But it's here now, temporarily in the cellar while I reorganize my collection to make room for it. These figures demand a vertical and burning-hot sun; that was their natural element. The effect is lost in the darkness of the cellar, where it's simply another lifeless mass and its grimace seems to reproach me for denying it light. The dealer had a spotlight focused directly on the sculpture, highlighting all the planes and lending a more amiable expression to my Chac-Mool. I must follow his example."

"I awoke to find the pipes had burst. Somehow, I'd carelessly left the water running in the kitchen; it flooded the floor and poured into the cellar before I'd noticed it. The dampness didn't damage the Chac-Mool, but my suitcases suffered; everything has to happen on a weekday. I was late to work."

"At last they came to fix the plumbing. Suitcases ruined. There's slime on the base of the Chac-Mool."

"I awakened at one; I'd heard a terrible moan. I thought it might be burglars. Purely imaginary."

"The moaning at night continues. I don't know where it's coming from, but it makes me nervous. To top it all off, the pipes burst again, and the rains have seeped through the foundation and flooded the cellar."

"Plumber still hasn't come; I'm desperate. As far as the City Water Department's concerned, the less said the better. This is the first time the runoff from the rains has drained into my cellar instead of the storm sewers. The moaning's stopped. An even trade?"

"They pumped out the cellar. The Chac-Mool is covered with slime. It makes him look grotesque; the whole sculpture seems to be suffering from a kind of green erysipelas, with the exception of the eyes. I'll scrape off the moss Sunday. Pepe suggested I move to an apartment on an upper floor, to prevent any more of these aquatic tragedies. But I can't leave my house; it's obviously more than I need, a little gloomy in its turn-of-the-century style, but it's the only inheritance, the only memory, I have left of my parents. I don't know how I'd feel if I saw a soda fountain with a jukebox in the cellar and an interior decorator's shop on the ground floor."

"Used a trowel to scrape the Chac-Mool. The moss now seemed almost a part of the stone; it took more than an hour and it was six in the evening before I finished. I couldn't see anything in the darkness, but I ran my hand over the outlines of the stone. With every stroke, the stone seemed to become softer. I couldn't believe it; it felt like dough. That dealer in La Lagunilla has really swindled me. His 'pre-Columbian sculpture' is nothing but plaster, and the dampness is ruining it. I've covered it with some rags and will bring it upstairs tomorrow before it dissolves completely."

"The rags are on the floor. Incredible. Again I felt the Chac-Mool. It's firm, but not stone. I don't want to write this: the texture of the torso feels a little like flesh; I press it like rubber, and feel something coursing through that recumbent figure . . . I went down again later at night. No doubt about it: the Chac-Mool has hair on its arms."

"This kind of thing has never happened to me before. I fouled up my work in the office: I sent out a payment that hadn't been authorized, and the director had to call it to my attention. I think I may even have been rude to my co-workers. I'm going to have to see a doctor, find out whether it's my imagination, whether I'm delirious, or what . . . and get rid of that damned Chac-Mool."

Up to this point I recognized Filiberto's hand, the large, rounded letters I'd seen on so many memoranda and forms. The entry for August 25 seemed to have been written by a different person. At times it was the writing of a child, each letter laboriously separated; other times, nervous, trailing into illegibility. Three days are blank, and then the narrative continues:

"It's all so natural, though normally we believe only in what's real . . . but this is real, more real than anything I've ever known. A water cooler is real, more than real, because we fully realize its existence, or being, when some joker puts something in the water to turn it red . . . An ephemeral smoke ring is real, a grotesque image in a fun-house mirror is real; aren't all deaths, present and forgotten, real . . . ? If a man passes through paradise in a dream, and is handed a flower as proof of having been there, and if when he awakens he finds this flower in his hand . . . then . . . ? Reality: one day it was shattered into a thousand pieces, its head rolled in one direction and its tail in another, and all we have is one of the pieces from the gigantic body. A free and fictitious ocean, real only when it is imprisoned in a seashell. Until three days ago, my reality was of such a degree it would be erased today; it was reflex action, routine, memory, carapace. And then, like the earth that one day trembles to remind us of its power, of the death to come, recriminating against me for having turned my back on life, an orphaned reality we always knew was there presents itself, jolting us in order to become living present. Again I believed it to be imagination: the Chac-Mool, soft and elegant, had changed color overnight; yellow, almost golden, it seemed to suggest it was a god, at ease now, the knees more relaxed than before, the smile more benevolent. And yesterday, finally, I awakened with a start, with the frightening certainty that two creatures are breathing in the night, that in the darkness there beats a pulse in addition to one's own. Yes, I heard footsteps on the stairway. Nightmare. Go back to sleep. I don't know how long I feigned sleep. When I opened my eyes again, it still was not dawn. The room smelled of horror, of incense and blood. In the darkness, I gazed about the bedroom until my eyes found two points of flickering, cruel yellow light.

"Scarcely breathing, I turned on the light. There was the Chac-Mool, standing erect, smiling, ocher-colored except for the flesh-red belly. I was paralyzed by the two tiny, almost crossed eyes set close to the wedge-shaped nose. The lower teeth closed tightly on the upper lip; only the glimmer from the squarish helmet on the abnormally large head betrayed any sign of life. Chac-Mool moved toward my bed; then it began to rain."

I remember that it was at the end of August that Filiberto had been fired from his job, with a public condemnation by the director, amid rumors of madness and even theft. I didn't believe it. I did see some wild memoranda, one asking the Secretary of the Department whether water had an odor; another, offering his services to the Department of Water Resources to make it rain in the

desert. I couldn't explain it. I thought the exceptionally
heavy rains of that summer had affected him. Or that living in that ancient mansion with half the rooms locked
and thick with dust, without any servants or family life,
had finally deranged him. The following entries are for
the end of September.

"Chac-Mool can be pleasant enough when he wishes
. . . the gurgling of enchanted water . . . He knows wonderful stories about the monsoons, the equatorial rains,
the scourge of the deserts; the genealogy of every plant
engendered by his mythic paternity: the willow, his way-
ward daughter; the lotus, his favorite child; the cactus, his
mother-in-law. What I can't bear is the odor, the nonhu-
man odor, emanating from flesh that isn't flesh, from sandals that shriek their antiquity. Laughing stridently, the
Chac-Mool recounts how he was discovered by Le
Plongeon and brought into physical contact with men of
other gods. His spirit had survived quite peacefully in
water vessels and storms; his stone was another matter,
and to have dragged him from his hiding place was un-
natural and cruel. I think the Chac-Mool will never
forgive that. He savors the imminence of the aesthetic.
"I've had to provide him with pumice stone to clean the
belly the dealer smeared with ketchup when he thought
he was Aztec. He didn't seem to like my question about
his relation to Tlaloc, and when he becomes angry his
teeth, repulsive enough in themselves, glitter and grow
pointed. The first days he slept in the cellar; since yesterday, in my bed."

"The dry season has begun. Last night, from the living
room where I'm sleeping now, I heard the same hoarse
moans I'd heard in the beginning, followed by a terrible
racket. I went upstairs and peered into the bedroom: the
Chac-Mool was breaking the lamps and furniture; he

sprang toward the door with outstretched bleeding hands, and I was barely able to slam the door and run to hide in the bathroom. Later he came downstairs, panting and begging for water. He leaves the faucets running all day; there's not a dry spot in the house. I have to sleep wrapped in blankets, and I've asked him please to let the living room dry out."*

"The Chac-Mool flooded the living room today. Exasperated, I told him I was going to return him to La Lagunilla. His laughter—so frighteningly different from the laugh of any man or animal—was as terrible as the blow from that heavily braceleted arm. I have to admit it: I am his prisoner. My original plan was quite different. I was going to play with the Chac-Mool the way you play with a toy; this may have been an extension of the security of childhood. But—who said it?—the fruit of childhood is consumed by the years, and I hadn't seen that. He's taken my clothes, and when the green moss begins to sprout, he covers himself in my bathrobes. The Chac-Mool is accustomed to obedience, always; I, who have never had cause to command, can only submit. Until it rains—what happened to his magic power?—he will be choleric and irritable."

"Today I discovered that the Chac-Mool leaves the house at night. Always, as it grows dark, he sings a shrill and ancient tune, older than song itself. Then everything is quiet. I knocked several times at the door, and when he didn't answer I dared enter. The bedroom, which I hadn't seen since the day the statue tried to attack me, is a ruin; the odor of incense and blood that permeates the entire house is particularly concentrated here. And I discovered bones behind the door, dog and rat and cat bones. This is

* Filiberto does not say in what language he communicated with the Chac-Mool.

what the Chac-Mool steals in the night for nourishment. This explains the hideous barking every morning."

"February, dry. Chac-Mool watches every move I make; he made me telephone a restaurant and ask them to deliver chicken and rice every day. But what I took from the office is about to run out. So the inevitable happened: on the first they cut off the water and lights for nonpayment. But Chac has discovered a public fountain two blocks from the house; I make ten or twelve trips a day for water while he watches me from the roof. He says that if I try to run away he will strike me dead in my tracks; he is also the God of Lightning. What he doesn't realize is that I know about his nighttime forays. Since we don't have any electricity, I have to go to bed about eight. I should be used to the Chac-Mool by now, but just a moment ago, when I ran into him on the stairway, I touched his icy arms, the scales of his renewed skin, and I wanted to scream.

"If it doesn't rain soon, the Chac-Mool will return to stone. I've noticed his recent difficulty in moving; sometimes he lies for hours, paralyzed, and almost seems an idol again. But this repose merely gives him new strength to abuse me, to claw at me as if he could extract liquid from my flesh. We don't have the amiable intervals any more, when he used to tell me old tales; instead, I seem to notice a heightened resentment. There have been other indications that set me thinking: my wine cellar is diminishing; he likes to stroke the silk of my bathrobes; he wants me to bring a servant girl to the house; he has made me teach him how to use soap and lotions. I believe the Chac-Mool is falling into human temptations; now I see in the face that once seemed eternal something that is merely old. This may be my salvation: if the Chac becomes human, it's possible that all the centuries of his life will accumulate in an instant and he will die in a flash of lightning. But this might also cause my death: the Chac won't want me to witness his downfall; he may decide to kill me.

"I plan to take advantage tonight of Chac's nightly excursion to flee. I will go to Acapulco; I'll see if I can't find a job, and await the death of the Chac-Mool. Yes, it will be soon; his hair is gray, his face bloated. I need to get some sun, to swim, to regain my strength. I have four hundred pesos left. I'll go to the Müllers' hotel, it's cheap and comfortable. Let Chac-Mool take over the whole place; we'll see how long he lasts without my pails of water."

Filiberto's diary ends here. I didn't want to think about what he'd written; I slept as far as Cuernavaca. From there to Mexico City I tried to make some sense out of the account, to attribute it to overwork, or some psychological disturbance. By the time we reached the terminal at nine in the evening, I still hadn't accepted the fact of my friend's madness. I hired a truck to carry the coffin to Filiberto's house, where I would arrange for his burial.

Before I could insert the key in the lock, the door opened. A yellow-skinned Indian in a smoking jacket and ascot stood in the doorway. He couldn't have been more repulsive; he smelled of cheap cologne; he'd tried to cover his wrinkles with thick powder, his mouth was clumsily smeared with lipstick, and his hair appeared to be dyed.

"I'm sorry . . . I didn't know that Filiberto had . . ."

"No matter. I know all about it. Tell the men to carry the body down to the cellar."

In a Flemish Garden

Sept. 19. That attorney Brambila gets the most hare-brained ideas! Now he's bought that old mansion on Puente de Alvarado, sumptuous, but totally impractical, built at the time of the French Intervention. Naturally, I thought it was just another of his many deals, and that he intended, as he had on other occasions, to demolish the house and sell the land at a profit, or at least to build an office and commercial property there. That is, that's what I thought at first. I was astounded when he told me his plan: he meant to use the house, with its marvelous parquet floors and glittering chandeliers, for entertaining and lodging his North American business associates—history, folklore, and elegance all in one package. And he wanted me to live for a while in his mansion, because this Brambila, who was so impressed with everything about the place, had noticed a certain lack of human warmth in these rooms, which had been empty since 1910, when the family fled to France. A caretaker couple who lived in the rooftop apartment had kept everything clean and polished—though for forty years there hadn't been a stick of furniture except a magnificent Pleyel in the salon. You felt a penetrating cold (my attorney friend had said) in the house, particularly noticeable in contrast to the temperature outside.

"Look, my handsome blond friend. You can invite anyone you want for drinks and conversation. You'll have all the basic necessities. Read, write, do whatever it is you do."

And Brambila took off for Washington, leaving me stunned by his great faith in my power to create warmth.

Sept. 19. That very afternoon, with one suitcase, I moved into the mansion on Puente de Alvarado. It is truly beautiful, however much the exterior with its Second Empire Ionic capitals and caryatids seems to refute it. The salon, overlooking the street, has gleaming, fragrant floors, and the walls, faintly stained by spectral rectangles where paintings once hung, are a pale blue somehow not merely old but antique. The murals on the vaulted ceiling (Zobenigo, the quay of Giovanni e Paolo, Santa Maria della Salute) were painted by disciples of Francesco Guardi. The bedroom walls are covered in blue velvet, and the hallways are tunnels of plain and carved wood, elm, ebony, and box, some in the Flemish style of Viet Stoss, others more reminiscent of Berruguete and the quiet grandeur of the masters of Pisa. I particularly like the library. It's at the rear of the house, and its French doors offer the only view of a small, square garden with a bed of everlasting flowers, its three walls cushioned with climbing vines. I haven't yet found the keys to these doors, the only access to the garden. But it will be in the garden, reading and smoking, that I begin my humanizing labors in this island of antiquity. Red and white, the everlastings glistened beneath the rain; an old-style bench of greenish wrought iron twisted in the form of leaves; and soft wet grass, partly the result of love, partly perseverance. Now that I'm writing about it, I realize that the garden suggests the cadences of Rodenbach . . . Dans l'horizon du soir où le soleil recule . . . la fumée éphémère et pacifique ondule . . . comme une gaze où des prunelles sont cachées; et l'on sent, rien qu'à voir ces brumes détachées, un douloureux regret de ciel et de voyage . . .

Sept. 20. In this house I feel very far removed from the "parasitical ills" of Mexico City. For less than twenty-four hours I've been inside these walls that emanate a sensitivity, a flow, suggestive of other shores. I've been invaded by a kind of lucid languor, a sense of imminence; with every moment I become increasingly aware of certain perfumes peculiar to my surroundings, certain silhouettes from a memory that formerly was revealed in brief flashes but today swells and flows with the measured vitality of a river. Amid the rivets and bolts of the city, when have I noticed the change of season? We don't notice the season in Mexico City: one fades into another with no change of pace, "the immortal springtime, and its tokens." Here the seasons lose their characteristic reiterated novelty of parameters with rhythms, rites, and pleasures of their own, of boundaries about which we entwine our nostalgia and our projects, of signs that nurture and solidify consciousness. Tomorrow is the equinox. Today, in this place, I have with a kind of Nordic indolence noted, not for the first time, the approach of autumn. A gray veil is descending over the garden, which I am observing as I write; overnight, a few leaves have fallen from the arbor, carpeting the lawn; a few leaves are beginning to turn golden, and an incessant rain is fading the greenness, washing it into the soil. The smoke of autumn hovers over the garden, as far as the walls, and one could almost believe one heard, heavy as deep breathing, the sound of slow footsteps among the fallen leaves.

Sept. 21. I finally succeeded in opening the French doors in the library. I went out into the garden. The fine rain continues, imperceptible and tenacious. If in the house I seemed to caress the skin of a different world, in the garden I touched its nerves. In the garden those silhouettes of memory, of imminence, that I noticed yesterday make my nerves tingle. The everlastings are not the flowers I know: these are permeated with a mournful perfume, as if they had been gathered from a crypt after years among dust and marble. The very rain stirs colorings in the grass I want to identify with other cities, other windows; standing in the center of the garden, I closed my eyes . . . Javanese tobacco and wet sidewalks . . . herring . . . beer fumes, the haze of forests, the trunks of great oaks . . . Turning in a circle, I tried to absorb the totality of this quadrangle of vague light that even in the rain seems to filter through yellow stained glass, to glimmer in braziers, made melancholy before it became light . . . and the verdant growth of the vines was not that of the burnt earth of the plateau; this was a different, soft, green shading into blue in the distant treetops, covering rocks with grotesque slime . . . Memling! Between the eyes of a Virgin and reflections of copper, I had seen this same landscape from one of your windows! I was looking at a fictitious, an invented landscape. This garden was not in Mexico! This misty rain . . . I ran into the house, raced down the hallway, burst into the salon, and pressed my nose to the window: on the Avenida Puente de Alvarado, a blast of jukeboxes, streetcars, and sun, the monotonous sun. A Sun God without shading or effigies in its rays, a stationary Sun Stone, a sun of shortened centuries. I returned to the library: the rain still fell on the old, hooded garden.

Sept. 21. I've been standing here, my breath misting the door panes, gazing out at the garden and the reflection of my blue eyes. Hours perhaps, staring at the small, enclosed space, fingering my beard absentmindedly. Staring at a lawn that minute by minute is buried beneath new leaves. Then I heard a muted sound, a buzzing that might have come from within me, and I looked up. In the garden, almost opposite mine, another head, slightly tilted, its eyes staring into mine. Instinctively, I leaped back. The face in the garden never varied its gaze, impenetrable in the deep shadows beneath its brows. The figure turned away; I saw only a small body, black and hunched, and I covered my eyes with my hands.

Sept. 22. There's no telephone in the house, but I could go out on the Avenida, call up some friends, go to the Roxy . . . After all, this is my city; these are my people! Why can't I leave this house; more accurately, my post at the doors looking onto the garden?

Sept. 22. I am not going to be frightened because someone leaped over the wall into the garden. I'm going to wait all evening—it continues to rain, day and night!—and capture the intruder . . . I was dozing in the armchair facing the window when I was awakened by the intense scent of the everlastings. Unhesitatingly, I stared into the garden—yes, there. Picking the flowers, the small yellow hands forming a nosegay. It was a little old woman, she must have been at least eighty. But how had she dared intrude? And how had she got in? I watched as she picked the flowers: wizened, slim, clad all in black. Her skirts brushed the ground, collecting dew and clover; the cloth

sagged with the weight, an airy weight, a Caravaggio texture. Her black jacket was buttoned to the chin, her torso
was bent over, hunched against the cold. Her face was
shadowed by a black lace coif which covered tangled white
hair.

I could see nothing but her bloodless lips, the paleness
of her flesh repeated in the firm line of a mouth arched
slightly in the faintest, saddest, eternal smile devoid of any
motivation. She looked up; her eyes were not eyes . . .
what seemed to emerge from beneath the wrinkled lids
was a pathway, a nocturnal landscape, leading toward an
infinite inward journey. This ancient woman bent down to
pluck a red bud; in profile, her hawk-like features, her
sunken cheeks, reflected like the vibrating planes of the
reaper's scythe. Then she walked away toward . . . ? No,
I won't say she walked through the vines and the wall,
that she evaporated, that she sank into the ground or ascended into the sky; a path seemed to open in the garden,
so natural that at first I didn't notice it, and along it as
if—I knew it, I'd heard it before—as if treading a course
long-forgotten, heavy as deep breathing, my visitor disappeared beneath the rain.

Sept. 23. I locked myself in the bedroom and bar-
ricaded the door with everything I could lay my hands on.
I was sure it would do no good, but I thought I could at
least give myself the illusion of being able to sleep with
tranquillity. Those measured footsteps, always as if on dry
leaves; I thought I heard them every moment. I knew
they weren't real, that is, until I heard the faintest rustle
outside the door, and then the whisper of something
passed beneath the door. I turned on the light; the corner
of an envelope was outlined against the velvety floor. For
a moment I held its contents in my hand: old paper, elegant, rosewood.

Written in a spidery hand, large, erect letters, the message consisted of one word:

TLACTOCATZINE

Sept. 23. She will come, as she did yesterday and the day before, at sunset. I will speak to her today; she can't escape me, I will follow her through the hidden entry among the vines . . .

Sept. 23. As the clock was striking six, I heard music in the salon; it was the magnificent old Pleyel, playing waltzes. As I approached, the sound ceased. I turned back to the library. She was in the garden. Now she was skipping about, pantomiming . . . a little girl playing with her hoop. I opened the door, went out, I don't know exactly what happened; I felt as if the sky, as if the very air descended one level to press down on the garden; the air became motionless, fathomless, and all sound was suspended. The old woman stared at me, always with the same smile, her eyes lost in the depths of the world; her mouth opened, her lips moved; no sound emanated from that pale slit, the garden was squeezed like a sponge, the cold buried its fingers in my flesh . . .

Sept. 24. After the apparition at dusk, I came to my senses sitting in the armchair in the library; the French doors were locked, the garden solitary. The odor of the everlastings has permeated the house; it is particularly intense in my bedroom. There I awaited a new missive, a new sign from the aged woman. Her words, the flesh of silence, were struggling to tell me something . . . At eleven that evening I could sense beside me the dull light of the garden. Again the whisper of the long, starched skirts outside my door; and the letter:

My beloved
The moon has risen and I hear it singing; everything
is indescribably beautiful.

I dressed and went downstairs to the library; a veil-
become-light enveloped the old woman, who was sitting
on the garden bench. I walked toward her, again amid the
buzzing of bumblebees. The same air, void of any sound,
enveloped her. Her white light ruffled my hair, and the
aged woman took my hands and kissed them; her skin
pressed against mine. I *saw* this; my eyes told me what
touch would not corroborate: her hands in mine were
nothing but wind—heavy, cold wind; I intuited the
opaque ice in the skeleton of this kneeling figure whose
lips moved in a litany of forbidden rhythms. The everlastings trembled, solitary, independent of the wind. They
smelled of the grave. Yes, they grew there, in the tomb:
there they germinated, there they were carried every evening in the spectral hands of an ancient woman . . . and
sound returned, amplified by the rain, and a coagulated
voice, an echo of spilled blood copulating still with the
earth, screamed:
    "Kapuzinergruft! Kapuzinergruft!"
    I jerked free from her hands and ran to the front door
of the mansion—even there I heard the mad sound of her
voice, the drowned dead echoing in the cavernous
throat—and I sank to the floor trembling, clutching the
doorknob, drained of the strength to turn it.
    I couldn't; it was impossible to open.
    It is sealed with a thick red lacquer. In the center, a coat
of arms glimmers in the night, a crowned double eagle,
the old woman's profile, signaling the icy intensity of permanent confinement.
    And that night I heard behind me—I did not know I
was to hear it for all time—the whisper of skirts brushing
the floor; she walks with a new, ecstatic joy; her gestures

are repetitious, betraying her satisfaction. The satisfaction
of a jailer, of a companion, of eternal prison. The satisfaction of solitude shared. I heard her voice again, drawing
near, her lips touching my ear, the breath fabricated of
spume and buried earth:

". . . and they didn't let us play with our hoops, Max;
they forbade us; we had to carry them in our hands during our walks through the gardens in Brussels . . . but I
told you that in a letter, the letter I wrote from Bouchot,
do you remember? Oh, but from now on, no more letters,
we'll be together forever, the two of us in this castle . . .
We will never leave; we will never allow anyone to enter
. . . Oh, Max, answer me, the everlastings, the ones I
bring in the evenings to the Capuchin crypt, to the Kapu-
zinergruft, don't they smell fresh? They're the same
flowers the Indians brought you when we arrived here:
you, the Tlactocatzine . . . *Nis tiquimopielia inin maxocht-
zintl* . . . Remember? Lord, we offer you these
flowers . . ."

And on the coat of arms I read the inscription:
Charlotte, Kaiserin von Mexiko

Mother's Day

For Teodoro Cesarman

Every morning Grandfather vigorously stirs his cup of instant coffee. He grasps the spoon as in other times my dear-departed grandmother Clotilde had grasped the pestle, or he himself, General Vicente Vergara, had grasped the pommel of the saddle now hanging on his bedroom wall. Then he uncorks the bottle of tequila and tilts it to fill half the cup. He refrains from mixing the tequila and the Nescafé. Let the clear alcohol settle by itself. He looks at the bottle of tequila and it reminds him how red was the spilled blood, how clear the liquor that set the blood boiling, inflaming it before the great encounters, Chihuahua and Torreón, Celaya and Paso de Gavilanes, when men were men and there was no way to distinguish between the exhilaration of drunkenness and the recklessness of combat, sí, señor, how could fear creep in when a man's pleasure was battle and the battle was his pleasure?

He almost spoke aloud, between sips of the spiked coffee. Nobody knew how to make a *café de olla* any more, the little jug of coffee tasting of clay and brown sugar, no, nobody, not even the pair of servants he'd brought from the sugar plantation in Morelos. Even they drank Nescafé, invented in Switzerland, the cleanest and most orderly nation in the world. General Vergara had a vision of snow-capped mountains and belled cows, but he said nothing, his false teeth still lay at the bottom of the glass before him. This was his favorite hour: peace, daydreams, memories, fantasies, and no one to gainsay them. Strange, he sighed, that he'd lived such a full life and now memory should come back to him like a sweet lie. He sat and thought about the years of the Revolution and the battles that had forged modern Mexico. Then he spit out the mouthful of liquid he'd been swishing between his lizard tongue and his toughened gums.

Later that morning I saw my grandfather in the distance, shuffling along in his carpet slippers as he always did, down the marble halls, wiping with a large kerchief the bleariness and involuntary tears from his cactus-colored eyes. Seeing him from that distance, almost motionless, I thought he looked like a desert plant. Green, rubbery, dry as the plains of the north, a deceptive ancient cactus harboring the sparse rains in its entrails from one summer to the next, fermenting them: moisture seeped from his eyes but never reached the white tufts on his head, wisps of dried corn silk. In his photographs, on horseback, he loomed tall. As he scuffed along, purposeless and old, through the marble rooms of the huge house in Pedregal, he looked tiny, lean, pure bone, the skin clinging desperately to his skeleton, a taut, creaky little old man. But not bowed, no sir, I'd like to see the man who dared . . .

Once again I was beset by the same uneasiness I felt every morning, the anguish of a cornered rat, the feeling that seized me every time I saw General Vergara pur-

poselessly wandering the rooms and halls and corridors
that Nicomedes and Engracia scrubbed on their knees,
rooms that at this hour of the morning smelled of soapy
scrub brushes. The servants refused to use electric appli-
ances. They said no with great humility and dignity, in the
hope that it would be noticed. Grandfather thought they
were right; he loved the smell of soapy scrub brushes, and
that's why, every morning, Nicomedes and Engracia
scrubbed meters and meters of Zacatecan marble, Mexican marble, even if the honorable Agustín Vergara, my
father, did say, with his finger to his lips, that it had been
imported from Carrara—don't tell anyone, it's against the
law, they'll hit me with an ad valorem, you can't even give
a decent party any more, if you do, you end up on the society page and then you pay for it, nowadays a man has to
live the austere life, even feel ashamed to have worked
hard all his life to give his family the things . . .

I ran out of the house, shrugging into my Eisenhower
jacket. In the garage I climbed into my red Thunderbird
and started the motor, the door rising automatically at the
sound, and gunned out blindly. Something, a flicker of
caution, told me that Nicomedes might be there on the
driveway between the garage and the massive door in the
wall surrounding our property, moving the garden hose,
manicuring the artificial-seeming grass between the flag-
stones. I imagined the gardener flying skyward, torn
apart by the impact of the car, and I accelerated. The
cedar entrance door, faded by summer rains, swollen and
creaking, also opened automatically as the Thunderbird
passed the twin electric eyes embedded in the rock and
zoomed out; the tires squealed as I swerved to the right. I
thought I saw the snowy peak of Popocatepetl, but it was a
mirage. I accelerated. It was a cold morning, and the natural fog of the high plateau was rising to meet the blanket
of smog imprisoned by the ring of mountains and the
pressure of the high cold air.

I kept accelerating until I reached the access to the ring road around the city. I breathed deeply, and drove calmly now. There was nothing to worry about: I could circle the city once, twice, a hundred times, as many times as I wanted, driving thousands of kilometers with a sensation of never moving, of being simultaneously at the point of departure and the destination, seeing the same cement horizon, the same beer ads, billboards for the electric vacuum cleaners Nicomedes and Engracia detested, for soaps and television sets; the same squat, greenish, miserable buildings, barred windows, protective steel curtains, the same paint shops, repair shops, small refreshment stands with the box at the entrance filled with ice and carbonated drinks, corrugated tin roofs, and, occasionally, the dome of a colonial church lost among a thousand rooftop water-storage tanks, a smiling, stellar cast of prosperous characters, rosy and freshly painted, Santa Claus, the Blond Queen of Beers, Coca-Cola's little white-haired elf with his bottle-cap crown, Donald Duck, and, below, a cast of millions, extras, vendors of balloons and gum and lottery tickets, young men in T shirts and short sleeved shirts gathered around jukeboxes, chewing, smoking, loafing, smart-assing; building-supply trucks, armadas of Volkswagens, a collision at the exit to Fray Servando, motorcycle policemen in cinnamon-colored uniforms, putting on the bite, one-upping, horns, insults. Again I burned rubber, feeling free, the second trip identical, the same run, the water tanks, Plutarco, gas trucks, milk trucks, squealing brakes, milk cans tipping over, rolling, bursting on the asphalt, against the safety barriers, on the red Thunderbird, a sea of milk, Plutarco's white windshield. Plutarco in the fog. Plutarco blinded by limitless whiteness, the blinding liquid invisible to him, making him invisible, milk bath, sour milk, watered milk, your mother's milk, Plutarco.

Sure, my name lent itself to jokes, what would you expect from a name that sounded like Prick? In school I'd heard all that—Whaaaa? Did I hear . . . ? Say that again? Two, four, six, eight, there's a Verga t'appreciate, Verga, Verga, rah, rah, rah! And when they called the roll, there was always some joker waiting to answer, Vergara, Plutarco, present and primed, or present but spent, or Pee-Wee Vergara here. Then there'd be blows at recess. And when I began reading novels, at fifteen, I discovered there was an Italian author named Giovanni Verga, almost like my name, but that would never make any impression on a gang of ruffians like those shits at the National Prep. I hadn't gone to parochial school—first, because Grandfather had said *never,* what did we think the Revolution had been about, and then my old man, the lawyer, agreed, there were too damn many people who were fiercely anti-clerical in public but good little Catholics at home, better for the image. But I wished I could have been like my grandfather Don Vicente, when someone'd made a joke about his name he'd had the joker castrated. You're all smoke and no fire, no lead in your pencil, no powder in your cannon, the prisoner had said, and General Vergara cut off his balls, and I mean yesterday! From that time on, they'd called him General Balls, Old Balls and Guts, when he's around hang on to your nuts, and similar refrains had circulated all during Pancho Villa's long campaign against the Federales, when Vicente Vergara, still a young man but already forged in the fire of battle, had fought alongside the Centaur of the North, before going over to the ranks of Obregón when he saw the cause was lost in Celaya.

"I know what they say. Beat the shit out of anyone who tells you your grandfather was a turncoat."

"But no one's ever said that to me."

"Listen to me, boy, it was one thing when Villa came out of nothing, out of the Durango mountains, when he alone banded together all the malcontents and organized the

Northern Division, which polished off the dictatorship of
that drunk Huerta and his Federales. But when he set
himself against Carranza and decent law-abiding folk, that
was another thing altogether. He wanted to keep on fighting, anything that came along, because he'd gone past the
point where he could stop. After Obregón defeated him
at Celaya, Villa's army evaporated and all his men went
back to their corn patches and their woods. Villa went and
searched them out, one by one, to convince them they had
to keep fighting, and they said no, look, General, they'd
come back home, they were back with their women and
kids again. Then the poor bastards would hear shots, turn
around and see their houses up in flames and their families dead. 'You don't have any house or woman or kids
now,' Villa would say. 'You may as well come along with
me.' "

"Maybe he truly loved his men, Grandfather."
"Don't ever let anyone tell you I was a turncoat."
"No one says that. Everyone's forgotten all that stuff."

    I thought a lot about what he'd said. Pancho Villa truly
loved his men; he couldn't imagine that the soldiers didn't
feel the same about him. In his bedroom, General
Vergara had a lot of yellowed snapshots, some just newspaper clippings. You could see him there with all the
leaders of the Revolution, he'd been with them all, served
them all, in turn. As the leaders changed, so did Vicente
Vergara's attire—peering through the crowd engulfing
Don Panchito Madero the day of his famous entrance into
the capital, the small and fragile and ingenuous and miraculous apostle of the Revolution who with a book had
overthrown the all-powerful Don Porfirio in a land of illit-
erates, don't tell me it wasn't a miracle, and there was
young "Chente" Vergara in his narrow-brimmed, rib-
bonless felt hat and his old-fashioned shirt without the
stiff collar, one more downtrodden wretch, perched on

the equestrian statue of Carlos IV, that day when even the earth trembled, as it had the day Our Lord Jesus Christ had died, as if the apotheosis of Madero were already his Calvary.

"After our love for the Virgin and our hatred of the gringos, nothing binds us together more than a treacherous crime, I tell you, and all the people rose up against Victoriano Huerta for murdering Don Panchito Madero."

And then Vicente Vergara, captain of the Dorados, Pancho Villa's personal guard, his chest crisscrossed with cartridge belts, in a sombrero and white pants, eating a taco with Pancho Villa alongside a train billowing smoke, and then the constitutionalist Colonel Vergara, very young and proper in his Stetson and his khaki uniform, sheltered by the patriarchal and aloof figure of Venustiano Carranza, the principal leader of the Revolution, inscrutable behind smoked lenses and a beard that came to the buttons of his tunic, this snapshot looked almost like a family photograph, a just but severe father and a respectful and well-motivated son, not the same Vicente Vergara as the Obregonist colonel who in Agua Prieta took part in the pronunciamento against Carranza's abuse of power, liberated now from the tutelage of the father figure riddled by gunfire as he slept in his bedroll in Tlaxcalantongo.

"They all died so young! Madero never reached forty, and Villa was forty-five, Zapata thirty-nine, even Carranza, who seemed like an old man, was barely sixty-one, and General Obregón, forty-eight. What would have happened, tell me, boy, if I hadn't survived out of sheer luck, what if it'd been my destiny to die young, it's just chance that I'm not buried somewhere out there in some little town overgrown with buzzards and marigolds, and you, you'd never have been born."

And this Colonel Vergara sitting between General Alvaro Obregón and the philosopher José Vasconcelos at a dinner, this Colonel Vergara with his Kaiser mustache and dark, high-collared uniform rich with military braid.

"A Catholic fanatic killed our General Obregón, my boy. Ahhhhh. I went to all their funerals, every one of 'em you see here, they all died a violent death, except I didn't get to Zapata's funeral, they buried him in secret so they could say he was still alive."

And a different General Vicente Vergara, now dressed in civilian clothes, about to bid farewell to his youth, very neat, very spit-and-polish, in his light gabardine suit and pearl stickpin, very serious, very solemn, because only such a man could be offering his hand to the man with a granite face and the eyes of a jaguar, the Maximum Leader of the Revolution, Plutarco Elías Calles . . .

"That was a man, my boy, a humble schoolteacher who rose to be President. There wasn't a man could look him in the eye, not one, not even men who'd survived the awful test of a fake firing squad, believing their hour had come and not blinking an eye, not even them. Your godfather, Plutarco. Yes, boy, your godfather. Look at him, and look at you there in his arms. There we all are, the day you were baptized, the day of national unity when General Calles returned from exile."

"But why did he have me baptized? Didn't he persecute the Church mercilessly?"

"What does one thing have to do with the other? Were we going to leave you nameless?"

"No, Grandfather, but you also say that the Virgin unites all us Mexicans, how can you explain that?"

"The Virgin of Guadalupe is a revolutionary Virgin; she appeared on Hidalgo's banners during the War of Independence, and on Zapata's in the Revolution, she's the best bitchin' Virgin ever."

"But, Grandfather, it was because of you I didn't go to parochial school."

"The Church is good for only two things, to be born

right and to die right, you understand? But between the cradle and the grave they don't have any business sticking their noses in what doesn't concern them, let them stick to baptizing brats and praying for souls."

The three of us who lived in the big house in Pedregal only saw each other at supper, which was still whatever my grandfather the General wished. Soup, rice, fried beans, sugary rolls, and cocoa-flavored gruel. My father, the Honorable Don Agustín Vergara, got his own back for these ranch-style suppers by dining from three to five at the Jena or the Rivoli, where he could order steak Diane and crepes suzette. One revolting thing about the suppers was a peculiar habit of Grandfather's. After we finished eating, the old man would remove his false teeth and drop them into a half glass of warm water. Then he would add a half glass of cold water. He'd wait a minute and pour half this glass into a third. Then again he'd add a portion of warm water to the first glass, pour half of it into the third, and fill the first with warm water from the second. Then he would remove the teeth from the first of the three turbid mixtures swimming with particles of stew and tortilla, steep them in the second and the third, and, having obtained the desired temperature, place the teeth in his mouth and clamp them shut the way you snap a padlock.

"Nice and warm," he'd say, "sonofabitch, a set of teeth like a lion's."

"It's disgusting," my father the lawyer Agustín said one night, wiping his lips with his napkin and tossing it disdainfully on the tablecloth.

I looked at my father in astonishment. He'd never said a word all the years my grandfather had been performing the denture ceremony. The Honorable Agustín had to hold back the nausea the General's patient alchemy aroused. As for me, my grandfather could do no wrong.

"You ought to be ashamed. That's disgusting," the lawyer repeated.

"Hoo, hoo, hoo!" The General looked at him with scorn. "Since when can't I do what I bloody well please in my own house? My house, I said, not yours, Tín, nor that of any of those fancy-dancy friends of yours."

"I'll never be able to invite them here, at least not unless I hide you under lock and key."

"So my teeth make you vomit, but not my dough? By the way, how're things going . . . ?"

"Bad, really really bad . . ." my father said, shaking his head with a melancholy we'd never seen in him before. He wasn't a grave man, only a little pompous, even in his frivolities. This sadness, however, dissipated almost immediately, and he stared at Grandfather with icy defiance and a hint of mockery we couldn't understand.

Later Grandfather and I avoided comment on all this when we went to his bedroom, which was so different from the rest of the house. My father, the Honorable Agustín, had entrusted the details of the decor to a professional decorator, who'd filled the big house with Chippendale furniture, giant chandeliers, and fake Rubenses, for which he'd charged us as if they were real. General Vergara said he didn't give a fig for all that stuff, and he reserved the right to furnish his room with the things he and his dead Doña Clotilde had used when they built their first house in the Roma district back there in the twenties. The bed was brass, and although the room had a modern closet, the General closed it off by installing an ancient, heavy mahogany mirrored wardrobe in front of the closet door.

He gazed at his ancient wardrobe with affection. "When I open it, I still smell the smell of my Clotilde's clothes, so hard-working, the sheets all ironed, everything stiff with starch."

In that room, there are all kinds of things that no one ever uses any more, like a marble-topped washstand with a porcelain washbasin, and tall pitchers filled with water. A copper spittoon and a wicker rocking chair. The General has always bathed in the evening, and I guess, because of my father's mysterious behavior, Grandfather asked me to come with him that night. The two of us went together to the bathroom, the General carrying his gourd dipper with its hand-painted flowers and ducklings and his castile soap, because he despised the perfumed soaps with unpronounceable names that everyone was using then; after all, he wasn't a film star or a pansy. I helped him with his bathrobe, his pajamas, and his fleece-lined slippers. After lowering himself into the tub of warm water, he soaped up his fiber brush and began to scrub himself vigorously. He told me it was good for the circulation of the blood. I told him I preferred a shower, and he replied that showers were for horses. Then, without his even asking, I rinsed him with his gourd dipper, pouring water over his shoulders.

"I've been thinking, Grandfather, about what you told me about Villa and his guard."

"And I've been thinking about your answer, Plutarco. You may be right. God knows, there're times we miss our friends. Mine have been dying off, all of them. And no one can take their place. When the friends you've lived with and fought with die, you're all alone, flat out alone."

"You remember times when there were real men, I never get tired of hearing about them."

"Well, you're my friend, aren't you? But it isn't the same."

"Why not pretend I was with you in the Revolution, Grandfather? Pretend that I . . . ."

I was overcome with a strange embarrassment, and the old man sitting in the tub, all soaped up a second time, lifted his sudsy eyebrows quizzically. Then he took my hand in his wet one and pressed it hard, before brusquely changing the subject.

"What's your old man up to, Plutarco?"

"Who knows? He never tells me anything. You know that, Grandfather."

"He's never been one to be impudent. I tell you it pleased me how he talked back to me at supper."

The General laughed and slapped the water. He told me my father had always been a lazy bastard who'd had everything served to him on a silver platter and who'd been lucky to find himself with a decent living when General Cárdenas had swept Calles's supporters out of government. As he washed his hair, Grandfather told how until then he'd lived off his salary as a government official. But Cárdenas had forced him to look elsewhere for income, to make his living in business. The haciendas, the old agricultural estates, weren't producing. The peasants had burned them down before going off to fight. He said that while Cárdenas was reapportioning the land, someone had to produce. So Calles's supporters had got together as small landowners and bought up the bits and pieces of the haciendas not affected by the land distribution.

"We sowed cane in Morelos, tomatoes in Sinaloa, and cotton in Coahuila. The country could eat and clothe itself while Cárdenas was setting up communal land holdings, which never caught on because what every man wants is his own little plot of land, registered in his own name, see? I was the one that got things rolling, your father just took over the management as I got older. He'd do well to remember that when he gets feisty with me. But I swear I enjoyed it. He must be growing a little backbone. What's he got on his mind?"

I shrugged. I'd never been interested in business or politics. Where was the risk and adventure there? Where a risk comparable to what my grandfather had lived through early in his life? Those were the things that interested me.

Compared to the jumble of photographs of revolutionary leaders, the picture of my grandmother Doña Clotilde is something apart. She has a whole wall to herself, and a table with a vase filled with daisies. I think if Grandfather were a believer he'd have put candles there, too. The frame is oval and the photograph is signed by the photographer, Gutiérrez, 1915, Guanajuato. This ancient young woman who was my grandmother looks like a little doll. The photographer had tinted the photograph a pale rose, and only the lips and cheeks of Doña Clotilde glow in a mixture of shyness and sensuality. Did she really look like that?

"Like something out of a fairy tale," the General says to me. "Her mother died when she was a baby, and Villa shot her father because he was a moneylender. Wherever he went, Villa canceled the debts of the poor. But he didn't stop at that. He ordered the moneylenders shot, to teach them a lesson. I think the only one who learned the lesson was my poor Clotilde. I carried away an orphan who was happy to accept the first man who offered his protection. There were lots of orphan girls in that part of the country who to survive ended up as whores for the soldiers or, if they were lucky, vaudeville entertainers. Later she came to love me very much."

"And did you always love her?"

Grandfather, deep in his bedcovers, nodded.

"You didn't take advantage of her, just because she couldn't protect herself?"

He glared at me and abruptly cut off the light. I felt ridiculous, sitting in the darkness, rocking in the wicker chair. For a while the only sound was the noise of the chair. Then I got up and started to tiptoe out without saying good night. But I was stopped by a single painful vision. I saw my grandfather lying there dead. One morning we'd wake up and he'd be dead, it was bound to happen, and I'd never be able to tell him I loved him, never again. He'd grow cold, and my words, too.

I ran to him in the darkness and said to him: "I love you very much, Grandfather."

"That's good, boy. The same goes for me."

"Listen, I don't want to have everything served to me on a silver platter like you say."

"Can't be helped. Everything's in my name. Your father just manages it. When I die, I'm leaving everything to you."

"I don't want it, Grandfather; Grandfather, I want to begin from the beginning, the way you did . . ."

"Times are different, what do you think you could do now?"

I half smiled. "I wish I could have castrated someone, like you did."

"Do they still tell that story? Well, yes, that's the way it was. Except that I didn't make that decision by myself, you know."

"You gave the order, cut off his balls, and I mean yesterday!"

Grandfather patted me on the head and said no one knows how such decisions are made, they're never made by one man alone. He remembered one night by the light of the bonfires, on the outskirts of Gómez Palacio before the battle of Torreón. The man who'd insulted him was a prisoner, and he was a traitor besides.

"He'd been one of us. He went over to the Federales and told them how many we were and what arms we had. My men would have killed him anyway. I just beat them to it. It was every man's will. And then it became mine. He gave me the opportunity when he insulted me. Now they tell that colorful story, ah, what a bastard that General Vergara was, Old General Balls himself. Sí, señor. No, oh, no. It wasn't that simple. They'd have killed him anyway, and rightly so, because he was a traitor. But he was a prisoner of war, too. And that's a question of military honor as I see it, boy. No matter how bad the fellow was, he was still a prisoner of war. I kept my men from killing him. I think killing him would have dishonored them. But I wouldn't have been able to stop them. And that would have dishonored me. My decision was theirs and theirs was mine. That's the way things happen. There's no way of telling where your will ends and your men's begins."

"I came back to tell you I wish I'd been born at the same time as you and could have ridden with you."

"It wasn't a pretty spectacle, oh no. That man bleeding to death till the dawn rose over the dust of the desert. Then the sun ate him up and the buzzards held his wake. We left that place knowing secretly that what we'd done we'd done together. But if they'd done it and not me, I wouldn't be the leader and they wouldn't feel easy going into battle. There's nothing worse than looking a poor solitary bastard in the eye and killing him just before you kill a lot of faceless men whose eyes yours will never meet. But that's the way it is."

"Oh, Grandfather, how I wish . . ."

"Don't get your hopes up. There'll never be another revolution like that in Mexico! That kind only happens once."

"And what about me, Grandfather?"

"I feel sorry for you, boy, here, hug me tight, son, I understand, I swear I understand . . . I'd give a lot to be young again and be with you! What hell we'd stir up, Plutarco, you and me together, ummmm, sonofabitch!"

I seldom spoke with my father the lawyer. I've already said that the three of us only got together for supper and the General had the leading role there. But occasionally my father would call me to his study to ask me how I was getting along in school, what grades I was getting, what career I intended to follow. If I'd told him I didn't know, that I was spending my time reading novels, that I'd like to go to some far-off world like Michel Strogoff's Siberia or d'Artagnan's France, that I would much rather know what I could never be than what I wanted to be, my father wouldn't have reprimanded me, he wouldn't even have been disappointed. He simply wouldn't have understood. I knew all too well his perplexed look when I said something that completely escaped him. That pained me more than it did him.

"I think I'll study law, Father."

"That's good, that's a good choice. But then you should specialize in business. Would you like to go to Harvard Business School? It's difficult to get in, but I can pull a few strings."

I didn't disabuse him, and stood staring at the volumes in his library, all identically bound in red. There was nothing interesting there except a complete set of the Official Register, which always begins with announcements of foreign decorations, China's Order of the Celestial Star; the medal of the Liberator, Simón Bolívar; the French Legion of Honor. Only when my father is away do I dare creep like a spy into his carpeted, paneled bedroom. There isn't a single personal memento, not even a photograph of my mother. She died when I was five, and I don't remember her. Once a year, on the tenth of May, the three of us go to the French Cemetery, where my grandmother Clotilde and my mother, Evangelina was her name, lie buried side by side. I was thirteen when one of my classmates at the Revolution High School showed me a photograph of a girl in a bathing suit. It was the first time I'd ever felt a twinge of excitement. Like Doña Clotilde in her photograph, I felt pleasure and shame at the same time. I blushed and my classmate, guffawing, said, Be my guest, it's your mommy. A band of silk crosses the breast of the girl in the snapshot, tying at her hip. The

legend reads "Queen of the Mazatlán Carnival." "My father says your old lady was quite a piece," my schoolmate
said, bellowing with laughter.

"What was my mother like, Grandfather?"

"Beautiful, Plutarco. Too beautiful."

"Why aren't there any pictures of her in the house?"

"Too painful."

"I don't want to be left out of the pain, Grandfather."

The General looked at me very strangely when I said
that. How could I forget that look and my words that
famous night when I was awakened by loud voices in a
house where never a sound is heard once my father fin-
ishes his dinner and drives off in his Lincoln Continental,
to return early the next morning, about six, to bathe and
shave and breakfast in his pajamas, as if he'd spent the
night in the house. Who was he fooling? Every once in a
while I saw his picture in the society section of the paper,
always in the company of a rich widow, fiftyish like him,
but he could be seen with her. I never got any farther
than a whorehouse on Saturday nights, alone, with no
friends. I would have liked a relationship with a real lady,
mature, like my father's lover, not the "proper" girls you
met at parties given by other families, filthy rich like us.
Where was my Clotilde to rescue, to protect, to teach, to
love me? What was Evangelina like? I dreamed about her
in her white satin Jantzen bathing suit.

I was dreaming about my mother when I was awakened
by voices shattering the normal routine of the house. I sat
up in bed and instinctively pulled on my socks so I could
creep downstairs without making any noise. Of course, in
my dream I'd heard Grandfather shuffling along the corridor, it hadn't been a dream, it was real, no, I was the
only one in this house who knew that dreams are real.
That's what I was thinking as I moved noiselessly toward
the living room; the voices were coming from there. The

Revolution wasn't real, it was my grandfather's dream, my mother wasn't real, she was my dream, and that's why they were true. Only my father never dreamed, that's why he lived a lie.

Lies, lies, my grandfather was shouting. I stopped just outside the living room and hid behind the life-size reproduction of the Victory of Samothrace the decorator had placed there as a guardian goddess of our hearth—the living room that no one ever entered. It was for show; not a footprint, not a cigarette butt, not a single coffee stain. And now it was the scene of this midnight battle between my grandfather and my father, who were shouting at each other, my grandfather the General in a voice you can imagine ordering, Cut off his balls, and I mean yesterday, blast him, shoot him, first we'll kill him and then we'll make inquiries, Old General Balls himself; my father the lawyer in a voice I'd never heard before.

I imagined that Grandfather, in spite of his anger, was enjoying the fact that his son was finally talking back to him. He was dressing him down the way he would a drunken corporal: had he had a whip in his hand, he'd have left a crossword puzzle on my father's face, there's nothing lower than a sonofabitch like you. And my father to the General: You're an old bastard. And my grandfather: There's only one bastard in this family, he'd turned over a solid, honest fortune to him, all he'd asked was for him to manage it with the help of the best lawyers and accountants, all he had to do was sign his name and collect the income, put a little in the bank and reinvest a little, what did he *mean* there was nothing left? Get off it, you old bastard, get off it, at least I won't go to prison, I never signed anything, I was cagey as hell, I let the lawyers and the accountants sign everything for me, at least I can say that everything was done behind my back, though I'll accept the responsibility for the debts, even though I was as much a victim of fraud as the men who lent me the money. Son of a fucking bitch, I handed over a sound, solid fortune to you, wealth that comes from the land is the only secure wealth, money's not worth the paper it's printed on unless it's based on land, you gibbering jackass, diddling around with play money, who asked you to build an empire out of pure air, shadow shareholders, worthless stock, a hundred million pesos with nothing to back them up, who asked you to go around thinking the more debts you accumulated the safer you were? you little bastard. Don't get in an uproar, General, I can assure you the lawsuit against the lawyers and accountants will proceed, they deceived me, too, I'll stick to that. You'll stick to it, your ass, you'll have to give them the land, the property in Sinaloa, your fields of tomatoes, tomatoes, tomatoes! God, how my father laughed, I'd never heard him laugh like that. What a fool you are, General, tomatoes, do you think we constructed this house and bought our cars and lived the good life on tomatoes? do you think I'm a fishwife from La Merced? what do you think does better in Sinaloa, tomatoes or poppies? it's all the same, red fields, from the air you can't tell they're not tomatoes, why should I keep it quiet any longer? do you want to know everything? if I have to turn over the land to pay the debts it will all come out. Then burn off the fields, fast, you fucker, plow it under and say that you were cleaned out by the blight, what are you waiting for? Do you think they'll let me get away with that? you stupid old bastard, the gringos who buy the product and commercialize it, my . . . my associates in California where they sell the heroin, what about them? will they just sit there with their arms crossed? oh, sure, now tell me where I'm going to get a hundred million pesos to pay off my investors, tell me, between the house and the cars I can scratch up about ten million, and there's a little more in the Swiss account. You poor devil, you couldn't even milk anything off drugs, and those Yankees made a sucker out of you.

Then the General grew silent and the lawyer made a drowning sound in his throat.

"When you married a whore, you dishonored only yourself," Grandfather said finally. "But now you've dishonored me."

That I didn't want to hear. Don't let them go on, I prayed in the shelter of the wings of the Victory. This was ridiculous, a scene from a bad Mexican film, a soap opera on the idiot box, me hiding behind a curtain listening to the grownups telling truths to each other, a classic scene between Libertad Lamarque and Arturo de Córdova. Grandfather stode from the living room, and I stepped out in front of him and clutched his arm. My father stared at us in stupefaction. I asked Grandfather, "Do you have any money on you?"

General Vergara looked me straight in the eye and caressed his belt. It was his snakeskin belt filled with hundred-peso gold coins. "Right. Let's go."

We left, my arm around the old man, as my father screamed at us from the living room: "I'll not give either of you the pleasure of seeing me defeated!"

The General shoved the enormous cut-glass urn in the vestibule; it fell and shattered. We left behind us a trail of plastic calla lilies, and roared off in the red Thunderbird, I in my pajamas and socks, the General very circumspect in his light gabardine suit, his maroon tie secured below the knot with the pearl stickpin, still caressing the beltful of gold. Oh, it was great to roar along the ring road at one in the morning—no traffic, no scenery, the open road to eternity. That's what Grandfather said. Hang on tight, General, I'm going to floor her to a hundred and twenty, I've ridden rougher broncs than this. Grandfather laughed. Let's find someone to tell your stories to, let's find someone who'll listen, let's blow all the gold pieces, let's take her around again, Grandfather. You bet, boy, right from zero, again.

In the Plaza Garibaldi, at one-fifteen in the morning: First things first, boy, we need some mariachis to follow us around all night, you don't ask how much, just whether they know how to play "La Valentina" and "On the Road to Guanajuato," okay, boys, strike up the bass guitar. Grandfather let out a yowl like a coyote: "Valentina, Valentina, listen to my plea," let's go to Tenampa and have a tequila or two, that's what I have for breakfast, boys, see who can hold the most, that's how I worked myself up to a pitch for the encounter in Celaya, when we Villistas sent our cavalry out to swamp Obregón, "One passion fires me, and that's what I feel for you," and before us stretched the enormous plain, and in the distance we could see the artillery and the motionless horses of the enemy, and here come banged-up trays loaded with beer, and we surged forward at a gallop, sure of victory, with the courage of wild tigers, and now the mariachis are looking at us with stony eyes, as if my grandfather and I didn't exist, and then from invisible wolves' dens on the plain there suddenly emerged a thousand bayonets, boys, Yaqui Indians faithful to Obregón had hidden in those holes, be careful, don't spill that cold brew, and everyone was staring at us as if we were crazy, a loudmouthed old man and a kid in his pajamas, what's with them? there they were, ramming their bayonets into the bellies of our horses, holding them firm until they ripped out the guts, those Yaquis with earrings in their ears and their heads tied in red kerchiefs soaked in the blood and guts and balls of our horses, another round? sure, the night is young, we were scared, sure, we were scared, who'd ever have imagined such a magnificent tactic from General Obregón, right then I began to respect him, I swear I did, when do you want us to sing? didn't you hire us to sing, señor? the mariachis stared at us, thinking, I'll bet they don't have a red cent, we fell back, we attacked with cannon, but we'd already been defeated by the maneuver, Celaya was a field of smoke and blood and dying horses, smoke spiraled from Delicados, a bored mariachi poured salt and squeezed lemon on my grandfather's closed fist, we blew off one of General Obregón's arms, things were going so bad I said to myself right there, we'll never make it against this guy, the mariachi shrugged his shoulders and poured salt on the mouthpiece of his trumpet and began to play, teasing out sad sounds, Villa is pure unleashed, undirected force, Obregón is intelligent force, he's the king bastard of them all, I was ready to crouch down on the battlefield to follow the trail, to look for the arm we'd blasted off Obregón and hand it back to him and say, General, you're the fucking end, here's your arm back and I'm sorry, ah, sonofabitch, though I guess you know what happened? you don't know? don't you want to know? well, General Obregón flipped a gold coin in the air, like that, and the arm flew off the ground and the bloody fist snatched the coin in midair, like that, uh, sonofabitch, gotcha', old buddy, now are you interested in my story? I gotcha', the way Obregón got us and got his arm back at Celaya, "Well, if I'm to die tomorrow, it may as well be today," I just want you to love me, boys, that's all, and be faithful, even if it's just for tonight.

Two in the morning, in the silver-toned Club of the Aztecs, the sensational Ricky Rola, queen of the cha-cha-cha, cuba libres for everyone, these boys are my buddies, whaddya mean they can't be seated, you sourass little lemon, just look at those sick green bags under his eyes, crummy little punk, he cleans out the latrines, shut that lemon you call a trap or I'll squeeze it for you, whaddya mean why is my grandson in his pajamas? why, that's all the clothes he has, the only time he goes out is at night because he's sacked out all day with your dear momma and he's all tired out, whaddya mean, your musicians will protest? my mariachis belong to the union too, sit down, boys, General Vergara's orders, what did you say, you prick, a waiter says at your service, General, get that, lemon-puss? I'll bet you piss vinegar, yellow and rose and blue lights, the Everlasting Lily, Queen of the Sentimental Bolero, they stuffed her into those sequins with a shoehorn, look, General, they lifted those knockers with a derrick after they played soccer with them, that baby could score goals all by herself, she must have a belly button the size of a bullring, they slapped eight layers of paint on her before she came out, General, look at those eyelashes, like black venetian blinds, you're for sale? you don't say, how much for those sad eyes, Bubbles? she's a hypocrite, who's she singing those pimp songs to, boys, we'll see about that, charge! troops! a hypocrite, plain and simple, you were making fun of me, let's have a macho song, get up there on the platform, boys, grab-ass, li'l ole Everlasting Lily, let's have those cantaloupes, Bubbles, what a screech, respect an artist, go take your bath, Sweatso, go wash off that clown face, stop yelling, it's for your own good, charge! troops! sing, General, "and on February the sixteenth, Wilson sends to our great nation ten thousand American troops," let's hear that sobbing guitar, let's hear that salty trumpet, "tanks and cannons and airplanes, all looking for Villa, all trying to kill him," get down you old asshole, after them, my gallant mariachis, and that pansy in the pajamas, giddown, no one plays here but union musicians, musicians, hell, slick-haired greaser gays in little bow ties and shiny tuxedo jackets, shiny? I'll shine your balls, you old coot, hear that, boys? they're trying to bully me and I won't take that, no, by the Holy Virgin, I won't take that, cut off their balls, Grandfather, right here on the spot, one foot through the bass drum, bass guitar smashing against the snares, rip the guts out of the piano the way they did the horses at Celaya, watch out, Grandpa, for the guy with the saxophone, a right to the belly, butt that bastard's bass drum, Plutarco, hard at it, troops, I want to see the blood of those low-born bastards running on the dance floor, the guy on the snares has a wig on, Plutarco, grab it, that's right, egghead, should I crack that before I crack his nuts? kick his ass, Plutarco, and run like hell, all of you, old Lemonade's called the cops, grab the harp, boys, not a key left in place, here, General, the singer's eyelashes, and I'm leaving this stack of gold pieces to pay for the damages.

A little after three in the house of La Bandida, where I was well known, and the Madame herself greeted us, what swanky pajamas, Plutarco, and she felt so honored that the famous General Balls . . . and what a great idea to bring the mariachis, and could they play "Seven Leagues"? she herself, La Bandida, would sing it because it was her own composition, Seven Leagues was Villa's favorite horse, serve the rum, come do your stuff, girls, they've just arrived from Guadalajara, all very young, you'll be, at the most, the second person to touch her in her life, General, but if you prefer I can bring you a brand-new virgin, as they say, that was a good idea you had, that's it, that's it, right on the General's knees, Judith, do what I tell you, ayyy, Doña Chela, he looks like something to throw to the lions, my grandpa has a fatter carcass than this, listen, you little bitch, this is my grandfather and I want you to respect him, you don't have to defend me, Plutarco, now this little flower of the night is going to see that Vicente Vergara's not something to throw to the lions, he *is* the lion, come along, little Judith, let's see if we can find your cot, we'll see who's the macho, what I want to see's the color of your money, there you are, catch it, I like you, a gold piece, Doña Chela, look, the old man's loaded, "when he heard the train whistle, he reared up on his hind legs and whinnied," take your pick, boys, my grandfather told the mariachis, remember you're my troops and don't haggle.

I sat in the parlor, waiting and listening to records. My grandfather and the mariachis between them had cornered the market on girls. I drank a cuba libre and counted the minutes. After thirty, I began to get worried. I went up to the second floor and asked where Judith worked. The towel girl took me to her door. I knocked and Judith opened it, a tiny little thing without her high heels, stark naked. The General was sitting on the edge of the bed, trouserless, his socks held up by old red garters. He stared at me, his eyes brimming with the moisture that sometimes fell unbidden from his ancient barrel-cactus head. He looked at me sadly.

"I couldn't do it, Plutarco, I couldn't do it."

I grabbed Judith by the nape of her neck, I twisted her arm behind her back, the bitch clawed my shoulder and shrieked, it wasn't my fault, I did his show for him, everything he asked me to, I did my job, I did my part, I didn't rob him, don't look at me like that, I'll give you your money back if you want, but don't look at me so sad, please, don't hurt me, let me go.

I twisted her arm harder, I pulled harder on her frizzy hair, in the mirror I saw the face of a wildcat, screaming, her eyes squeezed shut, high cheekbones, lips painted with silvery pomade, sharp little teeth, sweaty shoulder.

"Was this what my mother was like, Grandfather? A whore like this? Is that what you meant?"

I let her go. She ran from the room, covering herself with a towel. I went to sit beside Grandfather. He didn't answer me. I helped him get dressed. He muttered: "I hope so, Plutarco, I hope so."

"Did she put the horns on my father?"

"He looked like a stag when she got through with him."

"Why did she do it?"

"She didn't have to, like this girl does."

"Then she did it because she liked it. What's bad about that?"

"It was ingratitude."

"I'm sure my father couldn't please her."

"She should have tried to get into the movies, and not come to my house."

"So did we do her a big favor? It would have been better if my father'd done her a favor in bed."

"I only know she dishonored your father."

"Because she had to, Grandfather."

"When I remember my Clotilde . . ."

"I tell you she did it because she had to, just like that whore."

"Well, *I* couldn't do it, boy. Must be lack of practice."

"Let me show you, let me refresh your memory."

Now that I'm past my thirtieth year, I can remember that night when I was nineteen as if I were living it again, the night of my liberation. Liberation was what I felt as I fucked Judith, with all the mariachis, drunk as hell, in her bedroom, pumping and pumping to the strains of the ballad of Pancho Villa's horse, "in the station at Irapuato, broad horizons beckoned," my grandfather sitting in a chair, sad and silent, as if he were watching life being born anew, but not his, not his ever again, Judith red with shame, she'd never done it that way, with music and everything, frozen, ashamed, feigning emotions I knew she didn't feel, because her body belonged to the dead night, I was the only one who conquered, no one shared the victory with me, that's why it had no flavor, it wasn't like those moments the General had told me about, moments shared by all, maybe that's why my grandfather was so sad, and why so sad forever was the melancholy of the liberation I thought I'd won that night.

It was about six in the morning when we reached the French Cemetery. Grandfather handed over another of the gold coins he carried in his richly ornamented belt to a watchman numb with cold, and he allowed us to enter. Grandfather wanted to play a serenade to Doña Clotilde in her tomb, and the mariachis sang "On the Road to Guanajuato" on the harp they'd stolen from the cabaret: "Life is without meaning, there's no meaning in life." The General sang with them, it was his favorite song, it reminded him of so many things from his youth: "On the road to Guanajuato, you pass through many towns."

We paid the mariachis and said we'd get together again soon, friends to the death, and Grandfather and I went home. Even though there was little traffic at that hour, I had no desire to speed. The two of us, Grandfather and I, on our way home to Pedregal, that unwitting cemetery that rises to the south of Mexico City. Mute witness to cataclysms that went unrecorded, the black, barren land watched over by extinct volcanoes is an invisible Pompeii. Thousands of years ago, lava inundated the night with bubbling flames; no one knows who died here, who fled. Some, like me, think that perfect silence, that calendar of creation, should never have been touched. Many times, when I was a boy, when we lived in the Roma district and my mother was still alive, we passed by Pedregal on the way to visit the pyramid of Copilco, stone crown of stone. I remember how, spontaneously, each of us would fall silent when we saw that dead landscape, lord of its own dusk that would never be dissipated by the (then) luminous mornings of our valley, do you remember, Grandfather? it's my first memory. We were on our way to the country, because then the country was very close to the city. I always sat on a servant's lap, was she my nurse? Manuelita was her name.

On the way back to the house in Pedregal with my drunk and humiliated grandfather, I remembered the

construction of the university, how they polished the volcanic rock, Pedregal put on spectacles of green glass, a
cement toga, painted its lips with acrylic, encrusted its
cheeks with mosaic, conquered the blackness of the land
with an even blacker shadow of smoke. The silence was
broken. On the far side of the vast parking lot at the university they parceled out the Pedregal Gardens. They established a style that would unify the buildings and landscape of the new residential site. High walls, white, indigo
blue, vermilion, and yellow. The vivid colors of the Mexican fiesta, Grandfather, combined with the Spanish tradition of the fortress, are you listening? They sowed the
rock with dramatic plants, stark, with no adornment but a
few aggressive flowers. Door locked tight like chastity
belts, Grandfather, and flowers open like wounded geni-
tals, like the cunt of the whore Judith that you couldn't
fuck and I could, and what for, Grandfather?

We were approaching Pedregal Gardens, the mansions
that must all have been the same behind their walls, Japan
with a touch of Bauhaus, modern, one-floor, low roofs,
wide picture windows, swimming pools, rock gardens. Do
you remember, Grandfather? The perimeter of the development was encircled by walls, and access was limited to a
certain number of orange wrought-iron gates tended by
guards. What a pitiful attempt at urban chastity in a capital like ours, wake up, Grandfather, look at it by night,
Mexico City, voluntarily a cancerous city, hungry for un-
controlled expansion, a hodgepodge of styles, a city that
confuses democracy with possessions, and egalitarianism
with vulgarity, look at it now, Grandfather, how we saw it
that night we spent with the mariachis and the whores,
look at it now that you're dead and I'm over thirty, bound
by its broad belts of poverty, legions of unemployed, im-
migrants from the countryside, and millions of babies
conceived, Grandfather, between a howl and a sigh: our
city, Grandfather, it won't long tolerate oases of exclu-

siveness. Keeping Pedregal Gardens in good condition was like fixing your fingernails while your body rots of gangrene. The gates collapsed, the guards disappeared, the caprice of construction broke forever the quarantine of our elegant leprosarium, and my grandfather's face was as gray as the concrete walls of the ring road. He'd fallen asleep, and when we reached the house I had to lift him out of the car like a child. How light he was, emaciated, just skin and bones, and what a strange grimace of forgetfulness on a face laden with memories. I carried him to his bed. My father was waiting for me at the door.

He signaled me to follow him through the marble halls to the library. He opened the cabinet filled with crystal ware and mirrors and bottles. He offered me a cognac and I shook my head no. I prayed he wouldn't ask me where we'd gone, what we'd done, because I would have had to give him an answer he wouldn't understand, and that, as I've already said, hurt me more than it did him. I rejected the cognac as I would have rejected his questions. It was the night of my liberation and I wasn't going to lose it by acknowledging that my father had the right to interrogate me. I had my silver platter, hadn't I, why try once more to find out, for myself alone, what love was, what it was to be courageous, to be free.

"What is it you hold against me, Plutarco?"

"That you left me out of everything, even pain."

I felt sorry for my father as I said it. He stood there for a moment, then walked to the picture window overlooking an interior patio, glass-enclosed, a marble fountain in the center. He drew back the curtains with a melodramatic gesture at the very moment Nicomedes turned on the fountain; it was as if they'd rehearsed it. I felt sorry for him; these were gestures he'd learned at the movies. Every move he made he'd learned at the movies. Everything he did was learned, and pompous. I compared his actions to the spontaneous hell my grandfather knew how to raise. My father for years had been hobnobbing with gringo millionaires and marquises with invented titles. His own certificate of nobility was his appearance in the society pages, his English mustache carefully brushed upward, graying hair, discreet gray suit, a showy handkerchief sprouting from his breast pocket like the dry plants from the Pedregal. Like many vulgar rich Mexicans of his generation, he modeled himself on the Duke of Windsor, a large knot in the necktie, but they never found their Mrs. Simpsons. Pitiful creatures: hobnobbing with some vulgar Texan who'd come to buy a hotel in Acapulco, or a Spanish sardine seller who'd bought his aristocracy from Franco, people like that. He was a very busy man.

He parted the curtains and said he knew his arguments wouldn't sway me, that my mother had not taken proper care of me, she'd been dazzled by the social scene, it was the time when the European émigrés were arriving, King Carol and Madame Lupescu with valets and Pekingese, and for the first time Mexico City felt itself to be an exciting cosmopolitan capital, not a petty town of Indians and military coups. It was inevitable that it would impress Evangelina, a beautiful girl from the provinces who'd had a gold tooth when he first met her, one of those girls from the coast of Sinaloa who become women while still very young, tall and fair, with eyes like silk, and long black hair, whose bodies hold both night and day, Plutarco, night and day glowing in the same body, all the promises, all of them, Plutarco.

He'd gone to the carnival in Mazatlán with some friends, young lawyers like himself, and Evangelina was the Queen. She was paraded along the seawall called Olas Altas in an open car adorned with gladiolas, everyone was courting her, the orchestras were playing "Little sweetheart mine, pure as a newborn child," she'd preferred him, she'd chosen him, chosen happiness with him, life with him, he hadn't forced her, he hadn't offered any more than the others, the way the General had with your grandmother Clotilde, who had no recourse but to accept the protection of a powerful and courageous man. Not Evangelina. Evangelina had kissed him for the first time one night on the beach, and said, I like *you*, you're the tenderest, you have handsome hands. And I *was* the most tender, I was, Plutarco, that's the truth, I wanted to love. The sea was as young as she, they'd been born together that very minute, Evangelina your mother and the sea, owing nothing to anyone, no obligations, unlike your grandmother Clotilde. I didn't have to force her, I didn't have to teach her to love me, as your grandfather had to teach his Clotilde.

In his heart the General knew that, and his veneration for my mother Clotilde pained him, Plutarco, he was like the old saying, he never lost, but if he lost, he took it with him, my mother was part of his war booty, no matter how hard he tried to hide it, she hadn't loved him, she had had to learn to love him, but Evangelina chose me, I wanted to love, your grandfather wants people to love him, and that's why he determined that Evangelina should stop loving me, the reverse of what happened to him, do you understand? all day long he compared her to his sainted Clotilde, everything was my dear dead Clotilde wouldn't have done it that way, when my Clotilde was alive—my Clotilde, may she rest in peace—she knew how to run a household, she was modest, she never raised her voice to me, my Clotilde was so well-mannered, she'd never had her picture taken showing her legs, and the same, even more, when you were born, Plutarco, take my Clotilde, now there was a real Mexican mother, there was a woman who knew how to care for a baby.

"Why don't you nurse Plutarco? Are you afraid it'll ruin those beautiful boobs? Well, what do you want them for? To show the men? Carnival's over, miss, it's time to be a decent mother."

If my father succeeded in making me hate the memory
of my mother Clotilde, imagine how it exasperated
Evangelina, it's no wonder your mother felt isolated, and
then driven out of the house, going to the dentist, looking
for parties to go to, looking for another man, my Evangelina was so simple, leave your father, Agustín, let's go live
by ourselves, let's love each other the way we did at first,
and the General, don't let that woman get on your back,
you let her get her own way just once and she'll dominate
you forever, but in his heart he was hoping she would
stop loving me so I would have to force her to love me,
the way it had been with him, so I wouldn't have any advantage he hadn't had. So no one would have the freedom he'd missed. If he'd had to work hard for everything, then we'd have to, too—first me and then you,
that's how he sees things, his own way, he gave us everything on a silver platter as he always says, and there wasn't
going to be another Revolution where a man could win at
a stroke both love and valor, not any more, now we have
to prove ourselves in other ways, why should he pay for
everything and us for nothing? he's our eternal dictator,
don't you need see if we dare show we don't need him, that
we can live without his memories, his heritage, his tyranny
of sentiment. He wants people to love him, General Vicente Vergara is our father, by God, and we're obliged to
love him and emulate him, to see if we can do what he
did, now that it's more difficult.

You and I, Plutarco, what battles are we going to win?
what women are we going to tame? what soldiers are we
going to castrate? you tell me. That's your grandfather's
terrible challenge, realize that quickly or you'll find yourself broken the way he broke me, he laughs and says, let's
see whether you can do what I did, now that it can't be
done any longer, let's see whether you can find a way to
inherit something more difficult than my money.

"Violence with impunity."

Evangelina was so innocent, so without defenses, that's what galled me more than anything, that I couldn't blame her, but I couldn't forgive her either. Now that's something your grandfather never lived through. Only with such a feeling could I triumph over him forever, inside myself, though he supported me and went on mocking me. I'd done something more than he'd done, or something different. I still don't know which. Your mother didn't know either. She must have felt guilty of everything, except the one thing I blamed her for.

"Her irritating innocence."

My father had been drinking all night. Even more than Grandfather and me. He walked to the hi-fi and turned it on. Avelina Landín was singing something about silver threads among the gold. My father dropped into a chair, like Fernando Soler in the old Mexican film *Soulless Woman*. I no longer cared whether this, too, was something he'd learned.

"The medical report said your mother had died by choking on a piece of meat. As simple as that. Those things are easily arranged. Your grandfather and I tied a beautiful scarf around her neck for the funeral."

He gulped down the rest of his cognac, put the glass on a shelf, and stood for a long while staring at the palms of his hands, as Avelina sang about the silvery moon reflected on a lake of blue.

Of course, the business matters were resolved. My father's friends in Los Angeles covered the hundred-million-peso debt so the fields in Sinaloa would remain untouched. Grandfather took to his bed for a month after the binge we'd had together, but he was back in good form for the tenth of May, Mother's Day, when the three of us men who lived in the huge house in Pedregal went together, as we did every year, to the French Cemetery to leave flowers in the crypt where my grandmother Clotilde and my mother Evangelina are buried.

The marble crypt is like our mansion in miniature. They are both sleeping here, said the General in a broken voice, head bowed, sobbing, his face hidden in a handkerchief. I stand between my father and my grandfather, clasping their hands. My grandfather's hand is cold, sweatless, like a lizard's skin. My father's hand blazes like fire. My grandfather sobbed again, and uncovered his face. If I'd looked at him closely, I'm sure I would have asked myself for whom he wept so bitterly, and for whom he wept more, his wife or his daughter-in-law. But at that moment I was simply trying to guess what my future would be. We'd gone to the cemetery without mariachis this time. I would have liked a little music.

The Two Elenas

"I don't know where Elena gets those ideas. That's not the way she was brought up. Nor you either, Victor. The truth is that marriage has changed her. Yes, there's no doubt. I thought she was going to give my husband a heart attack. Those ideas are completely indefensible, and especially at the dinner table. My daughter knows very well that her father needs to eat in peace. If not, his blood pressure goes up immediately. That's what the doctor has told us. And, after all, this doctor knows what he's talking about. He doesn't charge two hundred pesos a visit for nothing. I beg you to talk with Elena. She pays no attention to me. Tell her we'll put up with everything. That it doesn't matter to us that she neglects her home to learn French. That it doesn't matter that she goes to those weird films in dens filled with bushy-haired freaks. And that we don't mind those clownish red stockings. But when she tells her father at dinnertime that by living with two men a woman can better complement herself . . .

Victor, for your own sake, you ought to get ideas like that out of your wife's head."

When she'd seen *Jules and Jim* at a film club, Elena had gotten the devilish idea that she should carry the battle to the Sunday dinners with her parents—the only obligatory gathering of the family. When we came out of the theater we took the MG and went to get something to eat at the Coyote Flaco in Coyoacán. Elena looked, as always, very beautiful in her black sweater and leather skirt and the stockings her mother didn't like. She was wearing, in addition, a gold chain with a carved jadeite pendant that, according to an anthropological friend, describes the Mixtec prince Uno Muerte. Elena, who is always so happy and carefree, looked intense that night: the color had risen to her cheeks and she barely spoke to the friends who ordinarily get together in that rather elite restaurant. I asked her what she wanted to eat and she didn't answer: instead, she took my closed hand in hers and stared at me intently. I ordered two garlic steak sandwiches as Elena shook out her pale pinkish hair and rubbed her neck.

"Victor, Nibelung, for the first time I realize that you men are right in being misogynists and that we are born for you to detest. I'm not going to pretend any longer. I've discovered that misogyny is the condition of love. I know now that I'm mistaken, but the longer I express certain needs, the more you are going to hate me and try to satisfy me. Victor, Nibelung, you must buy me an old-fashioned sailor suit like Jeanne Moreau's."

I told her that she seemed perfect to me as long as she continued to expect everything of me. Elena stroked my hand and smiled.

"I know you don't feel completely free, darling, but have faith. After you have given me everything I ask of you, you yourself will beg that another man share our lives. You yourself will ask to be Jules. You yourself will ask that Jim live with us and bear the load. Didn't the

Little Blond Jesus say it? Let us love one another . . .
Why not?"

I thought that Elena might be right as far as the future
was concerned; I knew that with her, after four years of
marriage, all the moral rules learned from childhood
tended simply to fade away. That's what I have always
loved about her: her naturalness. She never rejects one
rule to replace it with another, but only to open a kind of
door, like those in children's stories where every illustrated page announces a garden, a cave, an ocean one
reaches through the secret opening on the previous page.

"I don't want to have children for six years," she said
one night, resting against my legs in the big dark room of
our house while we listened to Cannonball Adderley
records, that same house in Coyoacán that we've decorated
with colonial woodcarvings of polychrome saints and
virgins and hypnotic-eyed colonial masks: "*You* never go
to Mass and nobody says a word. I'm not going either,
they can say whatever they please." And in the attic that
serves us as a bedroom, bathed on clear mornings in the
light from the distant volcanoes: "I'm going to have coffee
with Alejandro today. He's a great artist and he would
feel inhibited if you were there, and I need him to explain
a few things to me alone." And as she follows me across
the boards connecting the unlaid floors in the houses I'm
building in Desierto de los Leones: "I'm going to be gone
for ten days, taking a train around the country." And as
we have a hurried cup of coffee one midafternoon in the
Tirol, fluttering her fingers in greeting to some friends
passing by on Hamburgo: "Thanks for taking me to the
brothel, Nibelung. It seemed straight out of the time of
Toulouse-Lautrec, as innocent as a Maupassant story.
And you know? Now I've found out that that's not where
sin and depravation are, but elsewhere." And after a private showing of Buñuel's *The Exterminating Angel:* "Victor,

morality is everything that gives life, and immorality everything that refutes it, isn't that right?"

And now she repeated, nibbling a sandwich: "Aren't I right? If a *ménage à trois* gives us life and happiness and makes for better personal relations among the three of us than the relationship between the two of us, then isn't that moral?"

I nodded as I ate, listening to the sputtering of the meat cooking on the raised grill. Several friends were watching that their cuts were done just the way they like them, and then came to sit with us, and Elena began to laugh again and be her usual self. Unfortunately, I was inspired to scan the faces of our friends in turn, imagining each of them installed in my house, giving Elena the portion of affection, stimulus, passion, or intelligence that I, exhausted beyond my limits, was incapable of granting her. As I observed the nearest face, avidly disposed to listen to her (and at times I grow weary of hearing her), another amiably offering to fill in the lacunae in her reasoning (I prefer that her conversation *not* be logical or consistent), yet another, more inclined to formulate precise and, according to him, revealing questions (and I never use words—rather, gestures or telepathy to set Elena in motion), I took some consolation from telling myself that, after all was said and done, what little they could give her would be given beyond a certain boundary of my life with her, like dessert or a cordial, an appendage. That one, the one who combed his hair like Ringo Starr, asked her precisely and revealingly why she continued to be faithful to me, and Elena replied that today infidelity is mandatory, just as Communion every Friday used to be, and turned away from him. The nearer one, the one in a turtleneck shirt, interpreted Elena's reply, adding that, doubtlessly, my wife meant that fidelity was becoming the attitude of the rebel. And the one here by me, the one in the perfect

Edwardian frock coat, merely invited Elena with an intensely oblique glance to continue speaking: he would be the perfect audience. Elena raised her arms and asked the waiter for an espresso.

We walked beneath the ash trees through the cobbled streets of Coyoacán, holding hands, experiencing the contrast of the day's heat still clinging to our clothing and the moist coolness of the night that, following the afternoon shower, brought a glow to our eyes and color to our cheeks. Silently, our heads bowed, holding hands, we like to walk through the ancient streets that have been since the beginning a point of encounter, a common meeting ground of our inclination to assimilate what is around us. I think we have never spoken of this, Elena and I. Nor do we need to. What I do know is that it pleases us to collect old things, as if we were rescuing them from painful oblivion, or as if by touching them we gave them new life, or as if in seeking the right place, light, and ambience in our home we were in reality defending ourselves against a similar future oblivion. We still have the lion's-maw handle we found in a hacienda in Los Altos that we caress every time we open the door to our home, knowing that every caress consumes it; illuminated by a yellow light in the garden, we have the stone cross representing the four converging rivers of hearts torn out, perhaps, by the same hands that later worked the stone; and we have the black horses from some long-ago dismantled carrousel, like figureheads from the prows of brigantines that would lie forever on the ocean floor unless their wooden skeletons came to rest on some distant shore of solemn cockatoos and dying turtles.

While I look for some Cannonball records, Elena takes off her sweater and lights the fire. I serve two glasses of absinthe and lie down on the rug to wait for her. She lies with her head cradled on my legs, smoking, while we both listen to the slow sax of Brother Lateef, whom we met in

the Gold Bug in New York, looking like a Congolese witch
doctor dressed by Disraeli, his eyes sleepy and swollen like
two African boas, a segregated-Svengali beard, his purplish
lips joined to the saxophone that silences the black so that
he may speak with an eloquence foreign to his surely
hoarse everyday stammer: the slow notes are a kind of
mournful affirmation that will never say all they want to
say, since from beginning to end they are only a seeking,
an approximation, muted by a strange shyness; they give
joy and direction to the contact of our bodies, which
begins to follow the feeling of Lateef's instrument; pure
announcement, pure prelude, limited entirely to the pleasures of foreplay, which, because of the sax, become the
act itself.

"What American Negroes are doing is turning the tables on the whites," Elena says as we take our appointed
places at her parents' enormous Chippendale dining
table. "The love, the music, the vitality of the Negroes is
forcing the whites to justify themselves. See how the
whites are now physically persecuting the blacks, because
they have finally realized that, psychologically, the blacks
are persecuting *them*."

"Well, I'm just thankful that there're no Negroes here,"
says Elena's father, helping himself to the potato-leek
soup offered him in a steaming porcelain tureen by the
Indian servant who during the daytime waters the gardens at the big Lomas house.

"But what does that have to do with it, Papa? That's like
saying the Eskimos are thankful for not being Mexicans.
Everyone is what he is, and that's that. What's interesting
is watching what happens when we come across somebody
who makes us doubt ourselves. Somebody, nonetheless,
whom we know we need. Somebody we need because they
reject us."

"Come along now, eat. These conversations get more

idiotic every Sunday. The only thing I know is that you didn't marry a Negro, did you? Higinio, bring the enchiladas."

Don José observes Elena, his wife, and me with an air of triumph. Doña Elena, in an effort to revive the languishing conversation, relates all the past week's activities. I look around at the brocaded rosewood furniture, the Chinese vases, the billowy curtains and vicuña rugs in the rectilinear house through whose towering windows one sees the eucalyptus trees shivering in the barranca. Don José smiles as Higinio serves the enchiladas topped with rich cream, and his little green eyes fill with an almost patriotic satisfaction, the same satisfaction I have seen when the President waves the flag on the fifteenth of September. But not the same that makes them tender when he sits down in front of his private jukebox to smoke a cigar and listen to boleros—they are much more moist then. My eyes stop at the sight of Doña Elena's pale hand playing with the soft center of her roll as she wearily enumerates all the cares that have kept her busy since we last saw each other. I listen abstractedly to that cascade of comings and goings, canasta games, visits to the poor children's ward, novenas, charity balls, searches for new curtains, quarrels with the servants, long telephone conversations with her friends, the expected visits to priests, babies, dressmakers, doctors, watch repairmen, pastry cooks, cabinetmakers, and engravers. I am hypnotized by the long, pale, caressing fingers rolling the soft bread into little balls.

"I told them never to come to ask me for money again, because I don't make the decisions about anything. That I would gladly send them to your father's office and his secretary would take care of it . . ."

. . . the languid movements of the slim wrist and the bracelet with the gold and copper medallions of the Christ of the Cubilete, the Holy Year in Rome, and President

Kennedy's visit, that clink against each other as Doña Elena plays with the bread . . .

". . . enough that one gives them moral support, don't you agree? I looked for you Thursday to come to the new film at the Diana with us. I even sent the chauffeur on ahead to stand in line, you know what the lines are like on opening day . . ."

. . . the plump arm, the translucent skin, the veins like a second skeleton, of glass, outlined beneath the smooth whiteness.

". . . I invited your cousin Sandrita and went by to pick her up in the car, but we started playing with the new baby and lost track of time. He's simply precious. She's very hurt that you haven't even called to congratulate her. It wouldn't be any effort to call, Elenita . . ."

. . . the black neckline open on high breasts constrained like some kind of new animal captured on a new continent . . .

". . . after all, we're family. You can't deny your blood. She wanted you and Victor to come to the christening. It's next Saturday. I helped her pick out the little ashtrays they're going to give as a remembrance to the guests. Well, as you see, the time got away from us while we chatted, and the tickets went to waste."

I looked up. Doña Elena was looking at me. She lowered her eyelids and announced that coffee would be served in the living room. Don José excused himself and went to the library, where his electric jukebox plays his favorite records if a slug is put in the slot. We sat down to have our coffee and in the distance the jukebox snorted and began to play "Nosotros" while Doña Elena turned on the television but, placing a finger to her lips, indicated that there would be no sound. We watched the mute images before us: a giveaway program in which a solemn master of ceremonies guided the five contestants—two nervously grinning young girls with beehive hairdos, a very proper housewife, and two dark, mature, melancholy men—toward the check hidden in the crowded studio replete with vases of flowers, fake books, and music boxes.

Elena, sitting next to me in the shadows of this marble-floored, plastic-lilied living room, smiled. I don't know where she got my nickname or what it has to do with me, but she began playing word games with it as she stroked my hand: "Nibelung. No Belong. Noble Hung. Nip Along."

The gray, striped, undulating figures searched for the treasure before our gaze and Elena, curling up, dropped her shoes on the carpet and yawned, while Doña Elena, taking advantage of the darkness, looked at me with those wide, wide, dark-circled, questioning black eyes. She crossed her legs, arranging her skirt over her knees. From the library came snatches of the bolero: *"Nosotros, que tanto nos quisimos"*—We loved each other so—and what was perhaps a grunt or two of digestive stupor from Don José. Doña Elena turned from me to fix her great black eyes on the quavering eucalyptus trees beyond the picture window.

I followed the direction of her glance. Elena yawned and purred, leaning against my knees. I caressed her neck. Behind us, the barranca that crosses Lomas de Chapultepec like a savage wound seemed to glow with hidden light, secretly accentuated by the movement of the night that bent the backs of the trees and loosened their long, pale hair.

"Do you remember Veracruz?" the mother asked the daughter, smiling. But Doña Elena was looking at me. Elena agreed with a murmur, half asleep against my legs, and I answered: "Yes. We've been there many times together."

"Do you like it?" Doña Elena extended her hand and then let it fall in her lap.

"A lot," I said. "They say it's the last Mediterranean city. I like the food. I like the people. I like sitting for hours on end under the open arches, eating rolls and drinking coffee."

"That's where I'm from," she said. For the first time I noticed her dimples.

"Yes. I know."

"But I've lost the accent." She laughed, showing her gums. "I was married when I was twenty-two. After you live in Mexico City awhile, you lose the Veracruz accent. And when you met me, well, I was older."

"Everyone says you and Elena look like sisters."

Her lips were thin but aggressive. "No. I was just remembering the stormy nights on the Gulf. How the sun doesn't want to give up, you know, and gets all mixed up with the storm and everything is bathed in a very pale, very greenish light, and you're suffocating there behind the shutters, waiting for the rain to end. Rain doesn't cool things off in the tropics. It simply makes it hotter. I don't know why the servants had to close the shutters every time a storm was coming. It would have been so beautiful to let it come with the windows open wide."

I lighted a cigarette. "Yes, the rain brings out some very heady odors. The earth releases its perfumes of tobacco and coffee and ripe fruit . . ."

"The bedrooms, too." Doña Elena closed her eyes.

"What?"

"There weren't any closets in those days." Her fingers touched the slight wrinkles around her eyes. "There was a wardrobe in every room, and the servants used to place laurel and oregano leaves in among the clothing. Besides, there were some places the sun never reached, that never dried out. It smelled . . . moldy . . . how shall I say it, musty . . ."

"Yes, I imagine so. I've never lived in the tropics. Do you miss it?"

And now she rubbed her wrists, one against the other, exhibiting the protruding veins of her hands. "Sometimes. It's hard to remember. Can you imagine, though I got married when I was eighteen, everyone considered me an old maid already."

"And that strange light from the barranca reminded you of all those things?"

The woman rose. "Yes. They're the spotlights José ordered installed last week. They look pretty, don't you think?"

"*I* think Elena has gone to sleep."

I tickled Elena's nose; she awakened and we returned to Coyoacán in the MG.

"I'm really sorry about those dreadful Sundays," Elena said as I was leaving for work the following morning. "But what can we do? We have to maintain some link to the family and bourgeois life, even if only for the sake of contrast."

"What are you going to do today?" I asked as I rolled up my blueprints and picked up my portfolio.

Elena bit into a fig, crossed her arms, and stuck out her tongue at a cross-eyed Christ we found once in Guanajuato. "I'm going to paint all morning. Then I'm going to Alejandro's for lunch so I can show him my latest things. At his studio. Yes, it's finished now. Right over in Olivar de los Padres. In the afternoon I'll go to my French class. Perhaps I'll have some coffee and then I'll wait for you at the film club. They're showing that classic film of Western mythology: *High Noon*. I made a date to meet those young blacks tomorrow. They're Black Muslims and I'm *mad* to know what they really think. Do you realize that the only thing we know about them is what the newspapers say. Have you ever spoken to a North American Negro, Nibelung? Then tomorrow afternoon you mustn't think of bothering me. I'm going to shut myself up and read Ner-

val from cover to cover. Don't think for a minute that
Juan's going to make a fool of me again with all that jazz
about the 'soleil noir de la mélancolie,' calling himself a
widower, talking about how disconsolate he is . . . like
Nerval. I've caught on to him and tomorrow night I'm
going to *screw* him . . . thinks he knows literature! Oh
yes, he's giving a masquerade party. We all have to go
dressed as Mexican murals. Oh well, let's get all that
damned folklore over with, once and for all. Buy me some
lilies, Victor, Nibelung-of-my-heart, and, if you wish,
dress as the cruel conquistador Alvarado who branded Indian maidens with burning irons before possessing
them—*Oh, Sade, where is thy whip?* Oh yes, and Wednesday
Miles Davis is playing at the Bellas Artes. He's a little
passé, but at any rate, he excites me—it's a hormonorama.
Get the tickets. Ciao, love."

She kissed my neck, and because of the rolls of blueprints in my hands I couldn't embrace her, but I drove
away with the smell of figs on my neck and the image of
Elena, in my shirt, unbuttoned but tied at the level of her
belly button, tight torero stretch pants, barefoot, preparing to . . . ? was it to read a poem or paint a picture? It
occurred to me that we would have to go on a trip
together soon. That brought us closer than anything. I
reached the Periférico. I don't know why, but instead of
crossing the Altavista overpass toward Desierto de los
Leones, I entered the ring road and then accelerated. Yes,
I do that sometimes. I want to be alone, and race and
laugh when someone roars by, giving me the old "Up
yours, buddy!" And too, perhaps I wanted to keep for a
half hour Elena's image as she said goodbye, her naturalness, her golden skin, her green eyes, her endless projects, and to think how happy I am to be with her, how no
one could be happier by the side of such a lively, modern
woman, one who . . . who . . . who complements me so
well.

I passed a glass factory, a baroque church, a roller coaster, a grove of cypresses. Where have I heard that damn word? Complement. I circle the Petróleos fountain and start up the Paseo de la Reforma. All the cars are moving toward the center of the city reverberating there in the distance beyond an impalpable and suffocating veil. I drive to Lomas de Chapultepec, where at this hour only the servants and wives are home, where husbands have gone to work and children to school, where surely my other Elena, my complement, must await me in her warm bed; Elena of the distrustful, shadowy black eyes, and skin as white and ripe and cushiony and perfumed as clothing in a tropical chest.

A Pure Soul

Juan Luis, I am thinking about you as I take my seat on
the bus that will carry me to the airport. I came early in-
tentionally. I don't want to see the people who will actually fly with us until the last minute. This is the bus for the
Alitalia flight to Milan; it will be an hour before the Air
France passengers to Paris, New York, and Mexico board
their bus. I'm just afraid I will cry or get upset or do
something ridiculous, and then have to endure glances
and whispers for sixteen hours. There's no reason why
anyone has to know anything. You prefer it that way, too,
don't you? I shall always believe it was a private act, that
you didn't do it because . . . I don't know why I'm thinking these things. I don't have the right to explain anything
in your name. Nor, perhaps, in mine either. How will I
ever know, Juan Luis? Do you think I am going to insult
our memories by affirming or denying that perhaps, at
such and such a moment, or over a long period of time—I
don't know how or when you decided, possibly when you
were a child, why not?—you were motivated by dejection,

or sadness, or nostalgia, or hope? It's cold. That icy wind
that passes over the city like the breath of death is blowing
from the mountains. I half bury my face in my lapels to
retain my body heat, though the bus is heated and now is
smoothly pulling away, enveloped in its own vapor. We
leave the station at Cornavin through a tunnel and I know
I will not see again the lake and bridges of Geneva, since
the bus emerges onto the highway behind the station and
moves always away from Lake Leman on the road to the
airport. We are passing through the ugly part of the city
where the seasonal workers live who have come from Italy
and Germany and France to this paradise on which not a
single bomb fell, where no one was tortured or assassinated or betrayed. Even the bus adds to the sensation of
neatness and order and well-being that so attracted your
attention from the moment you arrived, and now as I
clean the steamy window with my hand and see these
wretched houses I think that, in spite of everything, people mustn't live too badly in them. Switzerland after a
while becomes too comfortable, you said in a letter; we
lose the sense of extremes that are so blatant and so as-
saulting in our country. Juan Luis: in your last letter you
didn't need to tell me—I understand without having lived
it myself: that was always our bond—that all that external
order, the punctuality of the trains, honor in every trans-
action, planning ahead in one's job, and saving all of one's
life, demanded an internal disorder as balance. I'm laughing, Juan Luis. Behind a grimace that struggles to hold
back the tears, I begin to laugh, and all the passengers
turn to look at me and whisper among themselves. This is
what I wanted to avoid; at least these people are going to
Milan. I laugh when I think how you left the order of our
home in Mexico for the disorder of your freedom in Switzerland. Do you understand? From security in the land of
bloody daggers to anarchy in the land of the cuckoo clock.
Isn't that funny? I'm sorry. I'm over it now. I try to com-

pose myself by looking at the snow-capped peak of the
Jura, the enormous sheer gray cliff that now seeks in vain
its reflection in the lake born of its waters. You wrote me
that in summer the lake is the eye of the Alps: it reflects
them, but it also transforms them into a vast submerged
cathedral, and you said that when you plunged into the
water you were diving in search of the mountains. Do you
know I have your letters with me? I read them on the
plane that brought me from Mexico and, during the days
I have been in Geneva, in my free moments. Now I will
read them on the return trip. Except that on this crossing
you will accompany me.

We have traveled so much together, Juan Luis. As children we went every weekend to Cuernavaca when my
parents still had that house covered with bougainvillea.
You taught me to swim and to ride a bicycle. On Saturdays we cycled into town, where I learned to know everything through your eyes. "Look at the kites, Claudia; look,
Claudia, thousands of birds in the trees; look, Claudia,
silver bracelets, fancy sombreros, lemon ice, green statues;
come on, Claudia, let's try the wheel of fortune." And for
the New Year's festivities they took us to Acapulco and
you woke me up very early in the morning and we ran to
Hornos Beach because you knew that the sea was at its
best at that hour. That was the only time the snails and oc-
topus, the dark sculptured driftwood, the old bottles,
could be seen hurled forth by the tide, and together we
gathered all we could, though we knew they wouldn't
allow us to take it back to Mexico City, and truly, all those
useless things would never have fit in the car. Strange that
every time I try to remember what you were like at ten, at
thirteen, at fifteen, I think of Acapulco. It must be because during the rest of the year we each went to a different school, and only at the shore, and when we celebrated the turning of one year to another, were all the
hours of the day ours. We played wonderful games there.

On the rock castles where I was a prisoner of the ogres and you scaled the walls with a wooden sword in your hand, yelling and fighting off imaginary monsters to free me. In the pirate galleons—a skiff—where, terrified, I waited for you to end your struggle in the sea with the sharks that menaced me. In the dense jungles of Pie de la Cuesta, where we advanced hand in hand in search of the secret treasure marked on the map we'd found in a bottle. To accompany your actions you hummed background music invented at that very moment: dramatic, a perpetual climax. Captain Blood, Sandokan, Ivanhoe: *your* personality changed with every adventure; I was always the princess besieged, nameless, indistinguishable from her nebulous prototype.

There was only one hiatus: when you were fifteen and I was only twelve and you were embarrassed to be seen with me. I didn't understand, because you looked the same as always to me: slim, strong, tanned, your curly chestnut hair reddened by the sun. But we were friends again the next year, going everywhere together, no longer picking up shells or inventing adventures, but seeking now to prolong a day that began to seem too short and a night forbidden to us, a night that became our temptation, symbol of the new possibilities in a recently discovered, recently begun life. We walked along the rocky Farallón after dinner, holding hands in silence, not looking at the groups playing guitar around a bonfire or at the couples kissing among the rocks. We didn't need to say how painful it was to be around anyone else. As we didn't need to say that the best thing in the world was to walk together in the evening, holding hands, without a word, in silent communion with our secret, that mystery that between us never gave rise to a joke or a snide remark. We were serious but never solemn, remember? And maybe we were good for each other without knowing it, in a way I've

never been able to explain exactly, but that had to do with
the warm sand beneath our bare feet, with the silence of
the sea at night, with the brushing of our thighs as we
walked together, you in your new long, tailored white
pants, I in my new full red skirt. We had changed our way
of dressing, and no longer took part in the jokes, the embarrassment, the violence of our friends. You know, Juan
Luis, that most of them still act as if they were fourteen—
the kind of fourteen-year-olds we never were. *Machismo* is
being fourteen all one's life; it is cruel fear. You know,
because you weren't able to avoid it. As we left our childhood behind and you tried out all the experiences common to your age, you began to avoid me. (I would look
out at you from my window, I watched you go out in a
convertible full of friends and come back late, feeling
sick.) And so I understood when, after years of scarcely
speaking to me, when I enrolled in Arts and Science and
you in Business, you sought me, not at home, which
would have been the natural thing, but at school, and you
asked me to have a cup of coffee one afternoon in the
Mascarones cellar café, hot and packed with students.

You caressed my hand and said, "Forgive me, Claudia."

I smiled and thought that all our childhood was suddenly returning, not to be prolonged, but rather to be
brought to an end, to a kind of recognition that would at
the same time dissipate those years forever.

"For what?" I replied. "I'm happy we can talk again.
That's all I want. We see each other every day, but each
time it was as if the other weren't there. Now I'm happy
we can be friends again, like before."

"We're more than friends, Claudia. We're brother and
sister."

"Yes, but that's an accident. Because we are brother and
sister we loved each other very much when we were children; but we've hardly spoken to each other since."

"I'm going away, Claudia. I've already told my father. He doesn't agree. He thinks I ought to get my degree. But I have to go away."

"Where?"

"I've got a job with the United Nations in Geneva. I can continue my studies there."

"You're doing the right thing, Juan Luis."

You told me what I already knew. You told me you were sick of whorehouses, of learning everything by rote, of the obligation to be *macho*, of patriotism, lip-service religion, the lack of good films, the lack of real women, girls your own age you could live with . . . It was quite a speech, spoken quietly across that table in the Mascarones café.

"It's not possible to live here. I mean it. I don't want to serve either God or the devil; I want to burn the candle at both ends. And you can't do it here, Claudia. Just wanting to *live* makes you a potential traitor; here you're obliged to serve, to take a position; it's a country that won't let you be yourself. I don't want to be 'decent.' I don't want to be courteous, a liar, *muy macho*, an ass-kisser, refined and clever. *There's no country like Mexico* . . . thank God! I don't want to go from brothel to brothel. When you do that, then all your life you are forced to treat women with a kind of brutal, domineering sentimentality because you never learned to really understand them. I don't want that."

"And what does Mother say?"

"She'll cry. It doesn't matter. She cries about everything, what else would you expect?"

"And what about me, Juan Luis?"

He smiled childishly. "You'll come to visit me, Claudia. Swear you'll come see me!"

I not only came to see you; I came to look for you, to take you back to Mexico. And four years ago, when we said goodbye, the only thing I said was: "Think about me. Find a way to be with me always."

Yes, you wrote me begging me to visit you; I have your letters. You found a room with bath and kitchen in the most beautiful spot in Geneva, the Place du Bourg-de-Four. You wrote that it was on the fifth floor, right in the middle of the old city. From there you could see steep roofs, church towers, small windows and narrow skylights, and in the distance the lake fading from sight toward Vevey and Montreux and Chillon. Your letters were filled with the joy of independence. You had to make your bed and clean and get your own breakfast and go down to the dairy next door for milk. And you had your drinks in the café on the plaza. You talked so much about that café. It is called La Clémence and it has an awning with green and white stripes and anyone who *is* anyone in Geneva goes there. It's tiny, six tables facing a bar; waitresses in black serve cassis and say "M'sieudame" to everyone. I sat there yesterday to have a cup of coffee and looked at all those students in their long mufflers and university caps, at Hindu girls with saris askew under winter coats, at diplomats with rosettes in their lapels, at actors who are trying to avoid paying taxes, who take refuge in chalets on the lake shore, at the young Germans, Chileans, Belgians, and Tunisians who work at the ILO. You wrote that there were two Genevas. The ordered conventional city that Stendhal described as a flower without perfume; that's the one where the Swiss live, the backdrop for the other, the city of transients and exiles, a foreign city of chance encounters, of glances and sudden conversations, without the standards the Swiss have imposed upon themselves that then free their guests. You were twenty-three when you arrived here, and I can imagine your enthusiasm.

"But enough of that [you wrote]. I must tell you that I am taking a course in French literature and that there I met . . . Claudia, I can't explain what I feel and I won't even try, because you have always understood me without needing words. Her name is Irene and you can't imagine how beautiful and clever, how *nice* she is. She's studying literature here, and she is French; strange that she is studying the same things you are. Maybe that's why I liked her immediately. Ha ha." I think it lasted a month. I don't remember. It was four years ago. "Marie-José talks too much, but she amuses me. We spent the weekend at Davos and she made me look ridiculous because she is a formidable skier and I'm not worth a damn. They say you have to learn as a child. I confess I got a little uptight and the two of us returned to Geneva Monday as we had left Friday, except that I had a sprained ankle. Isn't that a laugh?" Then spring came. "Doris is English and she paints. I think she has real talent. We took advantage of the Easter holidays to go to Wengen. She says she makes love to stimulate her subconscious, and she leaps out of bed to paint her gouaches with the white peaks of the Jungfrau before her. She opens the windows and takes deep breaths and paints in the nude while I tremble with cold. She laughs a lot and says that I am a tropical creature with arrested development, and serves me kirsch to warm me up." I laughed at Doris the whole year they were seeing each other. "I miss her gaiety, but she decided that one year in Switzerland was enough and she left with her paint boxes and her easels to live on Mykonos. So much the better. She amused me, but the kind of woman who interests me is not a woman like Doris." One went to Greece and another came from Greece. "Sophia is the most beautiful woman I have ever known, I swear it. I know it's a cliché, but she looks like one of the Caryatids. Although not in the common sense. She is a statue because she can be observed from all angles; I have her turn around, nude, in the center of the room. But the important thing is the air that surrounds

her, the space around the statue, do you understand? The
space she *occupies* that permits her to be beautiful. She is
dark, she has very thick eyebrows, and tomorrow, Claudia, she is leaving with some rich guy for the Côte d'Azur.
Desolate, but satisfied, your brother who loves you, Juan
Luis."

And Christine, Consuelo, Sonali, Marie-France, Ingrid
. . . The references were ever more brief, ever more dis-
interested. You became preoccupied with your work and
with talking a lot about your friends there, about their national idiosyncrasies, their dealings with you, with meet-
ings and salaries and trips and even retirement benefits.
You didn't want to tell me that that place, like all places,
in the end creates its own quiet conventions and that you
were falling into the pattern of an international official.
Until a postcard arrived with a view of Montreux and
your cramped writing telling about a meal in a fabulous
restaurant, and lamenting my absence, signed with two
signatures, your scrawl, and an illegible—but carefully
copied below—Claire.

Oh yes. You were gauging this one carefully. You didn't
present her like the others. First it was a new job you were
going to be recommended for. Then that it was involved
with the next meeting of the council. Then, after that,
how you enjoyed working with your new friends but that
you missed the old ones. Then, that the most difficult
thing was getting used to the document officials who
didn't know your work habits. Finally, that you had had
the luck to work with a "compatible" official, and in the
next letter: her name is Claire. And three months before,
you had sent me the postcard from Montreux. Claire,
Claire, Claire.

I answered: "Mon ami Pierrot." So you weren't going to
be honest with me any more. How long has it been Claire?
I wanted to know everything, I demanded to know everything. Juan Luis, hadn't we been best friends before we

were brother and sister? You didn't write for two months. Then came an envelope with a snapshot inside. The two of you with the tall jet of a fountain behind you, and the lake in summertime; you and she leaning against the railing. Your arm around her waist. She, so cute, her arm resting on a flower-filled stone urn. But it wasn't a good snapshot. It was difficult to decide about Claire's face. Slim and smiling, yes, a kind of Marina Vlady, slimmer but with the same smooth long blond hair. Low heels. A sleeveless sweater. Cut low.

You admitted it without explaining anything. First the letters relating facts. She lived in a *pension* on the rue Emile Jung. Her father was an engineer, a widower, and he worked in Neuchâtel. You and Claire were going swimming together at the beach. You had tea at La Clémence. You saw old French films in a theater on the rue Mollard. Saturdays you had dinner at the Plat d'Argent and each of you paid his own check. During the week, you ate in the cafeteria of the Palace of Nations. Sometimes you took the tram and went to France. Facts and names, names, names, like a guidebook: Quai des Berges, Gran' Rue, Cave à Bob, Gare de Cornavin, Auberge de la Mère Royaume, Champelle, Boulevard des Bastions.

Later conversations. Claire's preference for certain films, certain books, concerts, and more names, that river of nouns in your letters (*Drôle de Drame* and *Les Enfants du Paradis,* Scott Fitzgerald and Raymond Radiguet, Schumann and Brahms), and then Claire says, Claire thinks, Claire feels. Carné's characters live their freedom as if it were a shameful conspiracy. Fitzgerald invented the modes, the gestures, and the disillusion that continue to nourish us. The German Requiem celebrates all profane deaths. Yes, I replied. Orozco has died, and there is an enormous retrospective in the Bellas Artes. And so on, round and round, all of it written out, as I had asked you.

"Every time I listen to you, I say to myself that it's as if we realized that we need to consecrate everything that up till now has been condemned, Juan Luis; to turn things inside out. Who mutilated us, my love? There's so little time to recover everything that has been stolen from us. No, I'm not suggesting anything, you know. Let's not make plans. I believe as Radiguet does that the unconscious maneuvers of a pure soul are even more singular than all the possible combinations of vice."

What could I answer? Nothing new here, Juan Luis. Papa and Mama are very sad that you won't be here with us for their silver wedding anniversary. Papa has been promoted to vice president of the insurance company and he says that's his best anniversary present. Mama, poor thing, invents some new illness every day. The first television station is broadcasting. I'm studying for finals for my junior year. I dream a little about everything that's happening to you; I pretend to myself I get it out of books. Yesterday I was telling Federico everything you're doing and seeing and reading and hearing, and we think perhaps if we pass our exams we could come visit you. Aren't you planning to come back someday? You could during your next vacation, couldn't you?

You wrote that fall was different now you were with Claire. On Sundays you often went for walks, holding hands, in silence; the scent of decaying hyacinths still lingered in the parks, but now it was the odor of burning leaves that pursued you during those long walks that reminded you of ours years ago on the beach, because neither you nor Claire dared break the silence, no matter what came to your minds, no matter what the enigma of overlapping seasons with their juxtaposition of jasmine and dead leaves suggested to you. In the end, silence. Claire, Claire—you wrote me—you have understood everything. I have what I always had. Now I can possess it. I've found you again, Claire.

I said again in my next letter that Federico and I were studying together for an exam and that we were going to Acapulco for the last days of the year. But I crossed that out before I sent you the letter. In yours you never asked who Federico was—and if you could ask me today, I wouldn't know how to answer. When vacation came, I said I would not accept his calls any more; I wouldn't see him at school any more. I went alone, with my parents, to Acapulco. I didn't tell you anything about that. I didn't write for several months, but your letters continued to arrive. That winter, Claire came to live with you in the room on Bourg-de-Four. Why think about the letters that came after that? They're here in my purse. "Claire, everything is new. We had never been together at dawn. Before, those hours meant nothing; they were a dead part of the day, and now I wouldn't exchange them for anything. We've always been so close, during our long walks, at the theater, in restaurants, at the beach, making up adventures, but we always lived in separate rooms. Do you know what I used to do, alone, thinking about you? Now I don't waste those hours. I spend the whole night close to you, my arms around your waist, your shoulder pressed to my chest, waiting for you to wake. You know that, and you turn toward me and smile with your eyes closed, Claire, as I turn back the sheet, I forget the places you have warmed through the night and I ask myself if this isn't what we always wanted, from the beginning, when we played and walked in silence, holding hands. We had to sleep beneath the same roof, in our own house, isn't that true? Why don't you write me, Claudia? I love you, Juan Luis."

You may remember how I teased you. It wasn't the same thing to love on a beach or in a hotel surrounded by lakes and snow as it was to live together every day. Besides, you were working in the same office. You'd end up boring each other. The novelty would wear off. Waking up together. Actually, it wasn't very pleasant. She will see how you brush your teeth. You will see her take off her makeup, cream her face, put on her garter belt . . . I think you've done the wrong thing, Juan Luis. Weren't you searching for your independence? Why have you taken on such a burden? If that's what you had in mind, you might as well have stayed in Mexico. But apparently it's difficult to escape the conventions in which we have been brought up. In the long run, although you haven't followed the formula completely, you're doing what Mama and Papa and everyone else has always expected of you. You've become a man of routine. After all the good times we had with Doris and Sophia and Marie-José. What a shame.

We didn't write each other for a year and a half. My life didn't change at all. My studies became a little useless, repetitive. How can they *teach* you literature? Once they put me in touch with a few things, I knew that I would be going my own way, I would read and write and study on my own. I went on going to class just for the sake of discipline, because I had to finish what I had begun. It's so foolish and pedantic when they go on explaining things you already know, with phony diagrams and illustrations. That's the bad thing about being ahead of your teachers, and they're aware of it but hide it to keep their jobs. We were coming to Romanticism and I was already reading Firbank and Rolfe and I had even discovered William Golding. I had my professors a little scared, and my only satisfaction during that time was the praise I received at college: Claudia has real promise. I spent more and more time locked in my room, I arranged it to my taste, put my books in order, hung my reproductions, set up my record player, and Mama finally got tired of telling me that I should meet boys and go out dancing. They left me alone. I changed my wardrobe a little, from the cotton prints you knew to white blouses and dark skirts, tailored suits—

outfits that make me feel a little more serious, more severe, more distant.

It seems we've arrived at the airport. The radar antennas are revolving and I stop talking with you. It's going to be an unpleasant moment. The passengers are stirring. I take my handbag and makeup case and my coat. I sit waiting for the others to get off. It's humid and cold and the fog conceals the mountains. It isn't raining, but millions of unformed, invisible droplets hang in the air: I feel them on my skin. I smooth my straight blond hair. I enter the building and walk toward the airline office. I give my name and the clerk nods. He asks me to follow him. We walk along a long, well-lighted corridor and emerge into the icy afternoon. We move across a long strip of pavement that ends at a kind of hangar. I am walking with my fists clenched. The clerk does not attempt to make conversation. He precedes me, a little ceremoniously. We enter the storage room. It smells of damp wood, of straw and tar. There are many crates lined up in orderly fashion, as well as rows of barrels, and even a small dog in a cage, barking. Your box is partly hidden behind some others. The clerk points it out to me, bowing respectfully. I touch the edge of the coffin and for several moments I stand there without a word. My weeping is buried deep inside my belly, but it is as if I were crying. The clerk is waiting, and when he thinks it seemly, he shows me the various papers I have been negotiating for during the last few days, the permits and authorizations from the police, the department of health, the Mexican consulate, and the airline. He asks me to sign the final embarkation documents. I do it, and he licks the gummed back of some labels and affixes them to the coffin, sealing it. I touch the gray lid once more and we go back to the central building. The clerk murmurs his condolences and says goodbye.

After clearing the documents with the airline and the

Swiss authorities, I go up to the restaurant, with my
boarding pass in my hand, and I sit down and order a cup
of coffee. I am sitting next to a large window and I can
see the planes appearing and disappearing on the runway. They fade into the fog or emerge from it, but the
noise of their engines precedes them or lingers behind
like the wake of a ship. They frighten me. Yes, you know
I am deathly afraid of them and I don't want to think
what this return trip with you will be like, in the middle of
winter, showing in every airport the documents with your
name and the permits that allow them to pass you
through. They bring my coffee and I take it black; it's
what I needed. My hand does not tremble as I drink it.

Nine weeks ago I tore open your first letter in a year
and a half and spilled my cup of coffee on the rug. I
stooped hurriedly to wipe it up with my skirt, and then I
put on a record and wandered around the room looking
at book jackets, my arms crossed; I even read a few lines
of poetry slowly, stroking the covers of the book, sure of
myself, far removed from your still unread letter con-
cealed in the torn envelope lying on the arm of the chair.

> Sweet souvenirs of love now sadly pondered,
> Yes, sweet they seemed when God did so assign,
> In memory joined and bound, mine not to sunder,
> With memory, too, they work my death's design.

"Of course, we've quarreled. She goes out slamming the
door behind her and I almost weep with rage. I try to get
interested in something but I can't and I go out to look
for her. I know where she is. Across the street, at La
Clémence, drinking and smoking nervously. I go down
the creaking stairs and out into the plaza and she looks at
me across the distance and pretends not to notice. I cross
the garden and walk slowly up to the highest level of
Bourg-de-Four, my fingers brushing the iron banister; I
reach the café and sit down beside her in one of the

wicker chairs. We are in the open air; in summer the café spills out onto the sidewalk and one can hear the music from the carillon of St.-Pierre. Claire is talking with the waitress. They are making small talk about the weather in that odious Swiss singsong. I wait until Claire stubs out her cigarette in the ashtray and I do the same, so as to touch her fingers. She looks at me. Do you know how, Claudia? As *you* looked at me, high on the rocks at the beach, waiting for me to save you from the ogre. You had to pretend you didn't know whether I was coming to save you or to kill you in the name of your jailer. But sometimes you couldn't contain your laughter and the fiction was shattered for an instant. The quarrel began because of my carelessness. Claire accused me of being careless and of creating a moral problem for her. What were we to do? It would have helped if I had had an immediate answer. But no, I retreated into my shell, silent and uncommunicative, and didn't even try to avoid the situation and do something intelligent. There were books and records in the house, but I set myself to working some crossword puzzles.

"*You* have to decide, Juan Luis. Please."

"I'm thinking."

"Don't be stupid. I'm not referring to that. I'm talking about *everything*. Are we going to spend our whole lives classifying documents for the United Nations? Or are we just living some in-between step that will lead to something better, something we don't know about yet? I'm willing to do anything, Juan Luis, but I can't make the decisions by myself. Tell me our life together and our work is just an adventure, and it will be all right with me. Tell me they're both permanent; that will be all right, too. But we can't act any longer as if our work is transitory and our love permanent, or vice versa, do you understand what I'm saying?"

"How was I going to tell her, Claudia, that her problem

was completely beyond my comprehension? Believe me, sitting there in La Clémence, watching the young people riding by on bicycles, listening to the laughter and murmurs of those around us, with the bells of the cathedral chiming their music, believe me, little sister, I fled from this whole confining world. I closed my eyes and sank into myself, I refined in the darkness of my soul my most secret knowledge; I tuned all the strings of my sensitivity so that the least movement of my soul would set them vibrating; I stretched my perception, my prophecies, the whole trauma of the present, like a bow, so as to shoot into the future, which wounded, would be revealed. The arrow flew from the bow, but there was no bull's-eye, Claudia, there was nothing in the future, and all that painful internal construction—my hands felt numb from the effort—tumbled down like sand castles at the first assault of the waves, not lost, but returning to that ocean we call memory; to my childhood, to our games, our beach, to a joy and warmth that everything that followed could only imitate, try to prolong, fuse with projects for the future and reproduce with present surprise. Yes, I told her it was all right; we would look for a larger apartment. Claire is going to have a baby."

She herself wrote me a letter in that handwriting I had seen only on the postcard from Montreux. "I know how important you are to Juan Luis, how the two of you grew up together, and all the rest. I want very much to see you and I'm sure we will be good friends. Believe me when I say I already know you. Juan Luis talks so much about you that sometimes I get a little jealous. I hope you'll be able to come see us someday. Juan Luis is doing very well in his job and everyone likes him very much. Geneva is small but pleasant. We've become fond of the city for reasons you can guess and here we will make our life. I can still work a few months; I'm only two months pregnant. Your sister, Claire."

And the recent snapshot fell from the envelope. You've gained weight, and you call my attention to it on the back of the photo: "Too much fondue, Sis." And you're getting bald, just like Papa. And she's very beautiful, very Botticelli, with her long blond hair and coquettish beret. Have you gone mad, Juan Luis? You were a handsome young man when you left Mexico. Look at you. Have you looked at yourself? Watch your diet. You're only twenty-seven years old and you look forty. And what are you reading, Juan Luis, what interests you? Crossword puzzles? You mustn't betray yourself, please, you know I depend on you, on your growing with me, I can't go ahead without you. You promised you were going to go on studying there; that's what you told Papa. The routine work is tiring you out. All you want to do is get to your apartment and read the newspaper and take off your shoes. Isn't that true? You don't say it, but I know it's true. Don't destroy yourself, please. I have remained faithful. I'm keeping our childhood alive. It doesn't matter to me that you're far away. But we must remain united in what matters most, we mustn't concede anything to demands that we be anything other (do you remember?) than love and intelligence and youth and silence. They want to maim us, to make us like themselves; they can't tolerate us. Do not serve them, Juan Luis, I beg you, don't forget what you told me that afternoon in the Mascarones café. Once you take the first step in that direction, everything is lost; there is no return. I had to show your letter to our parents. Mama got very sick. High blood pressure. She's in the cardiac ward. I hope not to have to give you bad news in my next letter. I think about you, I remember you, I know you won't fail me.

Two letters came. First, the one you sent me, telling me that Claire had had an abortion. Then the one you sent Mama announcing that you were going to marry Claire within the month. You hoped we would all be able to come to the wedding. I asked Mama to let me keep her letter with mine. I put them side by side and studied your handwriting to see if they were both written by the same person.

"It was a quick decision, Claudia. I told her it was too soon. We're young and we have the right to live a while longer without responsibilities. Claire said that was fine. I don't know whether she understood everything I said to her. But you do, don't you?"

"I love this girl, I'm sure of it. She's been good and understanding with me even though at times I've made her suffer; neither of you will be ashamed that I would want to make it up to her. Her father is a widower; he is an engineer and lives in Neuchâtel. He approves and will come to the wedding. I hope that you, Papa, and Claudia can be with us. When you know Claire you will love her as much as I, Mama."

Three weeks later Claire committed suicide. One of your friends at work called us; he said that one afternoon she had asked for permission to leave the office; she had a headache; she went to an early movie and you looked for her that night, as always, in the apartment; you waited for her, and then you rushed about the city, but you couldn't find her; she was dead in the theater, she had taken the Veronal before she went in and she had sat alone in the first row, where no one would bother her; you called Neuchâtel, you wandered through the streets and restaurants once more, and you sat in La Clémence until they closed. It was the next day before they called you from the morgue and you went to see her. Your friend told us that we ought to come for you, make you return to Mexico; you were mad with grief. I told our parents the truth. I showed them your last letter. They were stunned for a moment and then Papa said he would never allow you in the house again. He shouted that you were a criminal.

I finish my coffee and a waiter points toward where I

am seated. A tall man, with the lapels of his coat turned up, nods and walks toward me. It is the first time I have seen that tanned face, the blue eyes and white hair. He asks if he may sit down and asks if I am your sister. I say yes. He says he is Claire's father. He does not shake hands. I ask him if he wants a cup of coffee. He shakes his head and takes a pack of cigarettes from his overcoat pocket. He offers me one. I tell him I don't smoke. He tries to smile and I put on my dark glasses. He puts his hand in his pocket again and takes out a piece of paper. He places it, folded, on the table.

"I have brought you this letter."

I try to question him with raised eyebrows.

"It's signed by you. It's addressed to my daughter. It was on Juan Luis's pillow the morning they found him dead in his apartment."

"Oh yes, I wondered what had become of that letter. I looked for it everywhere."

"Yes, I thought you would want to keep it." Now he smiles as if he already knew me. "You're very cynical. Don't worry. Why should you? There's nothing anyone can do now."

He rises without saying goodbye. The blue eyes look at me with sadness and compassion. I try to smile, and I pick up the letter. The loudspeaker:

". . . le départ de son vol numéro 707 . . . Paris, Gander, New York, et Mexico. . . . priés de se rendre à la porte numéro 5."

I take my things, adjust my beret, and go down to the departure gate. I am carrying my purse and the makeup case and the boarding pass in my hands, but I manage, between the door and the steps of the airplane, to tear the letter and throw the pieces into the cold wind, into the fog that will perhaps carry them to the lake where you dived, Juan Luis, in search of a mirage.

These Were Palaces

To Luise Rainer

No one believed her when she began saying that the dogs were coming closer, batty old bag, crazy old loon she was, muttering to herself all day long, what nightmares she must have; after what she'd done to her daughter she couldn't help but have bad nights. Besides, old people's brains get drier and drier until there's nothing left but a shriveled little nut rattling around like a marble in their hollow heads. But Doña Manuelita is so virtuous, she doesn't just water her own flowers, she waters all the flowers on the second floor, every morning you can see her carrying her green gasoline tin, her yellowed fingers sprinkling water over the big clay pots of geraniums lining the iron railing, every evening you see her slipping the covers over the bird cages so the canaries can sleep in quiet.

Some say, isn't Doña Manuelita the most peaceful person you've ever known? What makes people say bad things about her? Old, and all alone, she never does anything out of the ordinary, never calls attention to herself.

The flowerpots in the morning, the bird cages in the evening. About nine, she goes out to do her shopping at La Merced market, and on the way back she stops in the big square of the Zócalo and goes into the Cathedral to pray for a while. Then she comes back to the old palace, a tenement now, and fixes her meal. Fried beans, warmed-over tortillas, fresh tomatoes, mint and onion, shredded chilis: the odors wafting out of Señora Manuela's kitchen are the same as those borne on the smoke from all the meals cooked over old charcoal-burning braziers. All alone, she eats, and stares at the black grate awhile, and rests, she must rest. They say she's earned it. All those years a servant in a rich man's house, a lifetime, you might say.

After the siesta, about dusk, she goes out again, all stooped over, her basket filled with dry tortillas, and that's when the dogs begin to gather. It's only natural. As she walks along she throws them the tortillas, and the dogs know it and follow her. When she can get enough together to buy a chicken, she saves the bones and throws them to the dogs as they follow her down La Moneda Street. The butcher says she shouldn't do it, chicken bones are bad for dogs, they can choke on them, chicken bones splinter and pierce the intestines. Then all the badmouths say that's proof that Doña Manuelita is an evil woman, look at that, luring the dogs just to kill them.

She returns about seven, soaked to the bone in the rainy season, her shoes gray with dust when it's dry. That's how everyone always thinks of her, bone-white, shrouded in dust between October and April, and between May and September a soppy mess, her shawl plastered to her head, raindrops dripping from her nose and trickling down the furrows of her eyes and cheeks and off the white hairs on her chin. She comes back from her adventures in the black blouse and flapping skirts and black stockings she always hangs out in the night air to dry.

She's the only one who dares to dry her clothes at night.
What did I tell you, she's mad as a hatter, what if it rains,
then what good does it do? There's no sun at night. And
there are thieves. Never you mind. She hangs her soaked
rags on the communal clotheslines that stretch in all directions across the patio of the building. I'll let them hang in
the night air, the gossips imagine Doña Manuelita saying.
Because the truth is, no one's ever heard her speak. And
no one's ever seen her sleep. Suppositions. Doña Manuela's clothes disappear from the clothesline before anyone's up. She's never been seen at the washtubs, kneeling
beside the other women, scrubbing, soaping, gossiping.

"She reminds me of a lonely old queen, forgotten by everyone," little Luisito used to say before he'd been forbidden to see her, or even speak to her.

"When she's coming up the stone staircase, I can imagine how this was a great palace, Mother, how a long time
ago very powerful and wealthy gentlemen lived here."

"I don't want you to have anything to do with her any
more. Remember what happened to her daughter. You,
more than anyone, ought to remember."

"I never knew her daughter."

"She wants you to take her place. I won't have that, that
would be the last straw, the old witch."

"She's the only one who ever takes me out. Everyone
else is always too busy."

"Your little sister's big enough now. She can take you."

So, following his directions, Rosa María pushed little
Luisito in his wheelchair, wherever he wanted to go. Toward Tacuba Street if what he wanted to see were the old
stone and volcanic rock palaces of the Viceregency, wide
porticos studded with nail heads as big as coins, balconies
of wrought iron, niches sheltering stone Virgins, high gut-
ters and drains of verdigris copper. Toward the squat,
faded little houses along Jesús Carranza Street if, on the

other hand, it was his whim to think about Doña Manue-lita. He was the only one who'd ever been in the old woman's room and kitchen, the only one who could de-scribe them. There wasn't much to describe, that was the interesting thing. Behind the doors that were also win-dows—the wooden kitchen door hung with sheer curtains, the door to her room covered by a sheet strung on copper rods—there was nothing worthy of comment. Just a cot. Everyone else decorated their rooms with calendars, al-tars, religious prints, newspaper clippings, flowers, soccer pennants and bullfight posters, paper Mexican flags, snapshots taken at fairs, at the Shrine of the Guadalupe. But not Manuelita. Nothing. A kitchen with clay utensils, a bag of charcoal, food for her daily meal, and the one room with its cot. Nothing more.

"You've been there. What does she have there? What's she hiding?"

"Nothing."

"What does she do?"

"Nothing. Everything she does she does outside her room. Anyone can see her—the flowerpots, the shopping, the dogs and the canaries. Besides, if you don't trust her, why do you let her water your geraniums and cover your birds for the night? Aren't you afraid your flowers will wither and your little birds will die?"

It's hard to believe how slowly the outings with Rosa María go. She's thirteen years old but not half as strong as Doña Manuelita. At every street corner she has to ask for help to get the wheelchair onto the sidewalk. The old woman had been able to do it by herself. With her, if they went down Tacuba, Donceles, and Gonzales Obregón to the Plaza of Santo Domingo, it was little Luisito who did the talking, it was he who imagined the city as it had been in colonial times, it was he who told the old woman how the Spanish city had been constructed, laid out like a chessboard above the ruins of the Aztec capital. As a little boy, he told Doña Manuelita, they'd sent him to school, it had been torture, the cruel jokes, the invalid, the cripple, his wheelchair tipped over, the cowards laughing and running away, he lying there waiting for his teachers to pick him up. That's why he'd asked them not to send him, to let him stay home, kids can be cruel, it was true, it wasn't just a saying, he'd learned that lesson, now they left him alone reading at home, the rest of them went out to work, except his mother, Doña Lourdes, and his sister Rosa María, all he wanted was to be left to read by himself, to educate himself, please, for the love of God. His legs weren't going to get well in any school, he swore he'd study better by himself, honest, couldn't they take up a collection to buy him his books, later he'd go to a vocational school, he promised, but only when it could be among men you could talk to and ask for a little compassion. Children don't know what compassion is.

But Doña Manuelita knew, yes, she knew. When she pushed his wheelchair toward the ugly parts of their neighborhood, toward the empty lots along Canal del Norte, turning right at the traffic circle of Peralvillo, it was she who did the talking, and pointed out the dogs to him, there were more dogs than men in these parts, stray dogs without masters, without collars, dogs born God knows where, born of a fleeting encounter between dogs exactly like each other, a male and a bitch locked together after the humping, strung together like two links of a scabrous chain, while the children of the neighborhood laughed and threw stones at them, and then, separated forever, forever, forever, how was the bitch to remember her mate, when alone, in one of a hundred empty lots, she whelped a litter of pups abandoned the day after they were born? How could the bitch remember her own children?

"Imagine, little Luis, imagine if dogs could remember one another, imagine what would happen . . ."

A secret shiver filled with cold pleasure ran down little Luisito's spine when he watched the boys of Peralvillo stoning the dogs, chasing them, provoking angry barking, then howls of pain, finally, whimpering, as, heads bloody, tails between their legs, eyes yellow, hides mangy, they fled into the distance until they were lost in the vacant lots beneath the burning sun of all the mornings of Mexico. The dogs, the boys, all lacerated by the sun. Where did they eat? Where did they sleep?

"You see, little Luis, if you're hungry, you can ask for food. A dog can't ask. A dog must take his food anywhere he can find it."

But it was painful for little Luis to ask, and he did have to ask. They took up the collection and bought his books. He knew that a long time ago in the big house in Orizaba they'd had more books than they could ever read, books his great-grandfather had ordered from Europe and then gone to Veracruz to wait for, a shipment of illustrated magazines and huge books of adventure tales that he'd read to his children during the long nights of the tropical rainy season. As the family grew poor, everything had been sold, and finally they'd ended up in Mexico City because there were more opportunities there than in Orizaba, and because his father'd been given a place as archivist at the Ministry of Finance. The building where they lived was close to the National Palace and his father could walk every day and save the bus fare. Almost everyone who worked in the office wasted two or three hours a day coming to the Zócalo from their houses in remote suburbs and returning after work. Little Luis watched how the memories, the family traditions, faded away with the years. His older brothers hadn't graduated from secondary school, they didn't read, one worked for the Department of the Federal District and the other in the shoe department at the Palacio de Hierro. Of course, among them they made enough money to move to a little house in Lindavista, but that was a long way away, and besides, here in the old building on La Moneda they had the best rooms, a living room and three bedrooms, more than anyone else had. And in a place that had been a palace centuries ago little Luis found it easier to imagine things, and remember.

If only dogs could remember each other, Doña Manuelita said. But we forget, too, we forget other people and forget about our own family, little Luisito replied. At dinnertime he liked to remember the big house in Orizaba, the white façade with wrought-iron work at the windows, the ground behind the house plunging toward a decaying ravine odorous of mangrove and banana trees. In the depths of the ravine you could hear the constant sound of a rushing stream, and beyond, high above, you could see the huge mountains ringing Orizaba, looming so close they frightened you. It was like living beside a giant crowned with fog. And how it rained. It never stopped raining.

The others looked at him strangely; his father, Don Raúl, lowered his head, his mother sighed and shook hers, one brother laughed aloud, the other made a circling motion at his brow with his index finger. Little Luisito was "touched," where did he get such ideas, why he'd never been in Orizaba, he was born and bred in Mexico City, after all, the family'd come to the city forty years ago. Rosa María hadn't even heard him, she just kept eating, her shoe-button eyes were as hard as stone, and held no memories. How it pained little Luisito to beg for everything, for books and for memories. I don't forget, I collect postcards, there's the trunk filled with old snapshots, it's used as a chest, I know everything that's inside.

Doña Manuela knew all this, too, because little Luisito had told her, before they'd forbidden her to take him out for a walk. When she was alone in her room, lying on her cot, she tried to communicate silently with the boy, remembering the same things he remembered.

"Just imagine, Manuelita, how this building must have looked before."

That was little Luisito's other memory, as if the past of that big house now shared by twelve families complemented the memory of the one and only house, the house in Orizaba, the house that belonged to only one family, his family, when they'd had an important name.

"Just imagine, these were palaces."

The old woman made a great effort to remember everything the boy told her and then imagine, as he did and when he did, a majestic palace: the entryway before there was a lottery stand, the carved marble façade stripped of cheap clothing stores, the bridal shop, the photographer's shop, and the soft-drinks stand, free of the advertisements that disfigured the ancient nobility of the building. A clean, austere, noble palace, a murmuring fountain in the center of the patio instead of the clotheslines and washtubs, the great stone stairway, the ground floor reserved for the servants, the horses, the kitchens, the grain storerooms, and the smell of straw and jelly.

And on the main floor, what did the boy remember? Oh, great salons smelling of wax and varnish, harpsichords, he said, balls and banquets, bedchambers with cool brick floors, beds draped with mosquito netting, mirrored wardrobes, oil lamps. This is the way that Doña Manuelita, alone in her room, spoke with little Luis, after they'd been separated. This is the way she communicated with him, by remembering the things he remembered and forgetting about her own past, the house where she'd worked all her life until she was an old woman, General Vergara's house in the Roma district, twenty-five years of service, until they'd moved out to Pedregal. There hadn't been time to win the friendship of young Plutarco; the new mistress, Señora Evangelina, had died only a few years after marrying the General's son, and her mistress Clotilde before that; Manuela had been only fifty when she was fired, she reminded the General of too many things, that's why he fired her. But he was generous. He continued to pay her rent in the tenement on La Moneda.

"Live your last years in peace, Manuela," General Vergara had said to her. "Every time I see you I think of my Clotilde. Goodbye."

Doña Manuelita chewed on a yellowed, knotted finger as she remembered her employer's words, those memories kept intruding into the memories she shared with little Luisito, they had nothing to do with them, Doña Clotilde was dead, she was a saint, the General had been influential in Calles's government, so in the midst of the religious persecution Mass was celebrated in the cellar of the house; every day Doña Clotilde, the servant Manuelita, and Manuelita's daughter, Lupe Lupita, went to confession and received Communion. The priest would arrive at the house in lay clothes, carrying a kit like a doctor's bag containing his vestments, the ciborium, the wine and the hosts, a Father Téllez, a young priest, a saint, whom the sainted Doña Clotilde had saved from death, giving him refuge when all his friends had gone before the firing wall, shot in the early morning with their arms opened out in a cross; she'd seen the photographs in *El Universal.*

That's why she'd felt so bad when the General fired her, it was as if he'd wanted to kill her. She'd survived Doña Clotilde, she remembered too many things, the General wanted to be left alone with his past. Maybe he was right, maybe it was better for both of them, the employer and the servant, to go their own ways with their secret memories, without serving as the other's witness, better that way. She again gnawed at her finger. The General still had his son and grandson, but Manuelita had lost her daughter, she would never see her again, all because she'd brought her to this accursed tenement, she'd had to break her little Lupita's solitude, in her employer's home she'd never seen anyone, she had no reason ever to leave the ground floor, she could get around quite easily in her wheelchair. But in this building there was no escape, all the overhelpful people, all the nosy people, everyone carrying her up and down stairs, let her get some sun, let her get some air, let her get out on the street, they took her from me, they stole her from me, they'll pay for it. Doña Manuela's few remaining teeth drew blood. She must think about little Luisito. She was never going to see Lupe Lupita again.

"Take me out to the empty lots where all the dogs gather," little Luisito directed Rosa María.

Some masons were constructing a wall on the vacant lot along Canal del Norte. But they'd just begun to raise the cement partition on one side of the lot, and little Luisito told Rosa María to go down the other side, away from the workmen. There were no children today, but a gang of teenagers in jeans and striped jerseys, all laughing, they'd caught a dog as gray as the wall. The workmen were watching from a distance, wielding trowels and mortar, watching and elbowing one another from time to time. Beyond them, the sound of the armada of trucks choking the traffic circle of Peralvillo: buses, building-supply trucks, open exhausts, smoke, desperate horns, implacable noise. It had been in Peralvillo that little Luisito had been hit by the tram. The last streetcar in Mexico City, and it had to hit him. The teenagers clamped the dog's muzzle shut; while a few held its legs, one of them laboriously cut off its tail, a mass of blood and gray hairs, better to have chopped it off with a machete, quick and clean.

They hacked at the ragged stump, leaving threads of flesh and a jet of blood spurting into the animal's throbbing anus. But the other dogs of this pack that gathered every morning on the empty lots where the workmen had begun the wall hadn't run away. They were all there, all the dogs together, at a distance, but together, watching the gray dog's torture, silent, muzzles frothing, dogs of the sun, look, Rosa María, they're not running away, and they're not just standing there stupefied waiting for it to happen to them next, no, Rosa María, look, they're looking at each other, they're telling each other something, they're remembering what's happening to one of their own, Doña Manuelita's right, these dogs are going to remember the pain of one of their own pack, how one of them suffered at the hands of a bunch of cowardly teenagers, but Rosa María's shoe-button eyes were like stone, without memory.

About one o'clock Doña Manuelita peered through the curtains on her door as the girl returned, pushing her brother in his chair. Even from a distance she could see the dust on the girl's shoes and she knew that they'd gone to the empty lots where the dogs gathered. In the late afternoon the old woman covered her head with her shawl, filled her shopping bag with dry tortillas and old rags, and went out to the street.

A dog was waiting for her in the doorway. It stared at her with its glassy eyes and whined, asking her to follow. When they reached the corner of Vidal Alcocer, she was joined by five more dogs, and all along Guatemala, by dogs of every breed, brown, spotted, black, about twenty of them, milling around Doña Manuelita as she portioned out pieces of dry tortilla, already turning green. They surrounded her and then preceded her, showing her the way, they followed her, nudging her softly with their muzzles, their ears erect, until they reached the iron fence before the Sagrario, the chapel of the Metropolitan Cathedral. From a distance, the old woman could see the gray dog lying beside the carved wooden door beneath the baroque eaves of the portal.

Doña Manuela and her dogs stepped into the great stone-floored atrium, she sat beside the injured dog, you're the one they call Cloudy, aren't you, poor half-blind fellow, well, just be thankful you have that one blind eye as blue as the sky and you can see only half the world, dear God, just look what they've done to you, come here, Cloudy, here on my lap, let me bandage your tail, bastards, picking on you for their fun, sons of your poor bitching mothers, just because dogs can't defend themselves or talk or call for help, I don't know any more whether they do these things to dumb animals to keep from doing them to each other or whether they're only practicing what they plan to do tomorrow, who knows, who knows, let's see now, Cloudy, poor old puppy, why I've known you since the day you were born, left on a rubbish heap, blind in that eye since birth, your mother didn't have time to lick you clean, right away you were tossed into the garbage and that's where I found you, there now, is that better? poor fellow, the cowards would pick on you, on you the most helpless of all my dogs, let's go give thanks, let's go pray for the well-being of all dogs, let's go pray, there, in the house of the Lord our God, Creator of all things.

Quietly, bent over, petting the dogs, more stooped than usual, with sweet words, Doña Manuela entered the Cathedral of Mexico that afternoon with her twenty dogs surrounding her; they managed to reach the main altar, it was the best hour, no one around but a few devout old women and two or three peasants staring at the ceiling with their arms uplifted. Doña Manuelita knelt before the altar, praying aloud, a miracle, God, give my dogs a voice, give them some way to defend themselves, give them some way to remember each other and remember those who have tortured them, God, you who suffered on the cross, have mercy on these dumb animals, do not forsake them, give them the strength to defend themselves, since you did not give men mercy or teach them to treat these poor animals with tenderness. Oh, God, my Jesus, God and True Man, show that you are all of these, and give equally to all your creatures, not the same riches, no, not that, I'm not asking that much, only equal mercy so they can understand each other, or if not that, equal strength to defend themselves, don't give more love to some of your creatures than to others, God, because those you have loved least will love you less, and they will say you are the devil.

Several of the women praying shushed her and one exasperatedly asked for silence and another cried, Respect the House of God, and then acolytes and two priests came running toward the altar, aghast, what sacrilege, a mad woman and a pack of mangy dogs. None of this had any effect on Doña Manuela, she'd never experienced such exaltation, she'd never spoken such beautiful and heartfelt words, almost as beautiful as those her daughter, Lupe, knew how to speak. The old woman stood there, so happy, more than bathed, feeling embalmed in the afternoon light filtering down from the highest domes, multiplied in reflections from silver organ pipes, golden frames, humble vigil lights, and the glowing varnish of the rows of pews. And God, to whom she'd been speaking, was answering her, He was saying:

"Manuela, you must believe in me in spite of the fact that the world is cruel and unjust. That is the trial I send you. If the world were perfect, you would have no need to believe in me, do you understand?"

But now the priests and acolytes were dragging her away from the altar, shooing the dogs; one maddened acolyte was beating the animals with a crucifix and another was dousing them with incense to stupefy them. All the dogs began barking at once and Doña Manuela, pushed and pummeled, looked at the crystal coffins wherein lay the wax statues of Christs more ill-treated than she or the dog Cloudy. Blood from your thorns, blood from your side, blood from your feet and hands, blood from your eyes, Christ of my heart, look what they have done to you, what are our sufferings compared to yours? Then why won't you allow me and my dogs to speak of our little pains here in your house that was built large enough to hold all your pain and ours?

Flung to her knees on the flat stones of the atrium, surrounded by her dogs, she was humiliated because she'd been unable to explain the truth to the priests and the acolytes, and then she was ashamed as she looked up and met the staring, uncomprehending eyes of little Luisito and Rosa María. Their mother, Señora Lourdes, was with them. But her eyes, oh yes, her eyes had something to say: look! that's the proof of what kind of woman old Manuela is, just what I've always said, we'll have to cast her from our building the way the priest cast her from the temple. In the shocked recrimination of those eyes Doña Manuelita saw menace, gossip, everyone remembering once again what she'd been able to forget and make others forget by her discretion, her decency, her helpful everyday chores, watering the geraniums, covering the canaries' cages.

Luisito looked quickly from his mother's eyes to Señora Manuela's. With both hands on the wheels he pushed his chair to where the old woman lay sprawled. He held out his hand, offering her a handkerchief.

"Here, Manuela. You've hurt your forehead."

"Thank you, but don't get yourself in trouble over me. Go back to your mother. Look at the terrible way she's staring at us."

"It doesn't matter. Please forgive me."

"But for what, child?"

"Every time I go out to the vacant lots and see how they treat the dogs, I feel good."

"But, Luis, child."

"I think to myself, if it weren't for them I'd be the one getting the beating. As if the dogs stood between those boys and me, suffering in my place. I'm the biggest coward of all, aren't I, Manuela?"

"Who knows," the stunned woman murmured as she dried the blood from her head with Luis's handkerchief; who knows, as laboriously she struggled to her feet, placing one hand on the ground and the other on her knee, then crossing them over her bulging belly and then on the arm of the wheelchair, rising like a statue of rags fallen from the highest niche of the Sagrario; who knows, is there anything you can do to make the dogs forgive you?

I'm fourteen, almost fifteen, I can talk to them like a man, they always will call me little Luis because I'll never grow very big, I'll be stuck in my chair getting smaller and smaller until I die, but today I'm fourteen, almost fifteen, and I can talk to them like a man and they'll have to listen to me. He repeated these words over and over that night as before supper he pored over the photographs and postcards and letters stored in the trunk that now served as a chest, since everything had to do double duty in these tenements that used to be palaces and now sheltered down-on-their-luck families who lived there with former servants, they who'd been wealthy in Orizaba, and Manuelita, who had never been more than a servant in a wealthy house. Little Luis repeated those words to himself, sitting at his usual place at the table that was used for preparing and eating their meals, as well as for schoolwork and the extra accounting his father brought home so as to pay the bills every month.

Sitting in silence, waiting for someone to speak first, staring intently at his mother, daring her to begin, to tell here at the dinner table what had happened to Doña Manuela that afternoon, so yes, the gossip would begin here and tomorrow everyone in the building would know: they beat her and chased her from the Cathedral along with all her dogs. No one was saying anything, because, when she wished, Señora Lourdes knew how to impose an icy silence, to make clear to everyone that it was no time for joking, that she was reserving the right to announce something very serious.

She directed a bitter smile to each of them—to her husband, Raúl, to her two older sons, who were waiting impatiently to go to the movies with their sweethearts, to Rosa María, who could hardly keep awake—but she waited until everyone had served himself the simple rice with peas to tell again the same story, the one she always dragged out to prove how bad Doña Manuelita was, how she'd made her own daughter, Lupe Lupita, believe that when she was a little girl she'd had a bad fall and that she'd been crippled and would always have to be in a wheelchair, nothing but lies, why there was nothing wrong with her at all, nothing but the selfishness and evil of Doña Manuela, who wanted to keep the girl with her forever so she'd never be alone, even if it meant ruining her own daughter's life.

"Thanks to you, Pepe," Doña Lourdes said to her oldest son. "You suspected something and convinced her to get out of the wheelchair and try to walk, and you showed her how, thanks to you, my son, Lupe Lupita was saved from her mother's clutches."

"For God's sake, Mother, that's all over now, don't keep bringing it up, please," Pepe said, blushing, as he always did when his mother told the story, and stroking his thin black mustache.

"That's why I've forbidden Luis to have anything to do with Manuela. And now, this very afternoon . . ."

"Mother," Luis interrupted, "I'm almost fifteen, I'm fourteen years old, Mother, I can talk to you like a man." He looked at his father's face, drained by fatigue, at the sleepy face of Rosa María, a girl without memories, at the stupid faces of his brothers, at the impossible pride, the haughty apprehension of his mother's beautiful face, none of them had inherited those high, hard, everlasting bones.

"Mama, that time I fell down the staircase . . ."

"It was an accident. No one was to blame."

"I know that, Mother, that isn't the point. But what I remember is how everyone in the building peeked out to see what was going on. I cried out. I was so afraid. But everyone stayed right where they were, staring, even you. She was the only one who came running to help me. She hugged me, she looked to see if I was hurt, and ruffled my hair. I could see all their faces, Mother. I didn't see a single face that wanted to help me. Just the opposite, Mother. In that moment, everyone wanted me dead, everyone wished it, I guess, out of compassion—poor little fellow, take him out of his misery, it's better that way, what can life offer him? Even you, Mother."

"That isn't true, Luis, how could you make up such a vicious lie?"

"I'm not very bright, Mother. I'm sorry. You're right. Doña Manuela needs me because she lost her Lupe Lupita. She wants me to take her place."

"Of course she does. Have you just realized that?"

"No. I've always known it, but I couldn't find the words to say it until now. It's good to know you're needed, it's good to know that if it weren't for you another person would be terribly lonely. It's good to need someone, like Manuela needed her daughter, like I need Manuela, like you need someone, Mother, everyone does . . . Like Manuela and her dogs need each other, like all of us need something, need to do something, tell something, even if it isn't true, write letters and say that things haven't been going too badly for us, in fact that we're living in Las Lomas, isn't that right, and that Papa has a factory, that my brothers are lawyers, and that Rosa María is in boarding school in Canada, and I'm your pride and joy,

Mother, first in my class, a champion horseback rider, yes, me, Mother . . ."

Don Raúl laughed quietly, nodding his head. "That's what you always wanted, Lourdes, how well your son knows you."

The mother's eyes, proud and despairing, did not leave little Luis's face, denying, denying, with all the intensity her silence could muster. His father was shaking his head: "What a shame that I couldn't give you any of that."

"You've never heard me complain, Raúl."

"No," the father said, "never. But once, way back at the beginning, you told me the things you'd like to have had, only once, more than twenty years ago, but I've never forgotten, though you never said it again."

"I never said it again, I've never reproached you for anything." And Señora Lourdes's eyes were on little Luis, in wild supplication.

But the boy was talking about Orizaba now, about the big house, the photographs and postcards, he'd never been there, so he had to imagine it all, the balconies, the rain, the mountains, the ravine, the furniture in that once-opulent house, the friends of a family like that, the suitors, why do you choose one person over another to marry, Mother, aren't you ever sorry, don't you ever dream what life could have been like with another man, and then you write letters to make him think everything worked out, that you'd made the right choice? I'm fourteen, I can speak like a man . . .

"I don't know," said Don Raúl, as if coming back from a dream, as if he hadn't followed the conversation too closely. "The Revolution got us all off the track, some for the better and others for the worse. There was one way to be rich before the Revolution, and a different way after. We knew how to be rich in the good old days, but we were left behind, what can you do?" He laughed softly, the way he always laughed.

"I never mailed those letters, you know that very well," Doña Lourdes said to little Luis in a tight voice as she helped him to bed, as she did every night, the same bed beside Rosa María, who'd fallen asleep at the table.

"Thank you, Mother, thank you for not saying anything about Manuela and her dogs."

He kissed her affectionately.

All next day Doña Manuelita expected the worst and went around watching for signs of hostility. That's probably why, very early, as she was gathering up her clothing and then watering the geraniums, she knew many eyes were watching her, curtains were silently drawn back, half-opened shutters were hastily shut, dozens of dark eyes, some veiled by the drooping lids of age, some young and round and liquid, were watching her in secret, were waiting for her without saying so, were approving of those tasks she was doing as if seeking forgiveness for what had happened with Lupe Lupita. Doña Manuela finally realized that she was doing these chores so they would be grateful to her, so they would never again throw the business of Lupe in her face. More than ever, that day, she realized that, she knew the arrangement was of long standing, that everyone had come to an understanding without any need for words, they were grateful that she watered the flowers and covered the bird cages, no one was going to say anything about what happened in the Cathedral, no one would humiliate her, everyone would forgive her for everything.

Doña Manuela spent the whole day in her room. She'd convinced herself that nothing was going to happen, but experience had taught her to be wary, alert, keep on your toes, Doña Manuela, best to sleep with one eye open, eh? Brooding in her single room and her kitchen, she fell prey to a strange bitterness, something foreign to her. If they no longer thought ill of her, why hadn't they shown it before? Why, only now that she'd been humiliated in the Cathedral, did everyone in the building respect her? She didn't understand, she just didn't understand. Was it because the Señora Lourdes, Luis and Rosa María's mother, hadn't done any gossiping?

She lay on her cot, staring at the bare walls and thinking about her dogs, how thanks to her, through her, they transmitted their news, how they talked to one another and to her, Cloudy's been hurt, he's curled up by the Sagrario in bad shape, poor thing, let's go pray to God Our Savior and ask Him to keep them from chasing us or abusing us any more, Doña Manuela.

It was the same with her and little Luisito, each could sense what the other felt, if she knew what he was feeling, he must know as well what she felt, they had so many things in common, especially the wheelchair, Luisito's and Lupe Lupita's. Young Pepe, little Luis's brother, took Lupe Lupita from her wheelchair. Manuela had put her there to protect her, not because she herself needed a companion, a servant is always lonely by virtue of being a servant, no, that wasn't it, it was to save her from their appetites, the way they would look at her. General Vergara with his bad reputation, his son Tín, always chasing after servant girls, no, she didn't want them to lay a hand on her Lupe Lupita, no one would try anything with a cripple, they'd feel too disgusted or too ashamed, anyone should know that . . .

"I'm telling you this now, daughter, now that you've gone forever, it was to save you, I tried to save you from the terrible fate that lies in store for a servant's daughter when she is beautiful, ever since you were a little girl I tried to save you, that's why I named you as I did, twice Lupe, Lupe Lupita, twice virgin, twice protected, my little girl."

It was a very long day, but Doña Manuelita knew there was nothing to do but wait. The moment would come. She would receive a sign. She'd let herself feel what her friend Luisito was feeling. They had so much in common, the wheelchair, his brother Pepe, who'd ruined La Lupita, and left her with only one of her names, her little girl was gone forever.

"I'm telling you this now, Lupe, now that I'll never see you again . . . I tried to protect you because you were all your father left me. I loved that bastard more than I loved you, and when I lost him I loved you as I'd loved him."

Then she heard the first barking in the patio. It was after eleven but Doña Manuela hadn't eaten, lost as she'd been in her thoughts. Never, but never, had one of her dogs come into the patio, they knew all too well the dangers that awaited them there. Another barking joined the first. The old woman covered her head with her black shawl and hurried from the room. The canaries were restless. She'd forgotten to cover them so they could sleep. They stirred uneasily, not daring to sing, not daring to sleep, as during the eclipses that had occurred twice in Manuela's life. The moment the sun had disappeared, the animals and birds had fallen silent.

Tonight, on the other hand, there was a moon and spring-like warmth. Increasingly certain of the meaning of her life, of the role that was hers to play as she waited for death, Doña Manuelita carefully placed the canvas covers over the bird cages.

"There, sleep quiet, this isn't your night, this is my night, sleep now."

She completed the chore that everyone was grateful to her for performing, the chore she did so they would be grateful and could live in peace, and then she walked to the top of the great stone staircase. As she had known he would, little Luis was there in his wheelchair, waiting for her.

It was all so natural. There was no reason it should be

otherwise. Little Luis rose from his chair and offered his arm to Doña Manuela. He stumbled a little, but the old woman was strong, she lent him all her support. He was taller than either of them had supposed, fourteen, going on fifteen, a young man. Together they descended the staircase, little Luisito twice supported—by the stone balustrade and Manuelita's arm. These were the palaces of New Spain, Manuela, imagine the parties, the music, the liveried servants holding aloft sputtering candelabra, preceding the guests on nights of great balls, the scalding wax burning their hands and never a word of complaint. Come with me, Manuela, we'll go together, child.

Señora Manuelita's twenty dogs were in the patio, barking in unison, barking with joy, all of them, Cloudy, the mangy ones, the hungry ones, the bitches swollen with worms or with pregnancy, who knows, time would tell, the bitches who'd recently given birth to more dogs, teats dragging, more dogs to populate the city with orphans, with bastards, with little sons of the Virgin huddling beneath the baroque eaves of the Sagrario. Doña Manuela grasped little Luisito by his belt and took his hand, the dogs barked happily, looking at the moon as if the moonlit night was the first night of the world, before pain, before cruelty, and Manuela led Luisito, the dogs were barking, but the servant and the boy heard music, old old music, music heard centuries ago in this palace. Look at the stars, little Luisito, Lupe Lupita always asked, when do the stars go out? Would she still be asking, wherever she is? Of course she is, Manuela, of course she's asking, dance, Manuela, tell it all to me as we dance together, we're just alike, your daughter and I, Lupe Lupita and Luisito, isn't that right? Yes, yes, it's true, I see the two of you, yes, I see you now, a moonlit, starlit night just like this, dancing a waltz, the two of you together, just alike, waiting for what never comes, what never happens, children in a dream, caught in a dream: don't leave, my son, don't come out to look, stay there, it's better, stay there; but Lupita has gone, Manuela, you and I are left here in the building, it isn't Lupita and I, it's you and I, waiting, what are you waiting for, Manuela? What are you waiting for besides death?

How the dogs bark, that's why the moon's come out tonight, that's the only reason it came out, so the dogs would bark, and listen, Luisito, listen to the music and let me hold you up, how well you dance, child, forget it's me, pretend you're dancing with my beautiful Lupe Lupita, that you have your arm around her waist, and as you're dancing you smell her perfume, you hear her laughter, you look into her startled doe's eyes, and I'll pretend that I still know how to remember love, my only love, Lupe's father, a servant's love, in the dark, groping, rejected, the dark of the night, love that's a single word repeated a thousand times.

"No . . . no . . . no . . . no . . ."

Dazed by the dancing, intoxicated by her memories, Doña Manuelita lost her footing and fell. Little Luisito fell with her, their arms about each other, laughing, as the music faded and the barking increased.

"Shall we promise to help the dogs, little Luisito?"

"Let's promise, Manuela."

"You can speak up. The dogs can't. The dogs have to take what they can."

"Don't worry. We'll look after them always."

"It isn't true what they say, that I love the dogs because I didn't love my daughter. That isn't true."

"Of course it isn't, Manuela."

And only then did Doña Manuelita ask herself why in the midst of all the uproar of barking and music and laughter no one had looked out, no door had opened, no voice had protested. Did she also owe that to her friend little Luis? Did that mean no one was ever going to bother her again, not ever?

"Thank you, child, thank you."

"Imagine, Manuela, just think. Centuries ago these were palaces, great palaces, beautiful palaces, very wealthy people lived here, very important people, like us, Manuela."

Around midnight he felt very hungry and got out of bed without waking anyone. He went to the kitchen and, fumbling, found a hard roll. He smeared it with fresh cream and began to eat. Then suddenly he stopped, honor or duty, he didn't know which stopped him. Always before, he'd asked. Even for a roll spread thick with cream. This was the first time he'd taken without asking. He took the dry leftover tortillas and went out to the patio to throw them to the dogs. But they were not there any longer, nor Manuelita, nor the moon, nor the music, nor anything.

The Doll Queen

To María Pilar and José Donoso

I

I went because that card—such a strange card—reminded me of her existence. I found it in a forgotten book whose pages had revived the specter of a childish calligraphy. For the first time in a long while I was rearranging my books. I met surprise after surprise, since some, placed on the highest shelves, had not been read for a long time. So long a time that the edges of the leaves were grainy, and a mixture of gold dust and grayish scale fell on my open palm, reminiscent of the lacquer covering certain bodies glimpsed first in dreams and later in the deceptive reality of the first ballet performance to which we're taken. It was a book from my childhood—perhaps from the childhood of many children—that related a series of more or less truculent exemplary tales which had the virtue of precipitating us onto our elders' knees to ask them, over and over again: Why? Children who are ungrateful to their parents; maidens kidnapped by splendid horsemen and returned home in shame—as well as those who happily abandon hearth and home; old men who in exchange for

(115)

an overdue mortgage demand the hand of the sweetest, most long-suffering daughter of the threatened family . . . Why? I do not recall their answers. I only know that from among the stained pages came fluttering a white card in Amilamia's atrocious hand: *Amilamia wil not forget her good friend—com see me here wher I draw it.*

And on the other side was that sketch of a path starting from an X that indicated, doubtlessly, the park bench where I, an adolescent rebelling against prescribed and tedious education, forgot my classroom schedule to spend some hours reading books which, if not in fact written by me, seemed to be: who could doubt that only from my imagination could spring all those corsairs, those couriers of the tsar, those boys slightly younger than I who floated all day down a great American river on a raft. Clutching the side of the park bench as if it were the bow of a magic saddle, at first I didn't hear the sound of the light steps that stopped behind me after running down the graveled garden path. It was Amilamia, and I don't know how long the child would have kept me company in silence had not her mischievous spirit one afternoon chosen to tickle my ear with down from a dandelion she blew toward me, her lips puffed out and her brow furrowed in a frown.

She asked my name, and after considering it very seriously, she told me hers with a smile which, if not candid, was not too rehearsed. Quickly I realized that Amilamia had discovered, if discovered is the word, a form of expression midway between the ingenuousness of her years and the forms of adult mimicry that well-brought-up children have to know, particularly for the solemn moments of introduction and of leave-taking. Amilamia's seriousness was, rather, a gift of nature, whereas her moments of spontaneity, by contrast, seemed artificial. I like to remember her, afternoon after afternoon, in a succession of images that in their totality sum up the complete Amilamia. And it never ceases to surprise me that I cannot think of her as she really was, or remember how she actually moved—light, questioning, constantly looking around her. I must remember her fixed forever in time, as in a photograph album. Amilamia in the distance, a point at the spot where the hill began its descent from a lake of clover toward the flat meadow where I, sitting on the bench, used to read: a point of fluctuating shadow and sunshine and a hand that waved to me from high on the hill. Amilamia frozen in her flight down the hill, her white skirt ballooning, the flowered panties gathered on her legs with elastic, her mouth open and eyes half closed against the streaming air, the child crying with pleasure. Amilamia sitting beneath the eucalyptus trees, pretending to cry so that I would go over to her. Amilamia lying on her stomach with a flower in her hand: the petals of a flower which I discovered later didn't grow in this garden but somewhere else, perhaps in the garden of Amilamia's house, since the pocket of her blue-checked apron was often filled with those white blossoms. Amilamia watching me read, holding with both hands to the slats of the green bench, asking questions with her gray eyes: I recall that she never asked me what I was reading, as if she could divine in my eyes the images born of the pages. Amilamia laughing with pleasure when I lifted her by the waist and whirled her around my head; she seemed to discover a new perspective on the world in that slow flight. Amilamia turning her back to me and waving goodbye, her arm held high, the fingers moving excitedly. And Amilamia in the thousand postures she affected around my bench, hanging upside down, her bloomers billowing; sitting on the gravel with her legs crossed and her chin resting on her fist; lying on the grass, baring her belly button to the sun; weaving tree branches, drawing animals in the mud with a twig, licking the slats of the bench, hiding under the seat, breaking off the loose bark from the ancient tree trunks, staring at the horizon beyond the hill, humming with her eyes closed, imitating the voices of birds, dogs, cats, hens, horses. All for me, and yet nothing. It was her way of being with me, all these things I remember, but also her way of being alone in the park. Yes, perhaps my memory of her is fragmentary because reading alternated with my contemplation of the chubby-cheeked child with smooth hair that changed in the reflection of the light: now wheat-colored, now burnt chestnut. And it is only today that I think how Amilamia in that moment established the other point of support for my life, the one that created the tension between my own irresolute childhood and the wide world, the promised land that was beginning to be mine through my reading.

Not then. Then I dreamed about the women in my books, about the quintessential female—the word disturbed me—who assumed the disguise of Queen to buy the necklace in secret, about the imagined beings of mythology—half recognizable, half white-breasted, damp-bellied salamanders—who awaited monarchs in their beds. And thus, imperceptibly, I moved from indifference toward my childish companion to an acceptance of the child's grace and seriousness and from there to an unexpected rejection of a presence that became useless to me. She irritated me, finally. I who was fourteen was irritated by that child of seven who was not yet memory or nostalgia, but rather the past and its reality. I had let myself be dragged along by weakness. We had run together, holding hands, across the meadow. Together we had shaken the pines and picked up the cones that Amilamia guarded jealously in her apron pocket. Together we had constructed paper boats and followed them, happy and gay, to the edge of the drain. And that afternoon, amid shouts of glee, when we tumbled together down the hill and rolled to a stop at its foot, Amilamia was on my chest, her hair between my lips; but when I felt her panting breath in my ear and her little arms sticky from sweets around my neck, I angrily pushed away her arms and let her fall. Amilamia cried, rubbing her wounded elbow and knee, and I returned to my bench. Then Amilamia went away and the following day she returned, handed me the card without a word, and disappeared, humming, into the woods. I hesitated whether to tear up the card or keep it in the pages of the book: *Afternoons on the Farm.* Even my reading had become infantile because of Amilamia. She did not return to the park. After a few days I left on my vacation, and when I returned it was to the duties of the first year of prep school. I never saw her again.

II

And now, almost rejecting the image that is unfamiliar without being fantastic, but is all the more painful for being so real, I return to that forgotten park and stopping before the grove of pines and eucalyptus I recognize the smallness of the bosky enclosure that my memory has insisted on drawing with an amplitude that allows sufficient space for the vast swell of my imagination. After all, Michel Strogoff and Huckleberry Finn, Milady de Winter and Geneviève de Brabant were born, lived, and died here: in a little garden surrounded by mossy iron railings, sparsely planted with old, neglected trees, scarcely adorned by a concrete bench painted to look like wood which forces me to think that my beautiful wrought-iron green bench never existed, or was part of my ordered, retrospective delirium. And the hill . . . How believe the promontory Amilamia ascended and descended in her daily coming and going, that steep slope we rolled down together, was *this*. A barely elevated patch of dark stubble with no more height and depth than what my memory had created.

Com see me here wher I draw it. So I would have to cross the garden, leave the woods behind, descend the hill in three loping steps, cut through that narrow grove of chestnuts—it was here, surely, where the child gathered the white petals—open the squeaking park gate and instantly recall . . . know . . . find oneself in the street, realize that every afternoon of one's adolescence, as if by a miracle, one had succeeded in suspending the beat of the surrounding city, annulling that flood tide of whistles, bells, voices, sobs, engines, radios, imprecations. Which was the true magnet, the silent garden or the feverish city?

I wait for the light to change, and cross to the other side, my eyes never leaving the red iris detaining the traffic. I consult Amilamia's card. After all, that rudimentary map is the true magnet of the moment I am living, and just thinking about it disturbs me. I was obliged, after the lost afternoons of my fourteenth year, to follow the channels of discipline; now I find myself, at twenty-nine, duly certified with a diploma, owner of an office, assured of a moderate income, a bachelor still, with no family to maintain, slightly bored with sleeping with secretaries, scarcely excited by an occasional outing to the country or to the beach, feeling the lack of a central attraction such as my books, my park, and Amilamia once afforded me. I walk down the street of this gray suburb. The one-story houses, doorways peeling paint, succeed each other monotonously. Faint neighborhood sounds barely interrupt the general uniformity: the squeal of a knife sharpener here, the hammering of a shoe repairman there. The neighborhood children are playing in the dead-end streets. The music of an organ grinder reaches my ears, mingled with the voices of children's rounds. I stop a moment to watch them, with the sensation, as fleeting, that Amilamia must be among these groups of children, immodestly exhibiting her flowered panties, hanging by her knees from some balcony, still fond of acrobatic excesses, her apron pocket filled with white petals. I smile, and for the first time I am able to imagine the young lady of twenty-two who, even if she still lives at this address, will laugh at my memories, or who perhaps will have forgotten the afternoons spent in the garden.

The house is identical to all the rest. The heavy entry door, two grilled windows with closed shutters. A one-story house, topped by a false neoclassic balustrade that probably conceals the practicalities of the roof terrace: clothes hanging on a line, tubs of water, servants' quarters, a chicken coop. Before I ring the bell, I want to rid myself of any illusion. Amilamia no longer lives here. Why would she stay fifteen years in the same house? Besides, in spite of her precocious independence and aloneness, she seemed to be a well-brought-up, well-behaved child, and this neighborhood is no longer elegant; Amilamia's parents, without doubt, have moved. But perhaps the new tenants will know where.

I press the bell and wait. I ring again. Here is another contingency: no one is home. And will I feel the need to look again for my childhood friend? No. Because it will not happen a second time that I open a book from my adolescence and find Amilamia's card. I'll return to my routine, I'll forget the moment whose importance lay in its fleeting surprise.

I ring once more. I press my ear to the door and am startled: I can hear harsh, irregular breathing on the other side; the sound of labored breathing, accompanied by the disagreeable odor of stale tobacco, filters through the cracks in the door.

"Good afternoon. Could you tell me . . . ?"

When he hears my voice, the person moves away with heavy and unsure steps. I press the bell again, shouting this time: "Hey! Open up! What's the matter? Don't you hear me?"

No response. I continue to ring, with no result. I move back from the door, still staring at the tiny cracks, as if distance might give me perspective, or even penetration.

With my attention fixed on that damned door, I cross the street, walking backward. A piercing scream, followed by a prolonged and ferocious blast of a whistle, saves me in time. Dazed, I seek the person whose voice has just saved me. I see only the automobile moving down the street and I hang on to a lamppost, a hold that more than security offers me support as icy blood rushes through my burning, sweaty skin. I look toward the house that had been, that was, that must be, Amilamia's. There, behind the balustrade, as I had known there would be, are fluttering clothes hung out to dry. I don't know what else is hanging there—skirts, pajamas, blouses—I don't know. All I see is that starched little blue-checked apron, clamped by clothespins to the long cord swinging between an iron bar and a nail in the white wall of the terrace.

III

In the Bureau of Records I have been told that the property is in the name of a Señor R. Valdivia, who rents the house. To whom? That they don't know. Who is Valdivia? He is down as a businessman. Where does he live? Who are *you?* the young woman asked me with haughty curiosity. I haven't been able to show myself calm and assured. Sleep has not relieved my nervous fatigue. Valdivia. As I leave the Bureau, the sun offends me. I associate the aversion provoked by the hazy sun sifting through the clouds—thus all the more intense—with a desire to return to the humid, shaded park. No. It is only a desire to know if Amilamia lives in that house and why they won't let me enter. But what I must reject is the absurd idea that kept me awake all night. Having seen the apron drying on the flat roof, the apron in which she kept the flowers, I had begun to believe that in that house lived a seven-year-old girl I had known fourteen or fifteen years before . . . She must have a little girl! Yes. Amilamia, at twenty-two, is the mother of a girl who perhaps dresses the same, looks the same, repeats the same games, and—who knows—maybe even goes to the same park. And deep in thought, I arrive once more at the door of the house. I ring the bell and wait for the labored breathing on the other side of the door. I am mistaken. The door is opened by a woman who can't be more than fifty. But wrapped in a shawl, dressed in black and in flat black shoes, with no makeup and her salt-and-pepper hair pulled into a knot, she seems to have abandoned all illusion or pretense of youth. She observes me with eyes so indifferent they seem almost cruel.

"You want something?"

"Señor Valdivia sent me." I cough and run my hand over my hair. I should have picked up my briefcase at the office. I realize that without it I cannot play my role very well.

"Valdivia?" the woman asks without alarm, without interest.

"Yes. The owner of this house."

One thing is clear. The woman will reveal nothing by her face. She looks at me, impassive.

"Oh, yes. The owner of the house."

"May I come in?"

In bad comedies, I think, the traveling salesman sticks a foot in the door so they can't close the door in his face. I do the same, but the woman steps back and with a gesture of her hand invites me to come into what must have been a garage. On one side there is a glass-paneled door, its paint faded. I walk toward the door over the yellow tiles of the entryway and ask again, turning toward the woman, who follows me with tiny steps: "This way?"

I notice for the first time that in her pale hands she carries a chaplet, which she toys with ceaselessly. I haven't seen one of those old-fashioned rosaries since my childhood and I want to say something about it, but the brusque, decisive manner with which the woman opens the door precludes any gratuitous conversation. We enter a long, narrow room. The woman quickly opens the shutters. But because of four large perennials growing in glass-encrusted porcelain pots the room remains in shadow. The only other objects in the room are an old high-backed cane sofa and a rocking chair. But it is neither the plants nor the sparseness of the furniture that holds my attention.

The woman asks me to sit on the sofa before she sits down in the rocking chair. Beside me, on the cane arm of the sofa, there is an open magazine.

"Señor Valdivia sends his apologies for not having come himself."

The woman rocks, unblinking. I peer at the comic book out of the corner of my eye.

"He sends greetings and . . ."

I stop, waiting for a reaction from the woman. She continues to rock. The magazine is covered with red scribbles.

". . . and asks me to inform you that he must disturb you for a few days . . ."

My eyes search the room rapidly.

". . . A reassessment of the house must be made for tax purposes. It seems it hasn't been done for . . . You have been living here since . . . ?"

Yes. That is a stubby lipstick lying under the chair. If the woman smiles, it is while the slow-moving hands caress the chaplet. I sense, for an instant, a swift flash of ridicule that does not quite disturb her features. She still does not answer.

". . . for at least fifteen years, isn't that so?"

She does not agree. She does not disagree. And on the pale thin lips there is not the least trace of lipstick . . .

". . . you, your husband, and . . . ?"

She stares at me, never changing expression, almost daring me to continue. We sit a moment in silence, she playing with the rosary, I leaning forward, my hands on my knees. I rise.

"Well then, I'll be back this afternoon with the papers . . ."

The woman nods and in silence picks up the lipstick and the comic book and hides them in the folds of her shawl.

IV

The scene has not changed. This afternoon, as I write sham figures in my notebook and feign interest in determining the value of the dull floorboards and the length of the living room, the woman rocks, the three decades of the chaplet whispering through her fingers. I sigh as I finish the supposed inventory of the living room and ask for permission to see the rest of the house. The woman rises, bracing her long black-clad arms on the seat of the rocking chair and adjusting the shawl on her narrow, bony shoulders.

She opens the frosted-glass door and we enter a dining room with very little additional furniture. But the aluminum-legged table and the four aluminum-and-plastic chairs lack even the hint of distinction of the living-room furniture. The other window, with wrought-iron grill and closed shutters, must sometime illuminate this bare-walled dining room, devoid of either shelves or sideboards. The only object on the table is a plastic fruit dish with a cluster of black grapes, two peaches, and a buzzing corona of flies. The woman, her arms crossed, her face expressionless, stops behind me. I take the risk of breaking the order of things: clearly, these rooms will not tell me anything I really want to know.

"Couldn't we go up to the roof?" I ask. "That might be the best way to measure the total area."

The woman's eyes light up as she looks at me, or perhaps it is only the contrast with the shadows of the dining room.

"What for?" she says at last. "Señor . . . Valdivia . . . knows the dimensions very well."

And those pauses, before and after the owner's name, are the first indication that something has at last begun to trouble the woman, forcing her, in self-defense, to resort to a kind of irony.

"I don't know." I make an effort to smile. "Perhaps I prefer to go from top to bottom and not"—my false smile drains away—"from bottom to top."

"You will go the way I show you," the woman says, her arms crossed over her chest, a silver crucifix dangling over her dark belly.

Before smiling weakly, I force myself to realize that in these shadows my gestures are of no use, aren't even symbolic. I open the notebook with a creak of the cardboard cover and continue making notes with the greatest possible speed, never glancing up, taking down numbers and estimates for a job whose fiction—the light flush in my cheeks and the perceptible dryness of my tongue tell me—is deceiving no one. And as I cover the graph paper with absurd signs, with square roots and algebraic formulas, I ask myself what is keeping me from getting to the point, from asking about Amilamia and getting out of here with a satisfactory answer. Nothing. And yet I am certain, even if I obtained a response, I would not have the truth. My slim, silent companion is a person I wouldn't look at twice in the street, but in this almost uninhabited house with the coarse furniture, she ceases to be an anonymous face in the crowd and is converted into a stock character of mystery. Such is the paradox, and if memories of Amilamia have once again aroused my appetite for the imaginary, I shall follow the rules of the game, I shall exhaust appearances, and not rest until I have the answer—perhaps simple and clear-cut, immediate and obvious—that lies beyond the veils the señora of the rosary unexpectedly places in my path. Do I bestow a gratuitous strangeness on my reluctant hostess? If so, I'll only take greater pleasure in the labyrinths of my own invention. And the flies are still buzzing around the fruit dish, occasionally pausing on the damaged end of the peach, a nibbled bite—I lean closer, using the pretext of my notes—where little teeth have left their mark in the velvety skin and ocher flesh of the fruit. I do not look toward the señora. I pretend I am taking notes. The fruit seems to be bitten but not touched. I crouch down to see better, rest my hands on the table, move my lips closer as if wishing to repeat the act of biting without touching. I look down and see another sign near my feet: the track of two tires that seem to be bicycle tires, the print of two rubber tires that come as far as the edge of the table and then lead away, growing fainter, the length of the room, toward the señora . . .

I close my notebook.

"Let us go on, señora."

When I turn toward her, I find her standing with her hands resting on the back of a chair. Seated before her, coughing from the smoke of his black cigarette, is a man with heavy shoulders and hidden eyes: those eyes, scarcely visible behind swollen, wrinkled lids as thick and drooped as the neck of an ancient turtle, seem nevertheless to follow my every movement. The half-shaven cheeks, crisscrossed by a thousand gray furrows, sag from protruding cheekbones, and his greenish hands are folded under his arms. He is wearing a coarse blue shirt, and his rumpled hair is so curly it looks like the bottom of a barnacle-covered ship. He does not move, and the only sign of his existence is that difficult whistling breathing (as if every breath must breach a floodgate of phlegm, irritation, and abuse) I had already heard through the chinks of the door.

Ridiculously, he murmurs: "Good afternoon . . ." and I am disposed to forget everything: the mystery, Amilamia, the assessment, the bicycle tracks. The apparition of this asthmatic old bear justifies a prompt retreat. I repeat "Good afternoon," this time with an inflection of farewell. The turtle's mask dissolves into an atrocious smile: every pore of that flesh seems fabricated of brittle rubber, of painted, peeling oilcloth. The arm reaches out and detains me.

"Valdivia died four years ago," says the man in a distant, choking voice that issues from his belly instead of his larynx: a weak, high-pitched voice.

In the grip of that strong, almost painful, claw, I tell myself it is useless to pretend. But the waxen, rubber faces observing me say nothing, and so I am able, in spite of everything, to pretend one more time, to pretend I am speaking to myself when I say: "Amilamia . . ."

Yes; no one will have to pretend any longer. The fist that clutches my arm affirms its strength for only an instant, immediately its grip loosens, then it falls, weak and trembling, before lifting to take the waxen hand touching his shoulder: the señora, perplexed for the first time, looks at me with the eyes of a violated bird and sobs with a dry moan that does not disturb the rigid astonishment of her features. Suddenly the ogres of my imagination are two solitary, abandoned, wounded old people, scarcely able to console themselves in this shuddering clasp of hands that fills me with shame. My fantasy has brought me to this stark dining room to violate the intimacy and the secret of two human beings exiled from life by something I no longer have the right to share. I have never despised myself more. Never have words failed me so clumsily. Any gesture of mine would be in vain: shall I come closer, shall I touch them, shall I caress the woman's head, shall I ask them to excuse my intrusion? I return the notebook to my jacket pocket. I toss into oblivion all

the clues in my detective story: the comic book, the lipstick, the nibbled fruit, the bicycle tracks, the blue-
checked apron . . . I decide to leave the house without
saying anything more. The old man, from behind his
thick eyelids, must have noticed.

The high breathy voice says: "Did you know her?"

The past, so natural, used by them every day, finally
shatters my illusions. There is the answer. Did you know
her? How long? How long must the world have lived without Amilamia, assassinated first by my forgetfulness, and
then revived, scarcely yesterday, by a sad impotent memory? When did those serious gray eyes cease to be as-
tonished by the delight of an always solitary garden?
When did those lips cease to pout or press together thinly
in that ceremonious seriousness with which, I now realize,
Amilamia must have discovered and consecrated the objects and events of a life that, she perhaps knew intui-
tively, was fleeting?

"Yes, we played together in the park. A long time ago."

"How old was she?" says the old man, his voice even
more muffled.

"She must have been about seven. No, older than that."

The woman's voice rises, as she lifts her arms, seem-
ingly to implore: "What was she like, señor? Tell us what
she was like, please."

I close my eyes. "Amilamia is a memory for me, too. I
can only picture her through the things she touched, the
things she brought, what she discovered in the park. Yes.
Now I see her, coming down the hill. No. It isn't true that
it was a scarcely elevated patch of stubble. It was a hill,
with grass, and Amilamia's comings and goings had traced
a path, and she waved to me from the top before she
started down, accompanied by the music, yes, the music I
saw, the painting I smelled, the tastes I heard, the odors I
touched . . . my hallucination . . ." Do they hear me?
"She came waving, dressed in white, in a blue-checked

apron . . . the one you have hanging on the roof terrace . . ."

They take my arm and still I do not open my eyes.

"What was she like, señor?"

"Her eyes were gray and the color of her hair changed
in the reflection of the sun and the shadow of the
trees . . ."

They lead me gently, the two of them. I hear the man's
labored breathing, the crucifix on the rosary hitting
against the woman's body.

"Tell us, please . . ."

"The air brought tears to her eyes when she ran; when
she reached my bench her cheeks were silvered with
happy tears . . ."

I do not open my eyes. Now we are going upstairs.
Two, five, eight, nine, twelve steps. Four hands guide my
body.

"What was she like, what was she like?"

"She sat beneath the eucalyptus and wove garlands
from the branches and pretended to cry so I would stop
reading and go over to her . . ."

Hinges creak. The odor overpowers everything else: it
routs the other senses, it takes its seat like a yellow Mongol
upon the throne of my hallucination; heavy as a coffin, in-
sinuating as the slither of draped silk, ornamented as a
Turkish scepter, opaque as a deep, lost vein of ore, bril-
liant as a dead star. The hands no longer hold me. More
than the sobbing, it is the trembling of the old people that
envelops me. Slowly, I open my eyes: first through the
dizzying liquid of my corneas, then through the web of
my eyelashes, the room suffocated in that gigantic battle
of perfumes is disclosed, effluvia and frosty, almost flesh-
like petals; the presence of the flowers is so strong here
they seem to take on the quality of living flesh—the
sweetness of the jasmine, the nausea of the lilies, the tomb
of the tuberose, the temple of the gardenia. Illuminated

through the incandescent wax lips of heavy, sputtering candles, the small windowless bedroom with its aura of wax and humid flowers assaults the very center of my plexus, and from there, only there at the solar center of life, am I able to come to, and perceive beyond the candles, amid the scattered flowers, the plethora of used toys: the colored hoops and wrinkled balloons, cherries dried to transparency, wooden horses with scraggly manes, the scooter, blind hairless dolls, bears spilling their sawdust, punctured oilcloth ducks, moth-eaten dogs, frayed jumping ropes, glass jars of dried candy, worn-out shoes, the tricycle (three wheels? no, two, and not a bicycle's—two parallel wheels below), little wool and leather shoes; and, facing me, within reach of my hand, the small coffin supported on blue crates decorated with paper flowers, flowers of life this time, carnations and sunflowers, poppies and tulips, but like the others, the ones of death, all part of a compilation created by the atmosphere of this funeral hothouse in which reposes, inside the silvered coffin, between the black silk sheets, on the pillow of white satin, that motionless and serene face framed in lace, highlighted with rose-colored tints, eyebrows traced by the lightest pencil, closed lids, real eyelashes, thick, that cast a tenuous shadow on cheeks as healthy as in the park days. Serious red lips, set almost in the angry pout that Amilamia feigned so I would come to play. Hands joined over her breast. A chaplet, identical to the mother's, strangling that waxen neck. Small white shroud on the clean, prepubescent, docile body.

The old people, sobbing, are kneeling.

I reach out my hand and run my fingers over the porcelain face of my little friend. I feel the coldness of those painted features, of the doll queen who presides over the pomp of this royal chamber of death. Porcelain, wax, cotton. *Amilamia wil not forget her good friend—com see me here wher I draw it.*

I withdraw my fingers from the sham cadaver. Traces of my fingerprints remain where I touched the skin of the doll.

And nausea crawls in my stomach where the candle smoke and the sweet stench of the lilies in the enclosed room have settled. I turn my back on Amilamia's sepulcher. The woman's hand touches my arm. Her wildly staring eyes bear no relation to the quiet, steady voice.

"Don't come back, señor. If you truly loved her, don't come back again."

I touch the hand of Amilamia's mother. I see through nauseous eyes the old man's head buried between his knees, and I go out of the room and to the stairway, to the living room, to the patio, to the street.

V

If not a year, nine or ten months have passed. The memory of that idolatry no longer frightens me. I have forgotten the odor of the flowers and the image of the petrified doll. The real Amilamia has returned to my memory and I have felt, if not content, sane again: the park, the living child, my hours of adolescent reading, have triumphed over the specters of a sick cult. The image of life is the more powerful. I tell myself that I shall live forever with my real Amilamia, the conqueror of the caricature of death. And one day I dare look again at that notebook with graph paper in which I wrote down the data of the spurious assessment. And from its pages, once again, Amilamia's card falls out, with its terrible childish scrawl and its map for getting from the park to her house. I smile as I pick it up. I bite one of the edges, thinking that, in spite of everything, the poor old people might accept this gift.

Whistling, I put on my jacket and straighten my tie. Why not go see them and offer them this card with the child's own writing?

I am almost running as I approach the one-story house. Rain is beginning to fall in large isolated drops, bringing out of the earth with magical immediacy the odor of dewy benediction that stirs the humus and quickens all that lives with its roots in the dust.

I ring the bell. The rain gets heavier and I become insistent. A shrill voice shouts: "I'm coming!" and I wait for the mother with her eternal rosary to open the door for me. I turn up the collar of my jacket. My clothes, my body, too, smell different in the rain. The door opens.

"What do you want? How wonderful you've come!"

The misshapen girl sitting in the wheelchair places one hand on the doorknob and smiles at me with an indecipherable, wry grin. The hump on her chest makes the dress into a curtain over her body, a piece of white cloth that nonetheless lends an air of coquetry to the blue-checked apron. The little woman extracts a pack of cigarettes from her apron pocket and quickly lights a cigarette, staining the end with orange-painted lips. The smoke causes the beautiful gray eyes to squint. She fixes her coppery, wheat-colored, permanent waved hair, all the time staring at me with a desolate, inquisitive, hopeful but at the same time tearful expression.

"No, Carlos. Go away. Don't come back."

And from the house, at the same moment, I hear the high labored breathing of the old man, coming closer.

"Where are you? Don't you know you're not supposed to answer the door? Get back! Devil's spawn! Do I have to beat you again?"

And the rain trickles down my forehead, over my cheeks, and into my mouth, and the little frightened hands drop the comic book onto the wet paving stones.

The Old Morality

"Gloomy buzzards! Damned devouring crows! Get out of
here! You want my plants to dry up? Take the other road,
around Doña Casilda's house, let that old fanatic kneel to
you as you go by! Show a little respect for the house of a
Juárez Republican! Have you even seen me in your temple of darkness, you vultures! I've never asked you to visit
my house! Get out, get out of here!"

Leaning against the garden fence, my grandfather
shakes his cane. He must have been born with that cane. I
think he even takes it to bed with him, so as not to lose it.
The head of the cane looks just like Grandfather, except
it's a lion with a big mane and wide-stretched eyes that
look as if they could see many things at one time, and
Grandfather, well, yes, he has a lion's mane, too, and yellow eyes that stretch toward his ears when he sees the row
of priests and seminary students that file past our garden
to take the shortcut to the church. The seminary is a little
outside of Morelia and my grandfather swears they built it
on the road to our ranch just to annoy him. That isn't the

word he uses. My aunts say the words my grandfather uses are very immoral and that I shouldn't repeat them. It's strange that the priests always come by here, as if they liked hearing what he shouts, instead of taking the way around Doña Casilda's ranch. They went that way once and she knelt for their blessing and then invited them in for a cup of chocolate. I don't know why they'd rather come by here.

"One of these days I'm not going to take any more, you sons of bitches. Someday I'm going to sic the dogs on you!"

The truth is that my grandfather's dogs bark a lot when they're closed in, but as soon as they get past the fence they're as tame as anything. When the file of priests comes down the hill and they begin to cross themselves, the three German shepherds bark and howl as if the devil himself were coming. They must think it strange to see so many men wearing skirts, and clean-shaven too; they're so used to Grandfather's wild beard. He never combs it and sometimes I even think he roughs it up, especially when my aunts come to visit. What happens is, the dogs become very tame once they get out on the road, and they lick the priests' shoes and hands, and the priests get a funny little smile and look out of the corners of their eyes at Grandfather, who beats on the fence with his cane, hopping mad, so mad he gets his words tangled up. Though the truth is, I'm not sure but what it's something else the priests are looking at. Because Grandfather always waits for the men in skirts to go by with his arm tight around Micaela's waist, and Micaela, who is a lot younger than he is, squeezes up against Grandfather and unbuttons her blouse and laughs while she eats a big plump banana and then another and still another and her eyes shine as bright as her teeth when the priests go by.

"Doesn't it make you sick when you see my woman, you bloodsuckers?" Grandfather shouts, and squeezes Micaela tighter. "Do you want me to tell you where the heavenly kingdom is?"

He gives a big belly laugh and lifts up Micaela's skirts, and the priests begin to trot like scared rabbits, like the kind that sometimes come down from the woods close by the garden and wait for me to throw them some carrots. Grandfather and Micaela laugh and laugh, and I laugh just like them and take my grandfather's hand, he is laughing so hard he's crying, and I say: "Look, look, they're hopping like rabbits. You really scared them this time. Maybe they won't come back again."

My grandfather squeezes my hand in his, which is covered with bluish nerve lines and calluses as hard and yellow as the logs stored in the cave at the back of the garden. The dogs come back to the house and start barking again. And Micaela buttons her blouse and strokes Grandfather's beard.

But, almost always, things are calmer. Here we all like our work. My aunts say it is a sin that a thirteen-year-old boy should be working instead of going to school, but I don't know what they mean. I like to get up early and run to the big bedroom, where Micaela is looking at herself in the mirror, braiding her hair, mouth filled with hairpins, and Grandfather is still groaning in bed. Sure, what else could he expect, if you go to bed when the owls do and sleep only four hours, after playing cards with your friends till two o'clock in the morning . . . That's why at six o'clock, when I come into the bedroom, which is all cluttered with furniture, rocking chairs with little cushions for your head, great big wardrobes with mirrors so huge you can see all of yourself all at once, I crawl into the bed laughing. Grandfather pretends to be asleep for a while and thinks I don't know. I go along with the game and all of a sudden he growls like a lion, so loud it shakes the crystal candlestick, and then I pretend to be afraid and hide under those sheets that smell like nothing else in the world. Yes, sometimes Micaela says: "You're not a boy, you're like one of those dogs, they don't see anything, they just go where their noses lead them." She must be serious when she says that, because it's true that I go in the kitchen with my eyes closed and head straight for the pudding, for the honey pots and the squash-blossom sweets, for the bowl of *nata*—that thick skin from the milk—and the mangoes in syrup that Micaela is preparing. And without opening my eyes I stick my finger in the pot of stew and press my lips against the wicker tray where she is stacking up the warm tortillas. "Gosh, Grandfather," I said to him one day, "if I wanted to, I could go anywhere I want just by smelling and never get lost, I swear I could." Outside it's easy. As soon as the sun's up and the men are at the sawmill it's the odor of fresh resin that leads me to the shed where the workers stack the tree trunks and logs and then saw the planks the width and thickness they want. They all say hello and then, "Hey, Alberto, give us a hand," because they know that makes me proud, and they know that I know that they know. There are mountains of sawdust everywhere and it smells as if the real forest were here, because the wood never smells the same before or after, not when it's a tree or when it's a piece of furniture or a door or a beam in a house. One time there were bad things about Grandfather in the newspaper in Morelia, they called him a "land raper," and Grandfather went down to Morelia armed with his cane and busted the newspaperman's head and later he had to pay costs and damages: that's what the newspaper said. My grandfather is really quite a character, no doubt about it. If you could see him, the way he's like a wild bull with the priests and the newspapermen, and then so quiet and tame in the hothouse that's behind the house. No, he doesn't have plants there, but birds. Yes, he's a great bird collector, and I think one reason he loves me so much is because I inherited his taste for birds and I spend whole afternoons looking at them and bringing them seed and water and finally putting on their cage covers when they go to sleep after the sun goes down.

Birds are a serious business and Grandfather says you have to study a lot to look after them right. And he's right. These aren't just any old pigeons. I've spent hours reading the cards on each cage that explain where they're from and why they're so rare. There are two pheasants: the male has all the plumage and he's the vainest, too, while the female is dull and drab. And the Amazon cockatoo, very white with pale-blue circles under its eyes, as if it had been up all night. And an Australian bird, red, green, purple, and yellow. And the bird like flame, black and orange. And the whidah bird with a four-pointed tail that comes out once a year when it's looking for a mate and then drops out. And the silver pheasant from China, the color of a mirror, with a red face. And especially the magpies, which swoop down on anything shiny and then hide it so well you can't find it.

I know that I'd like to spend every afternoon looking at the prettiest birds, but then Grandfather comes and says to me: "All the birds know who all the others are, who their friends are, and how to entertain themselves playing. That's all they need to know."

Then later the three of us have dinner at the long, worn table that came from a convent, the only thing churchy, according to the old man, he'll allow in the house.

"And it's no skin off my nose," he says as Micaela serves us some peppers stuffed with beans and melted cheese, "that a refectory table should end up in a liberal's house. Señor Juárez converted the churches into libraries and the best proof that this poor country is going from bad to worse is that they've now taken out the books to put in the holy-water fonts again. At least I hope those hypocritical old aunts of yours wash the sleep out of their eyes each time they go to Mass."

"Well, they get washed pretty often, then." Micaela laughs as she passes the pulque jug to Grandfather. "They're so holy they never get out of the sacristy. They stink of old rags and piss."

Grandfather hugs her around the waist and we all laugh a lot and I make a drawing in my notebook of my dead mother's three sisters, making them look like the sharpest-nosed and nosiest birds in all Grandfather's collection. Then we all howl till our sides hurt and tears run down our faces and Grandfather's face looks like a tomato and then his friends arrive to play cards and I go up to sleep and early the next day I go into the bedroom where Grandfather and Micaela sleep and about the same things happen again and we're all very happy.

But today from the sawmill I hear the dogs barking and decide the priests must be passing by and I don't want to miss Grandfather's cuss words plopping like ripe tomatoes, but it seems strange for the priests to be going by so early and then I hear the loud horn and I know the aunts have arrived, I haven't seen them since Christmas, when they hauled me off to Morelia by force and I was bored as a clam while one of them played the piano and another sang and the other one offered little cups of punch to the bishop. I decide to pretend I don't know what's going on, but after a while I get curious to take a look at that automobile that's older than the hills and I come out of hiding like I'm just strolling around, whistling and kicking at the wood shavings and pieces of cork wood. Everyone has gone inside. But right in front of the gate there's that old machine with a spotted roof and velvet seats with hand-embroidered cushions. INRI, SJ, ACJM. I will ask Grandfather what those embroidered letters mean. Later. Now I feel sure that the old man is giving them something cool to drink, and so as not to worry him I tiptoe into the house and hide among the big flowerpots and plants where I can see them without their seeing me.

Grandfather is leaning with both hands on the head of his cane; his cigar is between his teeth, and he's puffing smoke like the express to Juárez. Micaela is standing with her arms crossed, laughing, in the kitchen door. The three aunts are sitting very stiffly all on the wicker sofa. All three are wearing black hats and white gloves and are sitting with their knees pressed tight together. Two of them are married and the one in the middle is an old maid, but there's no way of telling, because Aunt Milagros Tejeda de Ruiz is different from the others only in that she squints constantly, as if she had a cinder in her eye, and you can tell Aunt Angustias Tejeda de Otero only by the fact she wears a wig that's always slipping to one side, and Aunt Benedicta Tejeda, the spinster, looks only a little bit younger and she's the one who constantly touches her black lace handkerchief to the tip of her nose. But, aside from that, all three are thin, very light-skinned— almost yellow—with sharp noses and they all dress alike: in mourning all their lives.

"The mother was a Tejeda, but the father was a Santana like me, and that gives me the right!" Grandfather shouts, and blows smoke through his nose.

"The decent part comes from the Tejeda side, Don Agustín," says Doña Milagros, that eye gleaming like a beacon. "Don't you forget it."

"The decent part comes from my balls!" Grandfather shouts again and pours himself a glass of beer, growling at the aunts, who have covered their ears all at the same time. "Why should I try to explain anything to you cockatoos? I can save my breath for better things."

"Women!" screeches Doña Angustias, straightening her wig. "That prostitute you're living in sin with." "Alcohol," Señorita Benedicta murmurs, her eyes lowered. "It wouldn't surprise us to learn that the boy gets drunk every night." "Exploitation!" Doña Milagros shouts, scratching her cheek. "You make him work like a common laborer." "Ignorance"—Doña Angustias's eyes blink. "He's never set foot in a Christian school." "Sin"— Señorita Benedicta clasps her hands. "He's thirteen and he hasn't received Communion or even been to Mass." "Irreverence"—Doña Milagros points a finger at Grandfather. "Irreverence for the Holy Church and its priests, whom you attack so vilely every day." "Blasphemer!" Señorita Benedicta dries her eyes with the black handkerchief. "Heretic!" Doña Angustias shakes her head and the wig falls over her eyebrows. "Whoremonger!" Doña Milagros can no longer control the trembling of her eyelid.

"Adiós, Mama Carlota!" Micaela sings, flourishing her kitchen towel.

"Adiós—goodbye to the papist and the traitor!" Grandfather thunders, with his cane raised high: the three aunts take each other's hand and close their eye . 'For a family visit, this has already lasted too long. Go back to that antique you call a car and your rosaries and your incense and tell your husbands not to hide behind your skirts, because the only angelic thing about Agustín Santana is his name, and tell them he's waiting here for them when they really want to try to take the boy away. Godspeed to you, señoras, because only His grace can grant you that miracle. Giddap!"

But if Grandfather raises his cane, Doña Angustias retaliates by showing him a handful of papers. "You don't frighten us. Read this order from the juvenile judge. It is a court order, Don Agustín. The boy can no longer live in this atmosphere of shameless immorality. Two policemen will come this afternoon and take him to the home of our sister Benedicta: raising Alberto to be a little Christian gentleman will be a comfort to her in her lonely years. Let us go, sisters."

Aunt Benedicta's house is in the center of Morelia and from its balconies you can see a small plaza with iron benches and many yellow flowers. There is a church beside it; it is an old house and looks like all the other big houses in the town. There is an entry hall and a patio and the servants live downstairs: the kitchen is there also, and there two women fan charcoal stoves all day. Upstairs are the living rooms and the bedrooms, all opening onto a bare patio. You can imagine: Aunt Milagros said that I had to burn all my old clothes (my overalls, my boots, my sweatshirts) and that I have to dress the way I dress all the time now, in a blue suit and a stiff white sissy shirt. They put me with a stupid old professor to teach me how to talk fancy before classes begin after vacation, and I'm getting a pig's snout from so much pronouncing "u" the way the maestro wants it. Naturally, every morning I have to go with Aunt Benedicta to church and sit on the hard benches, but at least that's something different and sometimes I even enjoy it. Aunt and I eat by ourselves almost all the time, though sometimes the other aunts come with their husbands, who tousle my hair and say, "Poor little guy." And then I wander around the patio by myself or go to the bedroom they've given me. It has an enormous bed with a mosquito net. There's a crucifix over the head of the bed and a little bathroom right next to it. And I get so bored I can hardly wait for mealtimes, which are the least boring times, and for a half hour before mealtime I hang around the dining-room door, I visit the two women who fan the stoves, I find out what they're fixing and go back to stand guard by the door until one of the servants comes in to set the plates and silver at the two places and then my Aunt Benedicta comes out of her room, takes me by the hand, and we go into the dining room.

They say that Aunt Benedicta isn't married because she's very demanding and no man suits her; also that she's very old, she's already thirty-four. While we eat, I look at her to see if it shows that she's twenty years older than I am, but she goes right on sipping her soup without looking at me or talking to me. She never talks to me, and besides, since we sit so far apart at the table, we couldn't hear each other even if we shouted. I try to compare her with Micaela, who is the only woman I've ever been around, since my mother died when I was born and my father four years later and after that I lived with Grandfather and "that woman," as my aunts call her.

The thing about Señorita Benedicta is that she never laughs. And the only time she says anything it's to tell me something I already know or to give me orders when I'm already way ahead of her and doing the things she wanted without her telling me. She really gives me a hard time. I don't know whether the meals really are long or if they just seem long, but I try to entertain myself in different ways. One is to put a Micaela mask on my aunt's face, and this is very funny, I imagine her laughing her loud laugh and her head thrown back and her eyes always asking whether things are serious or a joke—that's Micaela—all this coming out of that high buttoned collar and black dress. Another is to talk to her in the language I invented myself, say, to ask her to pass me the coffee: "Hey-yeh, aunt-tant, asspay the offecay."

My aunt sighs and she must not be so awfully dumb, because she does what I ask, and only adds a lesson in manners: "One says *please*, Alberto."

But, as I was explaining, I get her goat in everything else. When she comes all serious to knock at my door to scold me for not being up yet, I answer her from the patio, all bathed and slicked up, so then she covers up her anger and says to me, more serious still, that it's time to go to church and I smile and show her the prayer book and she doesn't know what to say.

But she finally caught me one day, about a month after

I'd been living with her, and all because of that tattletale priest. They're preparing me for my First Communion and all the kids in catechism classes laugh that such a big boob doesn't know the first thing about who the Holy Spirit is. Besides that, they laugh just because it's me who's the big boob. Yesterday it was finally my turn to have a little talk alone with the priest to prepare me for confession. He talked a lot about sin and about how it wasn't my fault I didn't know anything about religion or had grown up in such an immoral atmosphere. He said not to worry but to tell him everything, because he'd never before had to prepare a boy as full of sin as I was, for whom perversion was an everyday thing, who couldn't even distinguish between good and evil. I racked my head trying to think what my worst sins could be and how the two of us were there in the empty church staring at each other without knowing what to say, and I started thinking about all the movies I'd seen and then I poured it out: how I had raided a ranch and carried off all the money and a few chickens besides, how I had grabbed and beat up a poor old blind man, how I had stabbed a policeman in the back, how I had forced a girl to strip and then bitten her on the face. The priest threw up his arms and crossed himself and said the worst anybody knew about Grandfather was nothing, and ran out as if I were the devil himself.

Well, my aunt really tore into my bedroom before I woke up. I thought the house was on fire. She slammed the doors open and shouted my name. I woke up and there she was, her arms in the air. Then she came and sat down on the bed next to me and told me that I had made fun of the priest and that that wasn't the worst. I had told all those lies in order to hide my true sins. I just looked at her as if she were out of her mind.

"Why don't you admit the truth?" she said, taking my hand.

"What do you mean, Aunt? Honest, I don't understand."

Then she ruffled my hair and squeezed my hand. "How you've seen your grandfather and that woman in improper postures."

I guess my dumb look didn't convince her, but I swear I didn't understand what she meant and even less when she kept on in a half-strangled voice, halfway between crying and screaming: "Together. In sin. Making love. In bed."

Oh, that. "Sure. They sleep together. Grandfather says that a man should never sleep alone or he'll dry up, and the same for a woman."

My aunt covered my mouth with her hand. She sat that way for a long time and I was on the point of suffocating. She looked at me in a real strange way, and then she got up and walked out very slowly, not saying anything, and I went back to sleep, but she didn't come back to get me up to go to Mass. She left me alone and I stayed in bed all morning until time for lunch, looking at the ceiling, thinking about nothing.

There are lots of lizards in the patio. I already know that when you look at them they turn the color of the stone or the tree to disguise themselves. But I know their trick and they can't get away from me. Today I've spent an hour following them, laughing at them because they think I don't know how to find them: you look for their eyes, shiny as painted pins. The whole point is not to lose sight of the eyes, because they can't disguise them, and since they open and close them all the time, it's like a signal turning on and off at the crossroads and that's the way I follow one and then another and when I want to—like now—I catch them and feel them throb in my fist, all smooth underneath and wrinkled on top and tiny, but with life, the same as anyone else. If only they knew I wouldn't hurt them, their throat wouldn't throb so, but that's the way things are. There's no way to make them understand. What scares them pleases me. I hold this one tight in my hand and my aunt is watching me from the corridor upstairs, not understanding what I'm doing. I run up the stairs and get there out of breath. She asks me what I've been doing. I act very serious so she won't get wind of anything. She's sitting fanning herself in the shade, since it's very hot. I stretch out my closed fist and she tries to smile; you can see it's an effort. She opens her hand to take mine and I put the lizard on her palm and force her fingers closed over it. She doesn't scream or get scared as I thought she would. She doesn't scold me or throw the lizard down. She just closes her fingers and her eyes tighter and looks like she wants to say something but can't and her nose trembles and she looks at me like nobody ever looked at me before, as if she wanted to cry and would feel better if she did. I tell her that the poor lizard is going to suffocate, and Señorita Benedicta leans toward the floor but can't let it go and finally opens her fingers and lets it run off along the paving stones and climb up the wall and disappear. And then her expression changes and her mouth twists and I see she's mad, but not really, so I smile and bury my head in my shoulders, try to look real innocent, and run back down to the patio.

I spend all afternoon in my room doing nothing. I feel tired and sort of sleepy like I'm getting a bad cold. It must be the lack of sun and fresh air in this dark old house. I begin to get sore about everything. I miss the sawmill, and Micaela's desserts, Grandfather's birds, the fun when the priests go by and the laughing at dinnertime and in the mornings when I go into their bedroom. I figure that up to now life in Morelia has been like a vacation, but I've been stuck here for a month and I'm getting tired of it.

I come out of my room a little late for dinner and my aunt is already sitting at the head of the table with her black handkerchief in her hand and when I take my place she doesn't scold me for coming in late—even though I did it on purpose. Just the opposite. She seems to be trying to smile and be pleasant. All I want is to throw a fit and go back to the ranch.

She hands me a covered plate and I uncover it. It's my favorite treat, *natas.*

"The cook told me you like it very much."

"Thank you, Aunt," I say, very serious.

We eat in silence and finally, when it's time to have our coffee and milk, I tell her I'm bored with living in Morelia and that I wish she would let me go back to live with Grandfather, which is where I like to live.

"Ingrate," my aunt says, and dries her lips with her handkerchief. I do not reply. "Ingrate," she repeats.

And she gets up and walks toward me, repeating that, and takes my hand and I'm sitting there very serious and she slaps me in the face with that long, bony hand and I swallow my tears and she slaps me again and suddenly she stops and touches my forehead and opens her eyes wide and says I have a fever.

It must be one of the world's worst, because I'm getting weak and my knees feel wobbly. My aunt takes me to my bedroom and says I must get undressed while she goes for the doctor. But really, all she does is flutter around while I take off the blue suit and white shirt and undershorts and get into bed, shivering.

"Don't you wear pajamas?"

"No, Aunt. I always sleep in my undershirt."

"But you have a fever!"

She rushes out like a madwoman and I lie there shaking and try to go to sleep and tell myself the fever's bad just to say something. The truth is that I go right to sleep and all Grandfather's birds come flying out together, stirring up a great commotion because they're all free at last: the blue sky fills with orange, red, and green lightning flashes, but this lasts only a short time. The birds are frightened, as if

they wanted to return to their cages. Now there are real
lightning flashes and the birds are stiff and cold in the
night. They're not flying any more, and they're turning
black. They are losing their feathers, no longer singing,
and when the storm passes and the dawn comes, they
have become the file of seminary students in their habits
on their way to church and the doctor is taking my pulse
and Aunt Benedicta seems very upset and I see the doctor
between dreams and my aunt says: "All right, now. Lie on
your back. I have to rub this liniment on you."

I feel the icy hands on my hot skin. Grandfather shakes
his cane and shouts cuss words at the priests. The liniment
smells very strong. He sics the dogs on the priests. Of
eucalyptus and camphor. The dogs just bark, frightened.
She rubs hard and my shoulders begin to burn. Grandfather shouts but his lips move in silence. Now she's rubbing
my chest and the smell is stronger. The dogs bark but
they don't make any sound either. I'm bathed in sweat
and liniment and everything burns and I want to go to
sleep but I know that I'm asleep at the same time I'm
wanting it. The cold hand rubs my shoulders and my ribs
and under my arms. And the dogs run loose, furious, to
sink their teeth into the seminary students, who turn into
birds at night. And my stomach burns as much as my
chest and my back and Aunt rubs and rubs to make me
better. The seminary students bare their teeth in a snarl
and laugh and open out their arms and fly away like buzzards, dying of laughter. And I'm so happy I laugh with
them, the sickness fills me with happiness and I don't
want her to stop making me better, I ask her to make me
feel better, I take her hands, the fever and the liniment
burn my thighs and the dogs run through the fields howling, like coyotes.

When I woke up, one night had passed and a morning
and the sun was just going down. The first thing I saw was
the shadows of the patio through the curtains on the

door. And then I realized that she was still sitting next to the head of the bed and she asked me to eat a little and put the spoon to my lips. I tasted the stewed oats and then looked at my aunt, with her hair falling over her shoulders and smiling as if she were grateful to me for something. I let her feed me the cereal as if I were a child, spoonful by spoonful, and I told her I was better and thanked her for making me feel better. She blushed and said that at last I was finding out that they loved me in this house, too.

I was in bed about ten days. First I read a mountain of novels by Alexandre Dumas, and ever since then I've thought that novels go with bronchitis like rain goes with planting time. But the curious thing is that my aunt went out to buy them as if setting out to commit a robbery and then hid them when she brought them to me, and I just shrugged my shoulders and as fast as I could began reading that wonderful story of the man who gets out of prison by pretending to be dead and they throw him in the sea and he washes ashore on the island of Monte Cristo. But I had never read so much before and I got tired and bored and lay thinking and counting the hours by watching the lights and shadows that came and went on the walls of my room. And anyone looking at me would have thought I was very calm, but inside me things were happening that I didn't understand. The thing was that I wasn't as sure as I had been before. If earlier they'd given me the chance to choose between going back to the ranch and staying here, I would have been way ahead of them, I would have hightailed it right back to be with Grandfather. And now I didn't know, I couldn't decide. And the question kept coming back no matter how I tried to avoid it and distract myself by thinking about other things. Of course, if anyone had asked me, I know what I would have answered: I'd be on my way back to the ranch. But inside me, no. I realized that, and also that it was the first time something like that had happened to me: that what I was thinking outside was different from what I was thinking inside.

I don't know what all that had to do with my aunt. I told myself, nothing. She looked the same, but she was different. She only came in to bring me my tray herself, or to take my temperature, or to see that I took my medicines. But I watched her out of the corner of my eye and I realized that the sadder she looked, the happier she was, and the happier she looked, the closer she was to crying, or you could see something was bothering her, and when she was sitting in the rocking chair fanning herself—when it seemed she was resting, quite free from care—the more I felt there was something she wanted, and the more she busied about and talked, the more I felt she didn't want anything, that she would have liked to leave my room and close herself up in her own.

Ten days passed and I couldn't stand the sweat and dirt and the grimy hair any more. Then my aunt said I was well and I could take a bath. I jumped out of bed very happy but, oh, boy, I almost fell from the dizziness that came over me. My aunt ran to take me by the arm and led me to the bathroom. I sat down, very dizzy, while she mixed the cold water with the hot, stirred it with her fingers, and let the tub fill up. Then she asked me to get into the water and I told her to leave and she asked me why. I said I was embarrassed.

"You're just a child. Pretend I'm your mother. Or Micaela. Didn't she ever give you a bath?"

I told her yes, when I was just a kid. She said it was the same thing. She said she was almost my mother, since she had taken care of me like a son while I was sick. She came to me and began to unbutton my pajamas and to cry and say how I had filled her life, how someday she would tell me about her life. I covered myself as best I could and got into the tub and almost slipped. She soaped me. She

began to rub me the way she had that night and she knew
how I liked that and I let her do it while she told me I
didn't know what loneliness was and repeated it over and
over and then said just last Christmas I had still been a
child and the water was very warm and my body felt
good, soapy, and she was cleansing me of the exhaustion
of my illness with caressing hands. She knew before I did
when I couldn't take any more and she herself lifted me
from the tub and looked at me and put her arm around
my waist.

I've been living here for four months now. Benedicta
asks me to call her "Aunt" in front of everyone else. I get
a kick out of slipping down the hallway mornings and
nights and yesterday the cook almost caught me. Sometimes I get very tired of it, especially when Benedicta cries
and yells and kneels before her crucifix with her arms
spread out wide. We never go to Mass or take Communion now. And nobody's said anything again about send-
ing me to school. But just the same, I still miss my life
with Grandfather and I have written a letter in which I
ask him to come after me, that I miss the sawmill and the
birds and the happy mealtimes. The only thing is, I never
send it. But I do keep adding things every day, and I
drop sly hints to see if he catches on. But I don't send the
letter. What I don't know how to describe very well is how
pretty Benedicta has become, how that stiff woman in
mourning who came to the ranch has changed. I'd like to
tell Micaela and Grandfather that they should see, that
Bendicta knows how to be affectionate, too, and she has
very smooth skin and, well, different eyes—bright and
very wide—and that she's very white. The only bad part is
that sometimes she moans and cries and twists so. We'll
have to see whether I ever send the letter. I got scared
today and even signed it, but I still haven't sealed it. Just a
while ago Benedicta and my Aunt Milagros were whisper-

ing in the living room behind the bead curtain that rattles when you go in and out. And then Aunt Milagros, with her trembling eyelid, came to my room and began to stroke my hair and ask me if I wouldn't like to come stay a while in her house. I just sat there, very serious. Then I thought about everything. I don't know what to think. I added one more paragraph to the letter I'm writing to Grandfather: "Come get me, please. It seems to me there's a lot more morality at the ranch. I'll tell you about it." And I put the letter in the envelope again. But I still can't decide whether to send it.

The Mandarin

To Graciela, Lorenza, and Patricia

I

Once Mexico City had been a city whose nights held the promise of the morning to come. Before going to bed, Federico Silva would walk out on the balcony of his house on Córdoba Street at two o'clock in the morning, when one could still smell the dampness of the earth of the coming day, breathe the perfume of the jacarandas, and feel the nearness of the volcanoes.

Dawn brought everything near, mountains and forests. Federico Silva closed his eyes in order to smell even better that unique odor of dawn in Mexico City: the sapid, green trace of the long-forgotten mud of the lake bed. To smell that odor was to smell the first morning. Only those who can perceive the nocturnal scent of the lost lake really know this city, Federico told himself.

That was a long time ago. Now his house stood only a block away from the huge sunken plaza of the Insurgentes metro station. An architect friend had compared that anarchical intersection of streets and avenues—Insurgentes, Chapultepec, Génova, Amberes,

(153)

and Jalapa—to the Place de l'Étoile in Paris, and Federico
Silva had had a good laugh. Actually, the Insurgentes intersection was more like a giant-sized stack of tortillas: a
busy thoroughfare, at times elevated above the flat roof-
tops of the bordering houses, then streets blocked with
cement posts and chains, then the stairways and tunnels
communicating with an interior plaza jammed with seafood restaurants and taco stands, itinerant vendors,
beggars, vagrant troubadours . . . and the students, shock-
ing numbers of youths lolling around while shoeshine
boys polished their shoes, eating sandwiches, watching the
slowly drifting smog, whistling and calling veiled obsceni-
ties at passing round-breasted, round-bottomed, skinny-
legged girls in miniskirts; the hip world, girls with
feathers and blue eyelids and silver-smeared mouths, boys
wearing leather vests over bare skin and yards of chains
and necklaces. And finally, the entrance to the metro: the
mouth of hell.

They had destroyed his morning-scented nights. The
air in his neighborhood became unbreathable, the streets
impassable. Under Federico Silva's nose—between the
wretched luxury of the Zona Rosa, a gigantic village's piti-
able cosmopolitan stage set, and the desperate, though
useless, attempt at residential grace in the Colonia
Roma—they had dug an infernal, unsalvageable trench, a
river Styx of gasoline vapors circulating above the human
whirlpool of the plaza, hundreds of young men whistling
and watching the smog drift by, sweating, loafing, sitting
in the filthy saucer of the sunken cement plaza. The
saucer of a cup of cold, greasy, spilled chocolate.

"Infamous!" he exclaimed impotently. "To think that
this was once a pretty, pastel-colored small town; you
could walk from the Zócalo to Chapultepec Park and have
everything you needed, government and entertainment,
friendship and love."

This was one of the standard tunes of this elderly bach-

elor clinging to forgotten things that no longer interested
anyone but him. His friends Perico and the Marqués told
him not to be so pigheaded. It was one thing, as long as
his mother had been alive (and God knows she took her
time in going), to respect the family tradition and keep
the house on Córdoba Street. But what was to be gained
now? He'd had stupendous offers to sell; the market
would top out; he ought to take advantage of the moment. He should know that better than anyone; he was a
landlord himself, that was his living: real estate.

Then they'd tried to force his hand by constructing tall
buildings on either side of his property; modern, they
called them, although Federico Silva insisted that one can
call modern only that which is built to last, not what's
slapped together to begin to disintegrate in two years'
time and fall down in ten. He felt ashamed that a country
of churches and pyramids built for eternity should end up
contenting itself with a city of shanties, shoddiness, and
shit.

They boxed him in, they stifled him, they blocked out
his sun and air, his view and his odors. And, in exchange,
they gave him a double helping of noise. His house, in-
nocently imprisoned between two cement-and-glass towers, began to tilt and crack under the excessive pressure.
One afternoon, while he was getting dressed to go out, he
watched a dropped coin roll until it came to rest against a
wall. Once in this same bedroom he'd played with his toy
soldiers, marshaled historic battles, Austerlitz, Waterloo,
even a Trafalgar in his bathtub. Now he couldn't fill the
tub because the water spilled over one edge.

"It's like living in the Leaning Tower of Pisa, but without the prestige. Just yesterday plaster fell on my head as
I was shaving, and the whole bathroom wall is cracked.
When will they learn that the spongy soil of our ancient
lake bed cannot support the insult of skyscrapers!"

It wasn't a truly old house, but the kind of mansion of

supposed French inspiration that was popular at the beginning of the century, and no longer built after the twenties. Actually, it more closely resembled a Spanish or Italian villa, with its flat roof, capricious stone designs on pale stucco, and grand entrance stairway leading to a foyer elevated above the dampness of the subsoil.

And the garden, a shady, moist garden, solace against the burning mornings of the high plateau; during the night a natural collector of the perfumes of the morning to come. What luxury: two large palm trees, a small gravel path, a sundial, an iron bench painted green, burbling water channeled toward beds of violets. With what animosity he regarded the ridiculous thick green glass with which the new buildings tried to defend themselves against the age-old Mexican sun. How much wiser the Spanish conquistadors, who had understood the importance of convent shadow and cool patios. Of course he would defend all this against the aggression of a city that first had been his friend and now had become his most ferocious enemy! The enemy of Federico Silva, known to his friends as the Mandarin.

His features were so markedly Oriental that they obscured the Indian mask underlying them. It happens with a lot of Mexican faces. The stigmas and accidents of known history recede to reveal the primal face, the face that goes back to Mongolian tundra and mountains. In this way Federico Silva was like the lost perfume of the ancient lake of Mexico: a sensitive memory, practically a ghost.

The hair of the man who wore this immutable mask was still so black it looked dyed. But because of the changes in the national diet he lacked the strong, white, enduring teeth of his ancestors. Black hair, in spite of the changes. But the essential benefits of chili peppers, beans, and tortillas, which contain sufficient calcium and vitamins to

make up for a limited diet, were no longer present in the
bodies of those generations that had forsaken them. Now
in that wretched cup-shaped plaza he watched the young
people eating junk—carbonated drinks and synthetic car-
amels and potato chips in cellophane bags, the garbage
food of the North added to the leper food of the South:
the trichina, the amoeba, the omnipotent microbe in every
slice of pork, tamarind-flavored soft drink, and wilting
radish.

In the midst of so much ugliness it was only natural that
he maintain his little oasis of beauty, his personal Eden
which nobody envied him anyway. Voluntarily, con-
sciously, he had remained on the edge of the mainstream.
He'd watched the caravans of fashion pass him by. He
preserved a few fashions, it was true. But what he chose
and he preserved. When something went out of style he
continued to wear it, he cultivated it and saved it from the
vagaries of taste. So his style was never out of style, his
suits, his hats and canes and Chinese dressing gowns, the
elegant ankle-high boots for his tiny Oriental feet, the
suave kid gloves for his tiny Mandarin hands.

He had been this way for years, since the forties, all the
time he was waiting for his mother to die and leave him
her fortune, and now, in turn, he would die, at peace, in
any way he wished, alone in his house, freed finally from
the burden of his mother, so extravagant and at the same
time so stingy, so vain, so painted, powdered, and be-
wigged till her dying day. The attendants at the funeral
parlor had outdone themselves. Feeling an obligation to
bestow in death a more colorful and lavish appearance
than life, they presented Federico Silva, with great pride,
with a raving caricature, an enameled mummy. The moment he saw her he'd ordered the casket sealed.

Family and friends had gathered during the days of the
wake for Doña Felícitas Fernández de Silva, and her

burial. Discreet, distinguished people everyone else re-
ferred to as aristocrats, as if, Federico Silva mused, an aristocracy were possible in a colony settled by fugitives,
petty clerks, millers, and swineherds.

"Let us content ourselves," he used to tell his old friend
María de los Angeles Negrete, "with being what we are,
an upper middle class that in spite of the whirlwinds of
history has managed through time to preserve its very
comfortable personal income."

The oldest name in this assemblage had acquired its
fortune in the seventeenth century, the most recent before 1910. An unwritten law excluded from the group the
nouveaux riches of the Revolution, but admitted those
damaged by the civil strife who'd then used the Revolution to recover their standing. But the customary, the
honorable, thing was to have been rich during the colonial
period, through the empire and the republican dicta-
torships. The ancestral home of the Marqués de Casa
Cobos dated from the times of the Viceroy O'Donojú, and
his grandmother had been a lady-in-waiting to the
Empress Carlota; Perico Arauz's ancestors had been min-
isters to Santa Anna and Porfirio Díaz; and Federico, on
the Fernández side, was descended from an aide-de-camp
to Maximilian, and through the Silvas from a magistrate
to Lerdo de Tejeda. Proof of breeding, proof of class
maintained in spite of the political upheavals of a country
known for its surprises, somnolent one day, in tumult the
next.

Every Saturday Federico joined his friends to play Mah-
Jongg, and the Marqués always told him, "Don't worry,
Federico. No matter how it shocks us, we must admit that
the Revolution tamed Mexico forever."

He hadn't seen the resentful eyes, the caged tigers lurk-
ing in the nervous bodies of the youths sitting watching
the smog drift by.

II

The day he buried his mother he really began to remember. Moreover, he realized that it was because of her disappearance that detailed memories were returning which had been buried beneath Doña Felícitas's formidable weight. That was when he remembered that once mornings could be perceived at midnight, and that he'd gone out on his balcony to breathe them, to collect the anticipated gift of the day.

But that was only one memory among many, the one most closely resembling a revived instinct. The fact is, he told himself, that the memory of old people is stimulated by the deaths of other old people. So he found that he was waiting for the death of some uncle or aunt or friend to be announced, secure in the knowledge that new memories would attend the rendezvous. In the same way, some day, they would remember him.

How would he be remembered? Meticulously grooming himself every morning before the mirror, he knew that he had changed very little over the last twenty years. Like Orientals, who, once they begin to age, never change until the day they die. But also because all that time he'd kept the same style of dress. No denying it, in hot weather he was the only person he knew who still wore a boater like the one made famous by Maurice Chevalier. With delight, savoring the syllables, he enunciated several foreign names for that hat: *straw hat, canotier, paglietta*. And in winter, a black homburg with the obligatory silk ribbon imposed by Anthony Eden, the most elegant man of his epoch.

Federico Silva always rose late. He had no reason to pretend that he was anything other than a wealthy rent collector. His friends' sons had fallen prey to a misplaced social consciousness, which meant they must be seen up and in some restaurant by eight o'clock in the morning,

eating hotcakes and discussing politics. Happily, Federico
Silva had no children to be embarrassed by being wealthy,
or to shame him for lying in bed till noon, waiting for his
valet and cook, Dondé, to bring him his breakfast so he
could drink his coffee and read the newspapers with tranquillity, shave and dress with calm.

Through the years he'd saved the clothes he'd worn as a
young man, and when Doña Felícitas died he gathered up
her extraordinary wardrobe and arranged it in several
closets, one corresponding to the styles that predated the
First World War, another for the twenties, and a third for
the hodgepodge style she'd dreamed up in the thirties
and then affected until her death: colored stockings, silver
shoes, boas of shrieking scarlet, long skirts of mauve silk,
décolleté blouses, thousands of necklaces, garden-party
hats, and pearl chokers.

Every day he walked to the Bellinghausen on Londres
Street, where the same corner table had been reserved for
him since the era of the hand-tailored suits he wore.
There he ate alone, dignified, reserved, nodding to passing acquaintances, picking up the checks of unaccompa-
nied ladies known to him or his mother, none of this
backslapping for him, no vulgarity, shouting, What's new!
What-a-sight-for-sore-eyes! or You've-made-my-day! He
detested familiarity. An almost tangible aura of privacy
surrounded his small, dark, scrupulous person. Let no
one attempt to penetrate it.

His familiarity was reserved for the contents of his
house. Every evening he took delight in looking at, admir-
ing, touching, stroking, sometimes even caressing his possessions, the Tiffany lamps and ashtrays, the Lalique
figurines and frames. These things gave him particular
satisfaction, but he enjoyed equally a whole room of Art
Deco furniture, round mirrors on silvered boudoir tables,
tall lamps of tubular aluminum, a bed with a headboard
of pale burnished metal, an entirely white bedroom: satin

and silk, a white telephone, a polar-bear skin, walls lacquered a pale ivory.

Two events had marked his life as a young man. A trip to Hollywood, when the Mexican consul in Los Angeles had arranged a visit to the set of *Dinner at Eight*, where he'd been shown Jean Harlow's white bedroom and even seen the actress from a distance: a platinum dream. And in Eden Roc he'd met Cole Porter, who'd just composed "Just One of Those Things," and Zelda and Scott Fitzgerald, who was writing *Tender Is the Night*. He'd had his picture taken with Porter that summer on the Riviera, but not with the Fitzgeralds. A photograph with a box camera that didn't need a flash. And in his room in the Hotel Negresco he'd had an adventure with a naked woman in the darkness. Neither knew who the other was. Suddenly the woman had been illuminated by moonlight as bright as day, as if the moon were the sun, a prurient, blinding spotlight stripped of the fig-leaf effect of the silver screen.

The visit to the Côte d'Azur was a constant topic of nostalgic reminiscences during the Saturday-afternoon reunions. Federico was a skilled Mah-Jongg player, and three of the habitual players, María de los Angeles, Perico, and the Marqués, had been with him that summer. It had all been memorable but that one event, the incident of the blond girl who resembled Jean Harlow. If one of the friends felt that another was about to venture into that forbidden territory, he warned him with a heavily charged look. Then everybody changed the subject, avoided talking about the past, and turned to their usual discussions of family and money.

"The two cannot be separated," Federico said as they played. "And as I have no immediate family, when I'm gone my money will be dispersed among distant branches of the family. Amusing, isn't it?"

He apologized for talking about death. But not about

money. Each of them had had the good fortune to appropriate a parcel of the wealth of Mexico at an opportune time—mines, forests, land, cattle, farms—and the luck to convert it quickly, before it had passed out of their hands, into the one secure investment: Mexico City real estate.

Half daydreaming, Federico Silva thought about the houses that so punctually produced his rents, the old colonial palaces on Tacuba, Guatemala, and La Moneda Streets. He'd never visited them. He was totally ignorant about the people who lived there. Perhaps one day he would ask one of his rent collectors to tell him who lived in the old palaces. What were the people like? Did they realize they were living in the noblest mansions of Mexico?

He would never invest in a new building like those that had blocked out his sun and made his house list to one side. That much he'd sworn to himself. Smiling, he repeated his oath as they walked to the dining table that Mah-Jongg Saturday in his home. Everyone knew that to be received by Federico Silva was a very special honor. Only he entertained with such detail, the seating plan in a red leather holder, the places set in accord to the strictest protocol—rank, age, former posts—and the card with the name of each guest at its precise place, the menu written out in the host's own hand, Dondé's impeccable service at the table.

That night as he glanced around the table, counting the absent, the friends who had preceded him in death, there was scarcely a flicker of expression on Federico Silva's Oriental mask. He rubbed his tiny porcelain Mandarin hands together: ah, there was no protocol as implacable as death, no priority more strict than that of the tomb. High overhead, the Lalique chandelier shed a vertical beam, perversely illuminating the Goyaesque faces of his table companions, the flesh of curdled custard, the deep fissures at the corners of the mouths, the hollow eyes of his friends.

Whatever became of the nude blond girl of that night in my room in the Hotel Negresco?

A Mayan profile thrust between Federico Silva and the lady seated at his right, his friend María de los Angeles Negrete, as Dondé began to serve the soup. The bridge of Dondé's nose began in the middle of his forehead and his tiny eyes were crossed.

"Isn't it extraordinary," Federico Silva commented in French. "Do you realize that this type of profile and crossed eyes was a mark of physical beauty among the Mayas? To achieve it they bound the infants' heads when they were born and forced them to follow the pendulum motion of a marble suspended on a thread. How is it possible that centuries later those artificially imposed characteristics continue to be transmitted?"

"It's like inheriting a wig and false teeth." María de los Angeles whinnied like a mare.

Dondé's profile between the host and his guest, his arm holding the soup tureen, the brimming soup ladle, the unexpected offense of Dondé's sweat, he'd warned him for the last time, bathe after you finish in the kitchen and before you begin to serve, sometimes it isn't possible, señor, there isn't enough time, señor.

"Yours, or my mother's, María de los Angeles?"

"What, Federico?"

"The wig. The teeth."

Someone jarred the ladle, Federico Silva, Dondé, or María de los Angeles, who knows, but steaming chickpea soup disappeared into the woman's bodice, screams, how could that have happened, Dondé, I'm sorry, señor. I swear, I didn't do it, ay! the curds-and-whey breasts of María de los Angeles, ay! the scalded tits, go take a bath, Dondé, you offend me, Dondé, my mother's wig and false teeth, the naked blonde, Nice . . .

He awakened with a fearful start, the anguish of a desperate effort to remember what he'd just dreamed, the certainty he would never recapture it, another dream lost forever. Drunk with sadness, he put on his Chinese dressing gown and walked out on the balcony.

He breathed deeply. He sniffed in vain for odors of the morning to come. The mud of the Aztec lake, the foam of the Indian night. Impossible. Like his dreams, the lost perfumes refused to return.

"Is anything the matter, señor?"

"No, Dondé."

"I heard the señor call out."

"It was nothing. Go back to sleep, Dondé."

"Whatever you say, señor."

"Good night, Dondé."

"Good night, señor."

III

"As long as I've known you, you've been a real stickler about what you wear, Federico."

He'd never forgiven his old friend María de los Angeles, who had once made fun of him by addressing him as Monsieur Verdoux. Maybe there *was* something Chaplinesque in antiquated elegance, but only when it disguised a diminishing fortune. And Federico Silva, as everyone knew, was not down on his luck. It was just that, like every person of true taste, he had the good sense to choose things that lasted. A pair of shoes, or a house.

"Save electricity. Go to bed early."

He would never, for example, wear spats and carry a cane at the same time. In his daily stroll down Córdoba Street to the Bellinghausen restaurant, he was careful to offset the showy effect of a brick-colored jacket with a Buster Brown belt he'd had made in 1933 by draping a nondescript raincoat over his arm with studied insouciance. And only on the infrequent days when it was really cold did he wear the derby, the black overcoat and white muffler. He was well aware that behind his back his friends whispered that the way he hung on to his clothes was really the most humiliating proof of dependence. With what Doña Felícitas had put him through, he had to make things last twenty or thirty years.

"Save electricity. Go to bed early."

But why after Doña Felícitas's death did he continue to wear the same old outfits? That was something they'd never asked him, now that he'd inherited the fortune. You could say that Doña Felícitas had deformed him, and he had turned necessity into a virtue. No, that wasn't it. His mother only pretended to be stingy. It all began with that sacred sentence—save electricity, go to bed early—said as if it were a sarcastic joke one night when she wanted to conceal her real intent, to save face, to pretend she didn't know her son was grown up, that he went out at night without asking her permission, that he dared leave her by herself.

"If I support you, the least I can expect is that you won't leave me here all alone, Feddie. I could die at any moment, Feddie. I know Dondé's here, but I am not thrilled at the idea of dying in the arms of a servant. Very well, Feddie. I suppose it must be, as you say, a very, very important engagement to cause you to abandon your own mother. Abandon, yes, that's the word. I pray to God you make up for the hurt you've caused me, Feddie. You know how. You promised me this year you'd follow Father Tellez's spiritual exercises. Please do that little favor for me, Feddie. I'm going to hang up now. I'm feeling very tired."

She replaced the white receiver. Sitting in the bed with the burnished metal headboard, surrounded with white cushions, covered with white furs, a great ancient doll, a milk-white Punchinella, lavishing powder on a floury face in which her blazing eyes, orange mouth, and red cheeks were obscene scars, flourishing with panache the white puff, enveloping herself in a choking, perfumed cloud of rice powder and aromatic talcum, her bare skull protected by a white silk cap. At night the wig of tight, shiny black curls reposed on a cotton-stuffed head on the silver boudoir table, like the wigs of ancient queens.

Sometimes Federico Silva liked to interject a touch of the fantastic into the Saturday conversations. Nothing more satisfying than an appreciative audience, and inevitably it was easy to frighten María de los Angeles. Federico Silva found this flattering. María de los Angeles was older than he, and he'd been in love with her as a boy; he'd wept when the precious little sixteen-year-old had chosen to go to the Country Club ball with older boys, not with him, the devoted little friend, the humble admirer of her blond perfection, her rose-colored skin, the filmy tulle and silken ribbons that veiled and encircled her desirable flesh. Oh, beautiful María de los Angeles. Now she looked like Goya's Queen María Luisa. He realized that in frightening her Federico Silva was still paying homage, just as he had at fifteen. But was the only possible homage gooseflesh?

"Supposedly, the guillotine was invented to spare the victim pain, you see. But the result was precisely the opposite. The speed of the execution actually prolongs the victim's agony. Neither the head nor the body has time to adjust. They feel they are still joined together, and the awareness that they are not takes several seconds to be comprehended. For the victim those seconds are centuries."

Did she understand? this long-toothed woman with the horse laugh and curds-and-whey breasts; the cruel overhead light from the Lalique chandelier could favor only a Marlene Dietrich, exaggerated shadows, funereal hollows, hallucinatory mystery. Beheaded by light.

"Without a head the body continues to move, the nervous system continues to function, the arms jerk and the hands implore. And the severed head, stimulated by a rush of blood to the brain, experiences extreme lucidity. The bulging eyes stare at the executioner. The accelerated tongue curses, remembers, denies. And the teeth clamp ferociously on the basket. Every basket at the foot of a guillotine looks as if it had been gnawed by an army of rats."

María de los Angeles exhaled a swooning sigh; the Marqués de Casa Cobos felt her pulse, Perico Arauz offered her a handkerchief dampened in cologne water. At two in the morning, after everyone had left, Federico Silva walked out onto his bedroom balcony wondering whose would be the next corpse, whose the next death, that would allow him to reclaim a bit more of his memories. One could also be a landlord of memory, but the only way to collect that rent was through another's death. What memories would his own death unleash? Who would remember him? He closed the French windows of his balcony and lay down on the white bed that had been his mother's. He tried to go to sleep by counting the people who would remember him. They might be the "best" people, but they were very few.

After the death of Doña Felícitas, Federico Silva began to worry about his own death. He instructed Dondé: "When you discover my body, before you notify anybody, put this record on the record player."

"Yes, señor."

"Look at it carefully. No mistakes, I'm putting it right on top."

"Don't worry, señor."

"And open this book on the table beside my bed."

"As you wish, señor."

He wanted to be found to the strains of Schubert's "Unfinished" Symphony, with Dickens's *The Mystery of Edwin Drood* open beside him. This was the least elaborate of his fantasies about his death. He decided to write four letters. In one he would describe himself as a suicide; in another,

as a man condemned to death; in the third, as incurably
ill; and in the fourth, as a victim of a human or natural disaster. This was the letter that presented the greatest dif-
ficulties. How could he synchronize the necessary three
factors: his death, mailing the letter, and the disaster, an
earthquake in Sicily, a hurricane in Key West, a volcanic
eruption in Martinique, an air crash in . . . ? He could
send the other three letters to people in places scattered
around the world asking them please to mail the letters
written and signed by him and addressed to his friends as
soon as they learned of his death: the suicide letter to
María de los Angeles, the condemned-man letter to Perico
Arauz, and the incurable-illness missive to the Marqués de
Casa Cobos. Confusion. Uncertainty. Eternal doubt. The
man about whose body we've gathered, the man we are
burying, was he actually our friend Federico Silva?

Nevertheless, the predictable confusion and uncertainty
of his friends were as nothing compared to his own. As he
reread the three letters, Federico realized that he knew
whom to send them to, but no one who would do him the
favor of mailing them. He had never again traveled
abroad following that trip to the Côte d'Azur. Cole Porter
had died smiling, the Fitzgeralds and Jean Harlow, weeping. To whom would he send the letters? In his mind's eye
he saw his bathing-suited young friends, Perico, the Marqués, and María de los Angeles, in Eden Roc forty years
ago. Where was the girl now who looked like Jean Harlow? She was his only secret ally. In death she could
atone for the pain and humiliation she had caused him in
life.

"And who the hell are you?"

"I myself don't know as I look at you."

"Sorry! I'm in the wrong room."

"No. Don't go. I don't know who you are."

"Let me go. Let me go or I'll scream."

"Please . . ."

"Let me go. Not even if you were the last man on earth. Filthy Chink!"

The last man. Carefully, he folded the letters before replacing them in their envelopes. A heavy hand fell on his fragile shoulder; a clatter of bracelets and chains, metal striking against metal.

"What's in the envelopes, old man? Your dough?"

"Is it him?"

"Sure it's him. He goes by the snack bar every day."

"I didn't recognize him in his darling Fu Manchu bathrobe."

"You'd know him with his cane."

"Or the cute little bibs over his shoes. Shit!"

"Hey, old man, don't get nervous. These are my buddies, the Barber, and Pocahontas. They call me Artist, at your service. We won't hurt you, I promise."

"What do you people want?"

"Only a lot of stuff you don't need."

"How did you get in here?"

"Ask the little fruit when he wakes up."

"What 'little fruit'?"

"The one who runs your errands."

"We put him out for a while. Like a light."

"I'm sorry to disappoint you. I don't keep any money in the house."

"I told you, we didn't come for your fucking money. Screw the money, old man."

"Come on, Artist. You're wasting time. Let's get going."

"Right on!"

"Barber, you entertain the walking dead here while Poca and I start collecting stuff."

"My party, Artie."

"Are the others downstairs?"

"The others? How many are there of you?"

"Christ, don't make me laugh, you old shit. Hey, he says how many are there? Christ!"

"Cuddle up to him, Pocahontas, and see how he likes that beautiful puss of yours. Give him a big smile, now; wiggle that cute little nose. That's the way, baby. Now tell him how many, what the fuck."

"Haven't you ever noticed us when you walk by the snack bar, old man?"

"No. Never. I don't lower myself to . . ."

"That's just it, baby. You should pay more attention to us. We pay attention to *you*. We've been paying attention to you for months. Right, Barber?"

"You said it. Day after fun-filled day. But let me tell you, Pocahontas, if I was you I'd feel pretty bad that the old shit didn't pick up on me, all decked out like that, all that pretty skin showing. Tongolele, you are *with* it!"

"Yeah, Fu Manchu, you sure put me down. You never once noticed me. But I bet you don't forget me now."

"All right, stop fooling around. Go see what you find in the closets, Poca. Then get the boys up here to carry out the furniture and lamps."

"On my way, Artist."

"And you, Barber, I want you to entertain his lordship here."

"Well, now, look here. I never had the pleasure of shaving such a distinguished gentleman, like they say."

"Artist! Would you look at all the old asshole's hats and shoes. He couldn't wear all these if he had a thousand legs."

"He's loaded, all right."

"What is it you want from me?"

"I want you to shut up so I can lather you nice and pretty."

"Keep your hands off my face."

"My, my. First you never noticed us, and now it's Keep your hands off my face. You sure are touchy, Fu."

"Get a load of this, but don't let it blow your mind."

"Knockout, Poca! Where'd you find the feather boas?"

"In the department store in the next room. He's got three closets stuffed full of old clothes. On my mother's grave, we hit the jackpot. Necklaces, hats, colored stockings. Anything, my lords, your heart desires!"

"You wouldn't dare. Keep your filthy hands off my mother's belongings!"

"Cool it, Fu. I told you, we're not going to hurt you. What the hell's it to you? It's just a lot of junk that doesn't mean anything to you, your lamps and ashtrays and doodads. Now what the fuck good do they do you?"

"You savages would never understand."

"Hey, you hear the bad word he called us?"

"Hell, that's not bad. It's a compliment. I wear a leather vest with nothing under it and you stick a few feathers in your hair, Poca baby, but tell me, does that make us look like dumb Indians? We're the Aztecs' revenge! Well, take a good look, you old turd, because you can kiss your furniture goodbye. And I'm taking your fancy clothes and Poca's taking your mommy's. That's what we came for."

"To steal my clothes?"

"Shit, yes. All of it, your clothes, your furniture, your silver, every-thing!"

"But why, what value can . . . ?"

"Now you put your finger on it. All this old stuff's back in style."

"And you're going to sell my possessions?"

"Are we! In Lagunilla market this stuff sells better than Acapulco Gold. What we are going to clear on all your pretties, old man!"

"But first, my beauty, you keep what you like best, the best necklace, the hippest feather boa, whatever grabs you, my little sweet-ass bitch."

"Don't start messing around with me, Artist. I've got my eye on that big white bed and if you get me all hot I might want to keep it for some extra slick dick tricks."

"How about a little right now?"

"Cut it out. Just take off. *You're* always hot."

"You, Barber, you entertain *him*."

"Does he look pretty? With his face all lathered up he looks like Santa Claus."

"Do not touch me again, sir."

"Whaaaat? Here, turn this way a little so I can give you a good shave."

"I told you, don't touch me."

"Tip your head a little to the left, be a good boy."

"Keep your hands off me, you're messing my hair!"

"Be good now, little fellow."

"You miserable beggars."

"What did you call us, fathead?"

"Us, beggars?"

"Beggars beg, old man. We take."

"You're a plague. Filth. Running sores."

"We're what? Hey, Artist, you think the old man's stoned?"

"No, it just burns him to be done in while we're riding so high."

"I'm the one who'll do the riding. I'll ride the whoring mothers of every one of you cockroaches. Pigs! Worms!"

"Whoa, there, Fu Manchu. You shut your mouth when it comes to my *mamacita*. I don't stand for that."

"Cool it, Barber."

"You, the one they call Barber, you . . ."

"Yes, you old bastard?"

"You are the most filthy son of a bitch I ever saw in my life. I forbid you to touch me again. If you want to touch something, make it your fucking mother's cunt!"

"Shit . . . Yeah, I think we've blown it . . ."

IV

Among Federico Silva's papers was a letter addressed to Doña María de los Angeles Valle, widow of Negrete. The executor delivered it to her, and before reading it the elderly lady reflected a moment about her friend, and her eyes filled with tears. Dead barely a week, and now this letter, written when?

She opened the envelope and removed the letter. It was undated, though it bore a place of origin: Palermo, Sicily. Federico wrote of a series of slight earthquakes that had taken place recently. The experts were forecasting a major earthquake, the worst in the island since the devastating quake of 1964. He, Federico, had a premonition that his life would end here. He had ignored the evacuation orders. His situation was unique: a desire for suicide annulled by a natural catastrophe. He was closed in his hotel room, watching the Sicilian sea, the "foamy" Sicilian sea, Góngora had called it, and how fine, how appropriate, to die in such a beautiful place, so removed from ugliness, lack of respect, and mutilation of the past . . . everything he most despised in life.

"Dear Friend. Do you remember the blond girl who caused the commotion in the Negresco? You may believe, and with some justification, that I am so simpleminded, that my life has been so monotonous, that I have lived that life under the spell of a lustful woman who did not wish to be mine. I am aware of the way that you, Perico, the Marqués, and all my other friends avoid that subject. Poor Federico. His one adventure ended in frustration. He grew old alongside a tyrant of a mother. And now he's dead.

"You will be correct insofar as the heart of the matter is concerned, but the outward appearances were not what they seemed. I have never told anyone this. When I begged that girl to stay, to spend the night with me in my room, she refused. She said, 'No, not if you were the last man on earth.' Those excruciating words—can you believe it?—saved me. I told myself that no one is the last man in love, only in death. Only death can say to us, 'You are the last.' Nothing, no one else, María de los Angeles.

"That sentence might have humiliated me but it did not intimidate me. I admit that I was afraid to marry. I felt a horror that I might prolong in my children what my mother had imposed upon me. You should know what I mean; our upbringing was very similar. I could not educate badly children I never had. You did. Forgive my frankness. The situation, I believe, authorizes it. Never mind; call my reluctance what you will—religious fear, ordinary avarice, sterile upbringing.

"Naturally, you pay for this cowardice when your parents have died and as is my case, you have no offspring. You have lost forever the opportunity to give your children something better, or at least something different from what your parents gave you. I don't know. What I do know is that you run the risk of dissatisfaction and error, whatever you do. At times, if you're a Catholic, as I am, and you find yourself forced to take a young girl to the doctor for an operation, or, even worse, you send by your servant the money for her abortion, you feel you have sinned. Those children one never had: did you spare them from coming into an ugly, cruel world? Or, quite the opposite, would they throw in your face that you never offered them the risks of life? Would they call you a murderer? A coward? I do not know.

"I fear that this less than forceful image of myself is the one each of you will remember. That is why I'm writing to you now, before I die. I had one love in my life, only one. You. The love I felt for you at fifteen lasted to the time of my death. I can tell you now. In you I centered the excuse for my bachelorhood and the needs of my love. I am not sure that you will understand. You were the only person I could love without betraying all the other aspects of my life and its demands. Being what I was, I had to love you as I did: faithfully, silently, nostalgically. But I was as I was because I loved you: solitary, distant, barely humanized, perhaps, by a certain sense of humor.

"I don't know whether I've made myself clear, or even whether I myself truly understood myself. We all think we know ourselves. Nothing is further from the truth. Think of me, remember me. And tell me whether you can explain to me what I am about to tell you. It may be the only puzzle of my life, and I will die without solving it. Every night before I go to bed I walk out on my bedroom balcony to take the air. I try to breathe the presages of the following morning. I had learned to identify the odors of the lost lake of a city equally lost. With the years it has become increasingly difficult.

"But that was not the real motive for my moments on the balcony. Sometimes, standing there, I begin to tremble, and I fear that once again the hour, the temperature, the eternal threat of storm—if only a dust storm—that hovers over Mexico City have made me react viscerally, like an animal, tamed in this clime, free in another, savage in some distant latitude. I fear, too, that with the darkness or the lightning, the rain or the dust storm, the ghost of the animal I might have been will return—or the son I never had. I carried a beast in my guts, María de los Ángeles. Can you believe it?"

The elderly woman wept as she returned the letter to its envelope. She paused for an instant, horrified, remembering the story about the guillotine that Federico liked to tell on Saturdays to frighten her. No. She'd refused to view the body with its neck slit from ear to ear by a straight-edge razor. Her morbid friends Perico and the Marqués had not been so fastidious.

The Cost of Living

To Fernando Benítez

Salvador Rentería arose very early. He ran across the roof terrace. He did not light the water heater but simply removed his shorts. The needling drops felt good to him. He rubbed himself with a towel and returned to the room. From the bed Ana asked him whether he wanted any breakfast. Salvador said he'd get a cup of coffee somewhere. The woman had been two weeks in bed and her gingerbread-colored face had grown thin. She asked Salvador whether there was a message from the office, and he placed a cigarette between his lips and said that they wanted her to come in person to sign.

Ana sighed and said: "How do they expect me to do that?"

"I told them you couldn't right now, but you know how they are."

"What did the doctor tell you?"

He threw the unsmoked cigarette through the broken pane in the window and ran his fingers over his mustache and his temples. Ana smiled and leaned back against the

tin bedstead. Salvador sat beside her and took her hand
and told her not to worry, that soon she would be able to
go back to work. They sat in silence, staring at the wooden
wardrobe, the large box that held tools and provisions,
the electric oven, the washstand, the piles of old newspapers. Salvador kissed his wife's hand and went out of the
room to the terrace. He went down the service stairs and
then crossed through the patios on the ground floor,
smelling the medley of cooking odors from the other
rooms in the rooming house. He picked his way among
skates and dogs and went out into the street. He entered a
store that occupied what had formerly been the garage to
the house, and the elderly shopkeeper told him that *Life
en Español* hadn't arrived yet, and he continued to move
from stand to stand, unlocking padlocks.

He pointed to a stand filled with comic books and said:
"Maybe you should take another magazine for your wife.
People get bored stuck in bed."

Salvador left. In the street a gang of kids were shooting
off cap pistols, and behind them a man was driving some
goats from pasture. Salvador ordered a liter of milk from
him and told him to take it up to number 12. He stuck his
hands in his pockets and walked backward, almost trot-
ting, so as not to miss the bus. He jumped onto the moving bus and searched for thirty centavos in his jacket
pocket, then sat down to watch the cypresses, houses, iron
grilles, and dusty streets of San Francisco Xocotitla pass
by. The bus ran alongside the train tracks and across the
bridge at Nonoalco. Steam was rising from the rails. From
his wooden seat, Salvador saw the provision-laden trucks
coming into the city. At Manuel Gonzalez, an inspector
got on to tear the tickets in half, and Salvador got off at
the next corner.

He walked to his father's house by way of Vallejo. He
crossed the small patch of dry grass and opened the door.
Clemencia said hello and Salvador asked whether his old

man was up and around yet, and Pedro Rentería stuck his head around the curtain that separated the bedroom from the tiny living room and said: "What an early bird! Wait for me. I just got up."

Salvador ran his hands over the backs of the chairs. Clemencia was dusting the rough pine table and then took a cloth and pottery plates from the glass-front cupboard. She asked how Anita was and adjusted her bosom beneath the flowered robe.

"A little better."

"She must need someone to look after her. If only she didn't act so uppity . . ."

They exchanged glances and then Salvador looked at the walls stained by water that had run down from the roof. He pushed aside the curtain and went into the messy bedroom. His father was cleaning the soap from his face. Salvador put an arm around his father's shoulders and kissed him on the forehead. Pedro pinched his stomach. They looked at each other in the mirror. They looked alike, but the father was more bald and curly-haired, and he asked what Salvador was doing out and about at this hour, and Salvador said he couldn't come later, that Ana was very sick and wasn't going to be able to work all month and that they needed money. Pedro shrugged his shoulders and Salvador said he wasn't going to ask for money.

"What I thought was that you might be able to talk to your boss; he might have something for me. Some kind of work."

"Well, yes, maybe so. Help me with these suspenders."

"It's just . . . well, look, I'm not going to be able to make it this month."

"Don't worry. Something will come along. Let me see if I can think of something."

Pedro belted his pants and picked up the chauffeur's cap from the night table. He embraced Salvador and led him to the table. He sniffed the aroma of the eggs Clemencia set before them in the center of the table.

"Help yourself, Chava, son. I'd sure like to help you. But, you know, Clemencia and I live pretty close to the bone, even if I do get my lunch and supper at the boss's house. If it wasn't for that . . . I was born poor and I'll die poor. Now, you've got to realize that if I begin asking personal favors, Don José being as tough as he is, then I'll have to pay them back somehow, and so long raise. Believe me, Chava, I need to get that two hundred and fifty out of him every payday."

He prepared a mouthful of tortilla and hot sauce and lowered his voice.

"I know how much you respect your mother, and I, well, it goes without saying . . . But this business of keeping two houses going when we could all live together and save one rent . . . Okay, I didn't say a word. But now, tell me, why aren't you living with your in-laws?"

"You know what Doña Concha's like. At me all day about how Ana was born for this and Ana was born for that. You know that's why we moved out."

"So, if you want your independence, you'll have to work your way. Don't worry. I'll think of something."

Clemencia wiped her eyes with the corner of her apron and sat down between father and son.

"Where are the kids?" she asked.

"With Ana's parents," Salvador replied. "They're going to stay there awhile, while she's getting better."

Pedro said he had to take his boss to Acapulco. "If you need anything, come to Clemencia. I've got it! Go see Juan Olmedo. He's an old buddy of mine and he has a fleet of taxis. I'll call him and tell him you're coming."

Salvador kissed his father's hand and left.

Salvador opened the frosted-glass door and entered a reception room in which a secretary and an accountant were sitting in a room with steel furniture, a typewriter, and an adding machine. He told the secretary who he was and she went into Señor Olmedo's private office and then asked him to come in. Olmedo was a very small, thin man; they sat down in leather chairs facing a low, glass-topped table with photographs of banquets and ceremonies beneath the glass. Salvador told Olmedo he needed work to augment his teacher's salary and Olmedo began to leaf through some large black notebooks.

"You're in luck," he said, scratching his sharp-pointed, hair-filled ear. "There's a very good shift here from seven to twelve at night. There are lots of guys after this job, because I protect my men." He slammed the big book shut. "But since you're the son of my old friend Pedrito, well, I'm going to give it to you. You can begin today. If you work hard, you can get up to twenty pesos a day."

For a few seconds, Salvador heard only the *tac-tac-tac* of the adding machine and the rumble of cars along 20 de Noviembre Avenue. Olmedo said he had to go out and asked Salvador to come with him. They descended in the elevator without speaking, and when they reached the street, Olmedo warned him that he must start the meter every time a passenger stopped to do an errand, because there was always some knothead who would carry his passenger all over Mexico City on one fare. He took him by the elbow and they went into the Department of the Federal District and up the stairs and Olmedo continued, telling him not to let just anyone get in.

"A stop here, a stop there, and the first thing you know you've gone clear from the Villa to Pedregal on a fare of one-fifty. Make them pay each time!"

Olmedo offered some gumdrops to a secretary and asked her to show him into the boss's office. The secretary thanked him for the candy and went into the boss's private office and Olmedo joked with the other employees

and invited them to have a few beers on Saturday and a
game of dominoes.

Salvador shook hands with Olmedo and thanked him,
and Olmedo said: "Is your license in order? I don't want
any trouble with Transit. You show up this evening, before seven. Ask for Toribio, he's in charge of dispatch.
He'll tell you which car is yours. Remember! None of
those one-peso stops; they chew up your doors. And none
of that business of several stops on one fare. The minute
the passenger steps out of the car, even to spit, you ring it
up again. Say hello to your old man."

He looked at the Cathedral clock. It was eleven. He
walked awhile along Merced and amused himself looking
at the crates filled with tomatoes, oranges, squash. He sat
down to smoke in the plaza, near some porters who were
drinking beer and looking through the sports pages.
After a time he was bored and walked toward San Juan de
Letrán. A girl was walking ahead of him. A package fell
from her arms and Salvador hurried to pick it up, and the
girl smiled at him and thanked him.

Salvador pressed her arm and said: "Shall we have a
lemonade?"

"Excuse me, señor, I'm not in the habit . . ."

"I'm sorry. I didn't mean to be fresh."

The girl continued walking ahead of him with short
hurried steps. She waggled her hips beneath a white skirt.
She looked in the shop windows out of the corner of her
eyes. Salvador followed her at a distance. Then she
stopped at an ice-cream cart and asked for a strawberry
ice and Salvador stepped forward to pay and she smiled
and thanked him. They went into a soft-drink stand and
sat on a bench and ordered two apple juices. She asked
him what he did and he asked her to guess and began to
shadowbox and she said he must be a boxer and he

laughed and told her he'd trained as a boy in the City Leagues but that actually he was a teacher. She told him she worked in the box office of a movie theater. She moved her arm and turned over the bottle of juice and they both laughed a lot.

They took a bus together. They did not speak. He took her hand and they got off across from Chapultepec Park. Automobiles were moving slowly through the streets in the park. There were many convertibles filled with young people. Many women passed by, dragging, embracing, or propelling children. The children were licking ice-cream sticks and clouds of cotton candy. They listened to the whistles of the balloon salesman and the music of a band in the bandstand. The girl told him she liked to guess the occupations of the people walking in Chapultepec. She laughed and pointed: black jacket or open-necked shirts, leather shoes or sandals, cotton skirt or sequined blouse, striped jersey, patent-leather heels: she said they were a carpenter, an electrician, a clerk, a tax assessor, a teacher, a servant, a huckster. They arrived at the lake and rented a boat. Salvador took off his jacket and rolled up his sleeves. The girl trailed her fingers in the water and closed her eyes. Salvador quietly whistled a few melodies as he rowed. He stopped and touched the girl's knee. She opened her eyes and rearranged her skirt. They returned to the dock and she said she had to go home to eat. They made a date to see each other the next evening at eleven, when the ticket booth closed.

He went into Kiko's and looked for his friends among the linoleum-topped, tubular-legged tables. He saw from a distance the blind man, Macario, and went to sit with him. Macario asked him to put a coin in the jukebox, and after a while Alfredo arrived and they ordered chicken tacos with guacamole, and beer, and listened to the song that was playing: "Ungrateful woman, she went away and left me, must have been for someone more a man than me." They did what they always did: recalled their adolescence and talked about Rosa and Remedios, the prettiest girls in the neighborhood. Macario urged them on. Alfredo said that the young kids today were really tough, carrying knives and all that. Not them. When you looked back on everything, they had really been pretty dumb. He remembered when the gang from the Poly challenged them to a game of soccer just to be able to kick them around and the whole thing ended in a scrap there on the empty lot on Mirto Street, and Macario had shown up with a baseball bat and the guys from Poly were knocked for a loop when they saw how the blind man clobbered them with a baseball bat. Macario said that was when everyone had accepted him as a buddy, and Salvador said that more than anything else it had been because of those faces he made, turning his eyes back in his head and pulling his ears back; it was enough to bust you up laughing. Macario said the one dying of laughter was him, because ever since he'd been ten years old his daddy had told him not to worry, that he'd never have to work, that the soap factory was finally going well, so Macario had devoted himself to cultivating his physique to be able to defend himself. He said that the radio had been his school and he'd gotten his jokes and his imitations from it. Then they recalled their buddy Raimundo and fell silent for a while and ordered more beer and Salvador looked toward the street and said that he and Raimundo always walked home together at night during exam time, and on the way back to their houses Raimundo asked him to explain algebra to him and then they stopped for a moment on the corner of Sullivan and Ramón Guzmán before going their own ways, and Raimundo would say: "You know something? I'm scared to go past this block. Here where our neighborhood ends. Farther on, I don't know what's going on. You're my buddy and that's why I'm telling you. I swear, I'm scared to go past this block."

And Alfredo recalled how when he graduated his family had given him an old car and they had all gone on a great celebration, making the rounds of the cheap nightclubs in the city. They had been very drunk and Raimundo said that Alfredo didn't know how to drive and began to struggle to take the wheel from Alfredo and the car had almost turned over at a traffic island on the Reforma and Raimundo said he was going to throw up, and the door flew open and Raimundo fell to the street and broke his neck.

They paid their bill and said goodbye.

He taught his three afternoon classes, and when he finished his fingers were stained with chalk from drawing the map of the republic on the blackboard. When the session was over and the children had left, he walked among the desks and sat down at the last bench. The single light bulb hung from a long cord. He sat and looked at the areas of color indicating mountains, tropical watersheds, deserts, and the plateau. He never had been a good draftsman: Yucatán was too big, Baja California too short. The classroom smelled of sawdust and leather bookbags. Cristobal, the fifth-grade teacher, looked in the door and said: "What's new?"

Salvador walked toward the blackboard and erased the map with a damp rag. Cristobal took out a package of cigarettes and they smoked, and the floor creaked as they fitted the pieces of chalk in their box. They sat down to wait, and after a while the other teachers came in and then the director, Durán.

The director sat on the lecture platform chair and the rest of them sat at the desks and the director looked at them with his black eyes and they all looked at him, the dark face and the blue shirt and maroon tie. The director said that no one was dying of hunger and that everyone was having a hard time and the teachers became angry and one said that he punched tickets on a bus after teaching two sessions and another said that he worked every night in a sandwich shop on Santa María la Redonda and another that he had set up a little shop with his savings and he had only come for reasons of solidarity. Durán told them they were going to lose their seniority, their pensions, and, if it came to that, their jobs, and asked them not to leave themselves unprotected. Everyone rose and they all left, and Salvador saw that it was already six-thirty and he ran out to the street, cut across through the traffic, and hopped on a bus.

He got off in the Zócalo and walked to Olmedo's office. Toribio told him that the car he was going to drive would be turned in at seven, and to wait awhile. Salvador closed himself in the dispatch booth and opened a map of the city. He studied it, then folded it and corrected his arithmetic notebooks.

"Which is better? To cruise around the center of the city or a little farther out?" he asked Toribio.

"Well, away from the center you can go faster, but you also burn more gasoline. Remember, *you* pay for the gas."

Salvador laughed. "Maybe I'll pick up a gringo at one of the hotels, a big tipper."

"Here comes your car," Toribio said to him from the booth.

"Are you the new guy?" yelled the flabby driver manning the cab. He wiped the sweat from his forehead with a rag and got out of the car. "Here she is. Ease her into first or sometimes she jams. Close the doors yourself or they'll knock the shit out of 'em. Here she is, she's all yours."

Salvador sat facing the office and placed the notebooks in the door pocket. He passed the rag over the greasy steering wheel. The seat was still warm. He got out and ran the rag over the windshield. He got in again and arranged the mirror to his eye level. He drove off. He raised the flag. His hands were sweating. He took 20 de Noviembre Street. A man immediately stopped him and ordered him to take him to the Cosmos Theater.

The man got out in front of the theater and his friend Cristobal looked into the side window and said: "What a surprise." Salvador asked him what he was doing and Cristobal said he was going to Flores Carranza's printing shop on Ribera de San Cosme and Salvador offered to take him; Cristobal got into the taxi but said that it wasn't to be a free ride for a buddy: he would pay. Salvador laughed and said that's all he needed. They talked about boxing and made a date to go to the Arena Mexico on Friday. Salvador told him about the girl he'd met that morning. Cristobal began talking about the fifth-grade students and they arrived at the printing plant, and Salvador parked and they got out. They entered through a narrow door and continued along a dark corridor. The printing office was in the rear and Señor Flores Carranza greeted them and Cristobal asked whether the broadsides were ready. The printer removed his visor and nodded and showed him the broadsides with red-and-black letters calling for a strike. The employees handed over the four packages. Salvador took two bundles and started ahead while Cristobal was paying the bill.

He walked down the long, dark corridor. In the distance, he heard the noise of automobiles along Ribera de San Cosme. Halfway along the corridor he felt a hand on his shoulder and someone said: "Take it easy, take it easy."

"Sorry," Salvador said. "It's very dark here."

"Dark? It's going to get black."

The man stuck a cigarette between his lips and smiled, but Salvador only said: "Excuse me." But the hand fell again on his shoulder and the fellow said he must be the only teacher who didn't know who *he* was, and Salvador began to get angry and said he was in a hurry and the fellow said: "The S.O.B., you know? That's me!"

Salvador saw that four cigarettes had been lighted at the mouth of the corridor, at the entrance to the building, and he hugged the bundles to his chest and looked behind him and another cigarette glowed before the entrance to the print shop.

"King S.O.B., the biggest fucking sonofabitch of 'em all, that's me. Don't tell me you never heard of *me!*" Salvador's eyes were becoming adjusted to the darkness and he could now see the man's hat and the hand taking one of the bundles.

"That's enough introduction, now. Give me the posters, teacher."

Salvador dislodged the hand and stepped back a few paces. The cigarette from the rear advanced. A humid current filtered down the corridor at the height of his calves. Salvador looked around.

"Let me by."

"Let's have those flyers."

"Those flyers are going with me, buddy."

He felt the burning tip of the cigarette behind him close to his neck. Then he heard Cristobal's cry. He threw one package, and with his free arm smashed at the man's face. He felt the squashed cigarette and its burning point on his fist. And then he saw the red saliva-stained face coming closer. Salvador whirled with his fists closed and he saw the knife and then felt it in his stomach.

The man slowly withdrew the knife and snapped his fingers, and Salvador fell with his mouth open.

The Son of Andrés Aparicio

To the memory of Pablo Neruda

THE PLACE

It had no name and so it didn't exist as a place. Other districts on the outskirts of Mexico City had names. Not this one. As if by oversight. As if a child had grown up without being baptized. Or worse: without even being given a name. It was as if by general agreement. Why name such a barrio? Perhaps someone had said, not really thinking, that no one would stay here very long. It was a temporary place, like the cardboard and corrugated tin shacks. Wind sifted through the badly fitting fiber walls; the sun camped on the tin roofs. Those were the true residents of the place. People came here confused, half dazed, not knowing why, maybe because this was better than nothing, because this flat landscape of scrub and pigweed and greasewood was the next frontier, one that came after the most recent place, a place that had a name. Here no name, no sewers, and the only light was an occasional light bulb where someone had tapped into the city power lines. No one had named the place because everyone pretended they were there temporarily. No one built on his own land. They were squatters, and though no one ever said it, they'd agreed among themselves that they wouldn't offer resistance to whoever came to run them off. They'd simply move on to the next frontier of the city. At least the time they spent here without paying rent would be time gained, time to catch their breath. Many of them had come from more comfortable districts with names like San Rafael, Balbuena, Canal del Norte, even Netzahualcóytl, where already two million people were living, want to or not, with its cement church and a supermarket or two. They came because not even in those lost cities could they make ends meet, but they refused to give up the last vestiges of decency, refused to go the way of the scavengers who picked over the dump or the paupers who sold stolen sand from Las Lomas. Bernabé had an idea. That this place had no name because it was like the huge sprawling city itself, that here they had everything that was bad about the city but maybe the best too, he wanted to say, and that's why it couldn't have a name of its own. But he couldn't say it, because words always came so hard to him. His mother still had a treasured old mirror and often gazed at herself in it. Ask her, Bernabé, whether she sees the place, the lost city with its scabrous winter crust, its spring dust devils, and in the summer the quagmires inevitably blending with the streams of excrement that run the entire year seeking an exit they never find. Where does the water come from, Mama? Where does all the shit go, Papa? Bernabé learned to breathe more slowly so he could swallow the black air trapped beneath the cold clouds, imprisoned within the encircling mountains. A defeated air that barely managed to drag itself to its feet and stagger across the plain, seeking mouths to enter. He never told anyone his idea because he couldn't get the words out. Every single one was locked inside him. Words were hard for him because nothing his mother said ever had any relation to reality, because his

uncles laughed and whooped it up as if they felt an obligation to enjoy themselves once a week before returning
to the bank and the gasoline station, but especially because he couldn't remember his father's voice. They'd
been living here eleven years. No one had bothered them,
no one had run them off. They hadn't had to offer resistance to anyone. Even the old blind man who'd serenaded
the power lines had died, he'd strummed his guitar and
sung the old ballad, *Oh, splendid, luminous electricity* . . .
Why, Bernabé? Uncle Rosendo said it was a bad joke.
They'd come temporarily and stayed eleven years. And if
they'd been there eleven years they'd be there forever.

"Your papa's the only one who got out in time, Bernabé."

THE FATHER

Everyone remembered his suspenders. He always wore
them, as if his salvation depended on them. They said he
hung on to life by his suspenders, and oh, if only he'd
been more like them he might have lasted a little longer.
They watched his clothes get old and worn, but not his
suspenders; they were always new, with shiny gilded clasps.
The old people who still used such words said that like his
gentility the suspenders were proverbial. No, his Uncle
Richi told him, stubborn as an old mule and fooling himself, that was your father. At school Bernabé had to fight
a big bully who asked him about his papa, and when Bernabé said he'd died, the bully laughed and said, That's
what they all say, everyone knows no papa never dies, no,
what happened was that your papa left you or worse
never even said you were his, he laid your mama and ran
off on her before you were even born. Stubborn but a
good man, Uncle Rosendo said, do you remember? when
he wasn't smiling he looked old and so he smiled the live-
long day though he never had any reason to, oh, what a

laugher Amparito's husband, laughing, always laughing, with nothing to laugh about, and all that bitterness inside because they'd sent him, a young agriculture student, a green kid, to be in charge of a co-op in a village in the state of Guerrero, just after he'd married your mama, Bernabé. When he got there he found the place burned out, many of the members of the co-op had been murdered and their crops stolen by the local political boss and the shippers. Your father wanted to file claims, he swore he was going to take it to the authorities in Mexico City and to the Supreme Court, what didn't he say, what didn't he promise, what didn't he intend to do? It was his first job and he went down there breathing fire. Well, what happened was that they no more than caught wind of the fact that outsiders were going to poke in and try to right all the injustices and crimes than they banded together, the victims the same as the criminals, to deny your father's charges and lay it all on him. Meddling outsider, come from Mexico City with his head filled with ideas about justice, the road to hell was paved by men like him, what all they didn't call him. They were bound together by years of quarrels and rivalries and by their dead. After all, time would work things out. Justice was rooted in families, in their honor and pride, and not in some butt-in agronomist. When the federal officials came, even the brothers and widows of the murdered blamed your papa. They laughed: let the government officials fight it out with the government agronomist. He never recovered from that defeat, you know. In the bureaucracy they were suspicious of him because he was an idealist and incompetent to boot, and he never got ahead there. Quite the opposite, he got stuck in a piddling desk job with no promotions and no raises and with his debts piling up, all because something had broken inside, a little flame had gone out in his heart is the way he told it, but he kept on smiling, hooking his thumbs in those suspenders. Who asked him to poke his nose in? Justice doesn't make good bedfellows with love, he used to say, those people loved one another even though they'd been wronged, their love was stronger than my promise of justice. It was as if you offered them a marble statue of a beautiful Greek goddess when they already had their ugly but oh, so warm and loving dark-skinned woman warming their covers. Why come to him? Your father Andrés Aparicio, smiling all the time, never forgot those mountains to the south and a lost village with no highway or telephone, where time was measured by the stars and news was transmitted only through memory and the one sure thing was that everyone would be buried in the same parcel of land guarded over by rose-colored angels and the withered yellow blossoms of the *cempazuchiles,* the flower of the dead, and they knew it. That village banded together and defeated him, you see, because passion unites more than justice, and what about you, Bernabé, who beat you up? where did you get that split lip and black eye? But Bernabé wasn't going to tell his uncles what he'd said to the big bully at school, or how they'd waded into each other because Bernabé hadn't known how to explain to the bully who his father Andrés Aparicio was, the words just wouldn't come and for the first time he knew vaguely, even though he didn't want to think about it too much, that if you weren't able to come up with words then you'd better be able to fight. But, oh, how he wished he could have told that sonofabitching bully that his father had died because it was the only dignified thing left to do, because a dead man has a kind of power over the living, even if he's a godforsaken corpse. Shit, you have to respect a dead man, don't you?

The Mother

She struggled to keep her speech refined, her at once sentimental and cold, dreamy and unyielding character might have been molded in her manner of speech, as if to make credible the language that no one spoke any longer in this lost barrio. Only a few old people, the ones who'd spoken of the proverbial gentility of her husband Andrés Aparicio, called on her, and she insisted on setting a proper table with a tablecloth and knives and forks and spoons, demanding that no one begin until everyone was served and that no one leave the table until she the wife, the señora, the lady of the house, rose to leave. She always said "please" when she asked for something and reminded others to do the same. She was always hospitable and made her guests welcome, when there had been guests still, and birthdays and saint's days and Christmas and even a crèche with pilgrims and candles and a piñata. But that was when her husband Andrés Aparicio was living and bringing home a salary from the Department of Agriculture. Now, without a pension, she couldn't manage, now only the old people came and chatted with her, using words like meticulous and punctual, with your permission and allow me, courtesy and thoughtlessness. But the old people were dying out. They'd come in huge enormous groups, three and sometimes four generations strung together like beads on a necklace, but in fewer than ten years all you saw were young people and children and looking for old people who spoke genteelly was like looking for a needle in the proverbial haystack. What would she have to say if all her old friends kept dying, she thought, gazing at herself in the baroque mirror she'd inherited from her mother when they all still lived on República de Guatemala before the rent freeze had been lifted and their landlord, Don Federico Silva, had mercilessly raised their rent. She hadn't believed his message, that his mother insisted, that Doña Felícitas was tyrannical and greedy, because later their neighbor Doña Lourdes told them that Señor Silva's mother had died and still he didn't lower the rents, what did you expect? When

Bernabé was old enough to think for himself, he tried to associate his mother's manners, the delicacy of the way she spoke in public, with tenderness, but he couldn't. The only times she became sentimental was when she spoke about poverty or about his father; but she was never more cold than when she spoke about those same subjects. Bernabé didn't know what his mother's theatrics meant but he did know that what she seemed to be saying had nothing to do with him, as if there were a great chasm between her acts and her words, don't ever forget Bernabé that you're well brought up, try not to mix with those ruffians at school, stay away from them, remember that you have a treasure beyond price, good family and good upbringing. Only twice did he remember his mother Amparo acting differently. Once when for the first time she heard Bernabé shout, You motherfucker, at another child in the street and when her son came into their hovel she collapsed against her dressing table, pressed her hands to her temples, and dropped the mirror to the floor, saying, Bernabé, I haven't given you what I wanted for you, you deserved better, look how you've had to grow up and where you've had to live, it isn't right, Bernabé. But the mirror didn't break. Bernabé never asked her what she meant. He knew that every time she sat before her dressing table with the mirror in her hand and cast sidelong glances at herself, stroking her chin, silently tracing the line of an eyebrow with a finger, erasing the tears of time from her eyes with the palm of her hand, his mother would speak, and this was more important to him than what she said, because for Bernabé speech was something miraculous, it took more courage to speak than to take a beating, because physical combat was merely a substitute for words. The day he came home after his fight with the bully at school he didn't know whether his mother was talking to herself or whether she knew he was creeping around behind one of the coarse cotton curtains the uncles had hung to mark off the rooms of the house that little by little every Sunday they were improving, replacing cardboard with adobe and adobe with brick until the place had a certain air of respectability, like the house they had when their father was the aide-de-camp to General Vicente Vergara, the famous the legendary Old General Iron Balls who often invited them to breakfast on the anniversary of the Revolution, on a cold morning toward the end of November. Not any longer; Amparito was right, the old people were dying off and all the young had sad faces. Not Andrés Aparicio, no, he was always smiling so he wouldn't look old. His proverbial gentility. He stopped smiling only once. A man from the barrio said something nasty to him and your father kicked him to death, Bernabé. We never saw him again. Oh, my child, look what they've done to you, Doña Amparo said finally, my poor child, my son, look how you've had to fight, and she stopped looking at herself in the mirror to look at her son my little sweetheart my dearest oh why do they pick on you my little saint and the mirror fell to the new brick floor and this time it shattered. Bernabé stared at her, un surprised by the tenderness she so infrequently displayed. She looked at him as if she understood that he understood that he shouldn't be surprised by something he always deserved or that Doña Amparo's tenderness was as temporary as the lost city where they'd lived the last eleven years without anyone coming with an eviction notice, a fact that so encouraged the uncles that they were replacing cardboard with adobe and adobe with brick. The boy asked his mother whether his father was really dead. She told him that she never dreamed about him. She answered with precision, letting him know that the cold and calculating side of her nature had not been overcome by tenderness. As long as she didn't dream about her dead husband, she didn't have to accept his death, she told him. That made all the difference, she let herself go, she wanted to be lucid and emotional at the same time, come give me a hug, Bernabé I love you, my little doll, listen carefully to what I say. Don't ever kill anyone for money. Never kill unless you know what you're doing. But if you do kill someone, do it with reason, with passion. It will make you clean and strong. Never kill anyone, my son, unless you buy a little life for yourself, my precious.

THE UNCLES

They were his mother's brothers and she called them the boys, though they were between thirty-eight and fifty years old. Uncle Rosendo was the oldest and he worked in a bank counting the old bank notes that were returned to the government to be burned. Romano and Richi, the youngest, worked in a gasoline station, but they looked older than Rosendo, because he spent most of the day on his feet and although they moved around a lot waiting on customers, lubricating cars, and cleaning windshields, they passed their time swilling soft drinks that swelled up their bellies. During all the spare time in the station located in a cloud of dust in the barrio of Ixtapalpa where you couldn't see anything clearly, not people not houses nothing but grimy cars and the hands of people paying, Romano drank Pepsis and read the sports pages while Richi played the flute, coaxing beautiful warm sounds from it and sipping from time to time on his Pepsi. They drank beer only on Sundays, before and after they went out to the barren field with their pistols to shoot rabbits and toads behind the shacks. They spent every Sunday this way, and Bernabé sitting on a pile of broken roof tiles watched from the back of the house. They laughed with a kind of slobbering glee, wiping their mustaches on their sleeves after every draught of beer, elbowing one another, howling like coyotes if they got a rabbit bigger than the rest. Then he watched them hug each other, clap each other on the back, and return dragging the bloody rabbits by the ears and Richi with a dead toad in each hand. While Amparo fanned the charcoal brazier and served them ears of corn sprinkled with chili pepper and rice cooked with tomatoes the brothers argued because Richi said that he was getting on toward forty and didn't want to die a big-bellied bastard, Amparito should forgive him, in some gas station even if it did belong to Licenciado Tín Vergara who did them the favor because the old General had ordered it and in a cabaret on San Juan de Letrán they were going to audition him to play flute in their dance band. Rosendo angrily picked up an ear of corn and Bernabé looked at his fingers leprous from counting all those filthy bank notes. He said that playing the flute was a queer's job, Amparito should forgive him, and Richi replied if he was so macho why hadn't he ever married and Romano rapped Richi's head half affectionately and half angrily because he wanted to get away from the station where Richi was his only company and Rosendo said it was because among the three of them they kept this household going, their sister Amparo and the boy Bernabé, that's why they never got married, they couldn't afford to feed any more than five mouths with what the three brothers earned and now only two if Richi went off with some dance band. They kept arguing and Richi said he'd earn more in the band and Romano said he'd blow it all on women just to prove something to the marimba players, and Rosendo said that no matter how small it was, with Amparo's permission, Andrés Aparicio's pension would help a little, all they had to do was declare him dead and Amparo wept and said it was her fault of course and would they forgive her. They all consoled her except Richi, who walked to the door and stood silently staring into the darkening dusk over the plain, ignoring Rosendo, who was again speaking as the head of the family. It isn't your fault Amparito but your husband could at least let us know whether or not he's dead. We've all worked at whatever we could, look at my hands, Amparito, do you think I enjoy it? but it was your husband who wanted to be something better (that was my fault, said Bernabé's mother) because a street sweeper or an elevator operator earns more than an office worker but your husband wanted to have a career so he could earn a pension (that was my fault, said Bernabé's mother), but to earn a pension you have to be dead and your husband just went up in smoke, Amparito. Outside it's all dark and gray said Richi from the door and Amparito said her husband had struggled to be a gentleman so we wouldn't sink so low. What's low about work, Richi asked with irritation, and Bernabé followed him out onto the quiet and sleeping plain into a dusk smelling of dried shit and smoking tortillas and a hint of the green, squat greasewood. Uncle Richi hummed Agustín Lara's bolero, *caballera de plata: hair of silver, hair of snow, skein of tenderness with one tress daring* . . . as airplanes descended in their approach to the international airport, the only lights those on a distant runway. God, I wish they'd hire me for the band, Richi said to Bernabé, staring at the yellowish fog, in September they're going to Acapulco to play for the national fiesta and you can come with me, Bernabé. We're not going to die without seeing the sea, Bernabé.

BERNABÉ

When he was twelve he stopped going to school, but didn't tell anyone. He hung around the station where his uncles worked and they let him clean the windshields as a part of the service; no matter if you only earn a few centavos, it's better than nothing. His absence went unnoticed at school, it didn't concern them. The classrooms were jammed with sometimes as many as a hundred children, and one fewer was a relief for everyone, even if no one noticed. They turned down Richi for the band and he told Bernabé flatly, at least come earn a few centavos, don't waste any more time or you're going to end up like your goddamn papa. He gave up playing the flute and signed Bernabé's grade cards so Amparo would think he was still in school and so a pact was sealed between the two that was the first secret relationship in Bernabé's life, because in school he was always too divided between what he saw and heard at home, where his mother always spoke of decency and good family and bad times, as if they'd known times that weren't bad, and when he tried to tell any of this at school he met hard, unseeing gazes. One of his teachers noticed and she told him that here no one offered or asked for pity because pity was a little like contempt. Here no one complained and no one was better than anyone else. Bernabé didn't understand but it made him mad that the teacher acted as if she understood better than anyone what only he could understand. Richi understood, come on Bernabé earn your coppers, just take a good look at what you can have if you're rich, look at that Jaguar coming into the station, jeez usually we get nothing here but rattletraps ah it's our boss the Honorable Tín passing by to see how business is and look at this magazine Bernabé wouldn't you like a babe like that all for yourself and I'll bet lawyer Tín's women look like that, look at those terrific tits Bernabé imagine lifting up her skirt and sliding between those thighs warm as milk Bernabé God I always get the short end of the stick look at this ad of Acapulco we're always shit on Bernabé look at the rich bastards in their Alfa Romeos, Bernabé, think how they must have lived when they were kids, think how they live now and how they'll live when they're old men, everything on a silver platter but you, Bernabé, you and me shit on from the day we're born, old men the day we're born, isn't that right? He envied his Uncle Richi, such a smooth talker, words came so hard for him and he'd already learned that when you don't have the words you get hard knocks, he left school to knock around in the city, which at least was dumb like him, isn't it true, Bernabé, that the big bully's words hurt more than his blows? Even if the city knocks you around, at least it doesn't talk. Why don't you read a book, Bernabé, the teacher who'd made him so mad asked, do you feel inferior to your classmates? He couldn't tell her that he felt uncomfortable when he read because books spoke the way his mother spoke. He didn't understand why but, from wanting it so much, tenderness was painful to him. In contrast, the city let itself be seen and loved and wanted, though in the end racing along Reforma and Insurgentes and Revolución and Universidad at rush hour, wiping windshields, hurling himself against the cars, playing them like bulls, hanging out with the other jobless kids and playing soccer with balls of wadded newspaper on a flat piece of ground like the one he'd grown up on, sweating the stench of gasoline fumes and pissing streams of sludge and stealing soft drinks on one corner and fried pork rind on another and sneaking into the movies drove him from his uncles and his mother, he became more independent and clever and greedy for all the things he was beginning to see, and everything beginning to speak to him, the damned words again, there was no way to escape them, buy me, take me, you need me, in every shop window, in the hand the woman extended from her car window to give him twenty centavos without a word of thanks for the swift and professional cleaning of her windshield, on the face of the rich young man who didn't even look at him as he said, keep your hands off my windshield, punk, in the wordless television programs he could see from the street through the glass of the show window, mute, intoxicating him with desires, as he stood as tall as he could and thought how he wasn't earning any more at fifteen than he had at twelve, cleaning windshields with an old rag on Reforma, Insurgentes, Universidad, and Revolución at the hour of the heaviest traffic and how he wasn't getting any closer to any of the things the songs and ads offered him and that his helplessness was stretching longer and longer and would never come to anything like his Uncle Richi's desire to play the flute in a dance band and spend the month of September in Acapulco skimming on water skis across a Technicolor bay, swooping from an orange hang glider above the fairy-tale palaces of the Hilton Marriott Holiday Inn Acapulco Princess. His mother, when she found out, was philosophical, she didn't scold him about anything any more, and she resigned herself to growing old. Her few remaining priggish friends, a widower pharmacist, a Carmelite nun, a forgotten cousin of former President Ruiz Cortines, saw in her gaze the tranquillity of a lesson well taught, of words well spoken. She could give no more of herself. She spent hours gazing down the empty road toward the horizon.

"I hear the wind, and the world creaks."

"Beautifully stated, Doña Amparito."

SUNDAY AFTERNOON RODEO

He came to hate his Uncle Richi because leaving school and cleaning windshields along the broad avenues hadn't made him rich or given him what everybody else had, if anything he was worse off than ever. That's why when Bernabé was sixteen his Uncles Rosendo and Romano decided to give him a very special present. Where do you think we've gone for a good time all these years without women of our own? they asked him, licking their mustaches. Where do you think we went after shooting rabbits and eating dinner with your mother and you? Bernabé said he guessed with whores, but his uncles laughed and said that only dumb shits paid for a woman. They took him to an empty factory on the abandoned silent road to Azcapotzalco with its putrid smell of gasoline where for a peso a head the watchman let them enter and his Uncle Rosendo and Uncle Romano pushed him before them into a dark room and closed the door. All Bernabé could see was a flash of dark flesh and then he had to feel. He took the first one he touched, each of them standing, her back against the wall and he leaning against her, desperate Bernabé, trying to understand, not daring to speak because what was happening didn't need words, he was sure that this desperate pleasure was called life and he seized it with open hands, moving from the hard and scratchy wool of a sweater to the softness of shoulders and the creaminess of breasts, from the stiff cotton of a skirt to the wet spider between the legs, from the thick laddered stockings to cotton-candy buttocks. He was distracted by his uncles' bellowings, their hurried and vanquished labors, but he realized that because he was distracted everything lasted longer, and finally he could speak, amazing himself, as he thrust his penis into this soft, melting, creamy girl who clung to him twice with her arms about his neck and her legs locked around his waist. What's your name, mine's Bernabé. Love me, she said, be sweet, be good, she said, be a doll, the same thing his mother said when she felt tender, oh, baby, oh, handsome, what a cock you've got there. Later they sat for a while on the floor but his uncles began whistling the way they did in the station, like a mule driver, hey, come on, kid, let's go, put your sword away, leave a little something for next Sunday, don't let these bulldoggers sap your strength, oooheee they're castrators, they'll eat you alive and spit out the pieces, by-eee by-eee now, who are you anyway, María Felix? Bernabé jerked the medal from the girl's neck and she screamed, but the nephew and the two uncles had already hurried from the Sunday-afternoon rodeo.

MARTINCITA

The following Sunday he came early and leaned against the fence by the factory entrance to wait for her. The girls arrived sedately, sometimes exaggerating their charade by wearing veils as if for Mass or carrying shopping baskets, some were more natural, dressed like today's servant girls in turtleneck sweaters and checked slacks. She was wearing the same cotton skirt and woolly sweater, rubbing her eyes, which smarted from the heavy yellow air of the Azcapotzalco refinery. He knew it was she, he'd kept playing with the little medal of the Virgin of Guadalupe, dangling it from his wrist, twirling it so the sun would flash into the eyes of his Lupe and her eyes would glint in return and she would stop and look and look at him and reveal, with a betraying gesture of hand to throat, that she was the one. She was ugly. Really ugly. But Bernabé couldn't turn back now. He kept swinging the medal and she walked over to him and took it without a word. She was repulsive, she had the flattened face of an Otomí Indian, her hair was frizzled by cheap permanents and the gold of her badly capped teeth mirrored the glitter of Our Lady of Guadalupe. Bernabé managed to ask her if she wouldn't like to go for a little walk but he couldn't say, It's true, isn't it, that you don't do it for money? She said her name was Martina but that everyone called her Martincita. Bernabé took her elbow and they walked along the path toward the Spanish Cemetery, which is the only pretty place in the whole area, with its huge funeral wreaths and white marble angels. Cemeteries are so pretty, said Martincita, and Bernabé imagined the two of them making it in one of the chapels where the rich buried their dead. They sat on a tomb slab with gilded letters and she took a lily from a flower holder, smelled it, and covered the tip of her snub nose with orange pollen, she laughed and then teased him with the white bloom, tickling her nose and then Bernabé's, who burst into sneezes. She laughed, flashing teeth like eternal noonday, and said that since he didn't talk much she was going to tell him the whole story, they all went to the factory for fun, there were all kinds, girls from the country like Martina and girls who'd lived a long time in Mexico City, that didn't have anything to do with it, what mattered was that everyone came to the factory because they enjoyed it, it was the only place they could be free for a while from servant-chasing bosses or their sons or the barrio Romeos who took advantage of a girl and then said, Why, I never laid eyes on you, and that's why there were so many fatherless babies, but there in the dark where you never knew each other, where there weren't any complications, it was nice to have their moment of love every week, no? honest, they all thought it was wonderful to make love in the dark, where no one could see their faces or know what happened or with who, but one thing she was sure of was that what interested the men who came there was the feeling that they were getting it from someone weak. In her village that's what always happens to the women of the priests, who were passed off as nieces or servants, any man could lay them saying, If you don't come through I'll tell that bastard priest. They say the same thing used to happen to the nuns when the big estate owners went to the convents and screwed the sisters, because who was going to keep them from it? That night when he was sixteen Bernabé couldn't sleep, he could think of only one thing: how well Martincita spoke, she didn't lack for words, how well she fucked too, she had everything except looks, what a shame she was such a pig. They made a date to meet in the Spanish Cemetery every Sunday and make love in the Gothic mausoleum of a well-known industrial family and she said there was something funny about him, he still seemed like a little boy and she thought there must be something about his home that didn't jibe with his being so poor and so tongue-tied, she didn't understand what it could be, even before she left home she'd known that only rich kids had a right to be little boys and grow up to be big, people like Martincita and Bernabé were born grown up, the cards are stacked against us, Bernabé, from the minute we're born, except you're different, I think you want to be different, I don't know. At first they did the things all poor young couples do. They went to anything free like watching the *charro* cowboys ride and rope in Chapultepec Park on Sundays and they went to all the parades during the first months they were lovers, first the patriotic parade on Independence Day in September, when Uncle Richi had wanted to be in Acapulco with his flute, then the sports parade on Revolution Day, and in December they went to see the Christmas lights and the old Christmas crèches in Bernabé's old house in the tenements on Guatemala Street, where his crippled friend Luisito lived. They barely said hello because it was the first time Bernabé had taken Martincita to meet anyone he knew and who knew his mother, Doña Amparito, and Doña Lourdes, the mother of Luis, and Rosa María didn't even speak to them and the crippled boy stared at them through eyes without a future. Then Martina said she'd like to meet Bernabé's other friends, Luisito frightened her because he was just like an old man in her village but he was never going to grow old. So they looked up the boys who played soccer with Bernabé and cleaned windshields and sold Chiclets and Kleenex and sometimes even American cigarettes on Universidad, Insurgentes, Reforma, and Revolución but it was one thing to run through the broad avenues joking and insulting one another and fighting over business and then spending their remaining energy on a field with a paper soccer ball and it was something else to go out with girls and talk like regular people, sitting in a cheap café facing a few silent pork rolls and pineapple pop. Bernabé looked at them there in the little café, they

were envious of Martina because he was really getting it
and not just in wet dreams or jerking off but they didn't
envy him because she was such a dog. Either to get back at
him or to show off or just to set themselves apart from
him the boys told them that some politician who drove
down Constituyentes every day on his way to the presidential offices on Los Pinos had wanted to impress a
watching presidential guard and had with a great flourish
given two of them tickets for the soccer match and the
rest of them had scraped together enough money to go
on Sunday and they were inviting him, but it would have
to be without her because the money wouldn't stretch that
far and Bernabé said no, he wasn't going to leave her all
by herself on a Sunday. They went with the boys as far as
the entrance of the Azteca Stadium and Martincita said
why didn't they go to the Spanish Cemetery, but Bernabé
just shook his head, he bought Martina a soft drink and
began to pace back and forth in front of the stadium like
a caged tiger, kicking the lampposts every time he heard
the shouting inside and the roar of *Goal!* So there was
Bernabé kicking lampposts and muttering, This fucking
life is beginning to get to me, when am I going to begin to
live, when?

WORDS

Martina asked him what they were going to do, she was
very truthful and told him she could deceive him and let
herself get pregnant but what good would that do if they
didn't come to an agreement first about their future. She
hinted around a lot like the time he suggested they hook a
ride to Puebla to the Fifth of May parade and managed to
get a supply truck to take them as far as the Church of
San Francisco Acatepec glittering like a thimble and from
there they walked toward the city of shining tiles and car-
amel candies, still blissful from their adventure together

and the clear landscape of pines and cool breezes from the volcanoes that was something new for Bernabé. She had come from the Indian plains of the state of Hidalgo and she knew what poor country looked like, but clean, too, not like the city filth, and watching the parade of the Zouaves and the Zacapoaxtlas, the troops of Napoleon and those of the Honorable Don Benito Juárez, she told him that she'd like to see him marching in a uniform, with a band and everything. His turn might come up in the lottery for the draft and everyone knew, said Martina with an air of being very much in the know, that they gave the draftees whatever education they needed and a career in the army wasn't a bad deal for someone who didn't even have a pot to pee in. Bernabé's words stuck in his throat because he felt he was different from Martincita but she didn't realize it, and looking at a display of sweets in a shop window he compared himself to her in the reflection and he thought he was handsomer, slimmer, even lighter of complexion, and his eyes had a kind of green spark, they weren't impenetrable like his sweetheart's black eyes, in which no white was visible. But since he didn't know how to tell her this, he took her to meet his mother. Martincita took it all to heart, she was thrilled and thought it was almost as good as a formal proposal. But all Bernabé wanted was to show her how different they were. Doña Amparito must have been waiting a long time for a day like this, an occasion that would make her feel young again. She took out her best clothes, a wide-shouldered tailored suit, her precious nylons and sharp-toed patent-leather shoes, she hung up some old photographs that proved the existence of ancestors, they hadn't sprung from nowhere, johnny-come-latelys, why certainly not, señorita, you see what kind of family you're hoping to get into and a photograph with President Calles in the center and to the left General Vergara and in the background the General's head groom, the father of Amparito, Ro-

mano, Rosendo, and Richi. But one look at Martincita,
and Doña Amparo was speechless. Bernabé's mother
could handle women like herself, women insecure of their
place in the world, but Martincita showed no sign of inse-
curity. She was a country girl and had never pretended to
be anything different. Doña Amparo glanced desolately at
the table set for tea and the mocha tea cakes she'd asked
Richi to bring from a distant bakery. But she didn't know
how to offer tea to this servant girl, not only a servant but
ugly ugly ugly, God help her but she was ugly, she could
even contend with a girl of that class if she were pretty,
but a servant and a scarecrow besides, what words could
deal with that? how could she say, Have a seat, señorita,
please forgive the circumstances but decency is something
one carries inside, something seen in one's manners, the
next time you come we can compare our family albums if
you would like, now wouldn't you like a drop of tea?
lemon or cream? a mocha tea cake, señorita? Bernabé
loves French pastry more than anything, he is a young
man with refined tastes, you know. She didn't offer her
hand. She didn't rise. She didn't speak. Bernabé pleaded
in silence, Speak, Mama, you know what words to say,
you're like Martincita that way, you both know how to
talk, I just plain can't get the words out. Let's go, Bernabé,
Martina said pridefully after five minutes of strained silence. Stay and have your tea with me, I know how much
you like it, Doña Amparo said, good afternoon, young
lady. Martina waited a couple of seconds, then wrapped
herself in her woolly sweater and hurried from the house.
They saw each other again, they spent one of their Sundays together all close and cuddling, and Martincita's
words, pretty and teasing but now with a hard and cutting
edge.

"Ever since I was a little girl I knew I couldn't be a little
girl. But not you, Bernabé, not you, I see that now."

PARTINGS

Bernabé tried once again, this time with the uncles, so many *r-r-r*'s Martina laughed, showing her gold teeth, Rosendo and Romano and Richi sitting with their pistols between their legs after a Sunday morning shooting rabbits and toads and then cutting pigweed leaves on the plain where the squat green greasewood grew. Richi said that the leaves of the pigweed were good for stomach cramps and frights and he elbowed his brother Rosendo and looked at Martincita, who was smiling, holding his nephew Bernabé's hand, and Romano told Bernabé that he was going to need some pigweed tea to get over his fright. The three uncles laughed maliciously and this time Martincita covered her face with her hands and ran from the house with Bernabé behind her, Wait for me, Martina, what's the matter? The uncles yelped like coyotes, licked their mustaches, hugged one another and clapped each other's shoulders weak with laughter: Listen, Bernabé, where'd you pick up the little stray? she looks like something you'd throw to the lions, our nephew with a reject like that? you shouldn't be screwing with her, let us get you something better where'd you scare her up, kid? don't tell us from the Sunday-afternoon rodeo? Oh, what a blockhead you are, nephew, no wonder your mother's been so upset. But Bernabé didn't know how to tell them how well she spoke and that she was loving besides, that she had everything except beauty, he wanted to tell them that but he couldn't, I'll miss her, he watched her run across the flat ground, stop, look back, wait for the last time, decide, Bernabé, I don't give you a bellyache or haunt your dreams, I cuddle you, I fondle you, I give you all my sweetness, decide, Bernabé, Bernabé my love. A real asshole, nephew; it's one thing to get a free lay from some servant girl on Sundays just to get your hard off but it's something else again who you show to the world and that's the very reason you're going to need money, Bernabé, stay here, don't be stupid, let her go, you don't marry the first little bitch you go to bed with, certainly not a pig with a dish face like your Martincita, my God, what an ass you are, Bernabé, it's about time for you to grow up and be a man and earn yourself a wad so you can take girls out, we've never had any children, we've given everything to you, we're counting on you, Bernabé, what do you need? a car, money, clothes? how are you going to buy clothes? what are you going to say to the hot mommas, nephew? how are you going to attract them? be bold as a bullfighter, Bernabé, remember they're the heifers, you're the torero and you have to make them charge, you need style, Bernabé, class like the song says, come on, Bernabé, learn how to fire the pistol, it's time now, come along with your old uncles, we've sacrificed ourselves for you and your mother, don't fight it, forget her, Bernabé, do it for us, it's time for you to get ahead, kid, you were spinning your wheels with that dog, boy, don't tell us we sacrificed ourselves for nothing, look at my hands peeling like a scabby old mutt, look at your Uncle Romano's big belly and he's got a matching spare tire of grease and fumes in his head, what does he have to look forward to? and look at your Uncle Richi's glazed eyes who never got to go to Acapulco he's bleary-eyed from dreaming, you want to be like that, kid? You need to go your own way, claw your way up, Bernabé, I'm an old man now and I'm telling you whether you like it or not we're growing apart, the way you just parted from your sweetheart you're going to have to part from your mother and us, with some pain a little more a little less but you get used to everything, after a while partings will seem normal, that's life, life is just one parting after another, it's not what you keep but what you leave behind that's life, you'll see, Bernabé. He spent that afternoon alone without Martina for the first time in ten months, wandering through the streets of the Zona Rosa, staring at the cars, the suits, the restaurant entrances, the shoes of the people going in, the neckties of the people coming out, his gaze flashing from one thing to another without really focusing on anything or anyone, fearing the bitterness the bile in his guts and balls that would make him kick out at the well-dressed young men and hip-swinging girls going in and out of the bars and restaurants on Hamburgo and Genova and Niza the way he'd kicked the lampposts outside the stadium. He tramped up and down Insurgentes that Sunday, a street jammed with automobiles returning from Cuer-navaca, bumpers crashing, balloon vendors, sandwich shops jammed too, he fantasized he could kick the whole city until there was nothing left but pieces of neon light and then grind up the pieces and swallow them and I'll be seeing you, Bernabé. That was when his Uncle Richi, with whom he'd been angry even before he made fun of Mar-tincita, waved excitedly from an open-air oyster stand near the bridge on Insurgentes.

"I've got it made, nephew. They've hired me as flute player and I'm off to Acapulco with the band. To prove I keep my word I want you to go with me. To tell you the truth, I think I owe it all to you. My boss wants to meet you."

El Güero

He didn't have to go to Acapulco with his Uncle Richi because the Chief gave him a job on the spot. Bernabé didn't meet him immediately, he only heard a deep and unctuous voice, like on the radio, from behind the glass office doors. Tell the boys to take care of him. In the dressing rooms they looked him up and down, some thumbed their noses at him, some gestured up yours and continued dressing, carefully arranging their testicles in close-fitting undershorts. A tall dark-skinned youth with a

long face and stiff eyelashes brayed at him and Bernabé
was about to take a swing at him but another man they
called El Güero because of his light hair came over and
asked him what he would like to wear, the Chief offered a
new wardrobe to new arrivals and he told him too that he
shouldn't pay any attention to the Burro, the poor thing
only brayed to say his name, not to insult anyone. Bernabé remembered what Martina had said in Puebla, Join
the army, Bernabé, they'll give you an education, you'll
learn to take orders, then they'll promote you and if they
discharge you, you buy a gun and go into business for
yourself, she joked. He told El Güero that a uniform
would be fine, he didn't know how to dress, a uniform was
fine. El Güero said it looked as if he was going to have to
look after him and he picked out a leather jacket, some
jeans still stiff from the factory, and a couple of checked
shirts. He promised that as soon as he got a girl he'd get
him a dress suit, but this would do for now and for the
workouts a white T-shirt and watch out for your balls,
eggs in a basket because sometimes the blows fell hot and
heavy. They took him to a kind of military camp that
didn't look like a camp from the outside, with a lot of gray
trucks always waiting in front and sometimes men dressed
in civilian clothes who tied a white handkerchief on their
arm as they entered and removed it when they came out.
They slept on campaign cots and from the crack of dawn
went through training exercises in a gym that smelled of
eucalyptus drifting through the broken windowpanes.
First were the rings and parallel bars, the horizontal bar
and box horse, the weights and the horse. Then came
poles, rope climbing, tree trunks across barrancas and
sharpshooting, and only at the end of the training,
bludgeons, rubber hoses, and brass knuckles. He looked
at himself naked in the full-length mirror in the dressing
room, as if sketched with an iron nib, hair that curled naturally not with curling irons like poor straight-haired

Martincita's, fine bony mestizo features with a real profile, not like Martincita's pushed-in face, a profile to his face and his belly and a profile between his legs and a green pride in his eyes that hadn't been there before. The Burro went by braying and laughing at the same time, with a lasso longer than his, and both things angered Bernabé. Again El Güero held him back and reminded him that the Burro didn't know any other way to laugh, that he announced himself with his braying the way that he, El Güero, announced his presence with his transistor, with the music that always preceded him, when you hear music, that's where your Güero is. One day Bernabé felt the earth change beneath his sneakers. It was no longer the soft earth of Las Lomas de Chapultepec, sandy and sprinkled with pine needles. Now all the training exercises were held in a huge hand-ball court, where they learned to run hard, fight hard, move on hard pavement. Bernabé concentrated on the Burro to work up his anger, to turn nimbly and land a karate chop on the nape of the enemy's neck. He jammed a knee into the tall lanky youth with stiff eyelashes, which put him down for the count, but after ten minutes the Burro came to, brayed, and continued as if nothing had happened. Bernabé felt as if the moment for action was near. El Güero said no, he'd done well in training, worked like all get-out and he deserved a vacation. He sat him in a coppery Thunderbird and said have a good time with the cassettes, you can choose the music and if you get bored turn on this small TV, we're off to Acapulco, Bernabé, I'm going to give you a taste of what life's all about, *I was born to dance the rumba, down in Veracruz, I was born in silv'ry moonlight, I play it fast and loose,* choose anything you want. Not really, he said to himself later, I didn't choose anything, they chose for me, the blond American girl was waiting for me in that big bed with the glittery bedspread, the bellboy dressed like an organ grinder's monkey was waiting to carry my suitcases, and another just like him to bring my breakfast to my room and fill my refrigerator, the only thing they didn't give me were the sun and the sea, because they were already there. He looked at himself in the hotel mirrors but he didn't know whether they looked back. Other than Martincita, he didn't know whether or not women liked him. El Güero told him if he wanted to pay he'd have to make a lot of money so it wouldn't feel like he was receiving a tip; look at this Thunderbird, Bernabé, it may be secondhand but it's mine, I bought it with my own dough, he laughed and told him that they wouldn't be seeing so much of each other now, it was time to turn him over to Ureñita, old Dr. Ureñita himself, what a drag he was with a face like a sour old maid and ugly as a constipated monkey, he wasn't like El Güero, who knew how to enjoy life, hey, baby, *ciao,* he said, spitting on each hand and then slapping the saliva on the hood bright as a new coin before he roared off in his Thunderbird.

UREÑITA

"What rank did you reach young man?"

"I don't seem to remember."

"Don't be asinine. Second? Third?"

"Whatever you say, Señor Ureña."

"Oh yes, Bernabé, I'll be having plenty to say. That's why I'm here. We get knuckleheads like you by the ton here. Well, never mind. That's our raw material. We'll see what we can do to refine it, to make an exportable product."

"Whatever you say, Señor Ureña."

"Presentable, I mean. Dialectics. Our friends think we have no history and no ideas because they see dolts like you and they laugh at us. So much the better. Let them believe what they will. That way we will occupy all the history they vacate. Do you understand what I'm saying?"

"No, maestro."

"They've filled our country's history with lies in order to weaken it, in order to make it putty, then they tear off a little piece and then another and at first no one notices. But one day you wake up and you no longer have the great, free, unified nation you dreamed of, Bernabé."

"I dreamed of?"

"Yes, even you, though you don't know it. Why do you think you're here with me?"

"El Güero told me to come. I don't know anything."

"Well, I'm going to make you understand, you simpleton. You are here to assist at the birth of a new world. And a new world can only be born of tumultuous, hate-filled beginnings. Do you understand? Violence is the midwife of history."

"If you say so, Señor Ureñita."

"Don't use the diminutive. Diminutives diminish. Who told you to call me Ureñita?"

"No one, I swear."

"Poor muddlehead. If I wanted I could analyze you blindfolded. This is what they send us. We owe that to John Dewey and Moisés Sáenz. Tell me, Bernabé, do you have a fear of getting buried in poverty?"

"I'm already there, Señor Ureña."

"You are mistaken. There are worse things. Imagine your poor old mother scrubbing floors, still worse, imagine her streetwalking."

"You imagine yours, prof."

"You do not offend me. I know who I am and what my worth is. And I know who you are, shitty *lumpen*. Do you think I don't know your kind? When I was a student I went to the factories, to try to organize the workers, to awaken their radical consciousness. Do you think they paid me any heed?"

"All the way, maestro."

"They turned their backs on me. They refused to hear

my message. They didn't want to face reality. And there you have it. Reality punished them, it avenged itself on them, on all of you, poor devils. You haven't wanted to face reality, that's the problem, you've tried to punish reality with dreams and you've failed as a revolutionary class. And yet here I am trying to form you, Bernabé. I warn you; I don't give up easily. Well, I've said what I had to say. They've vilified me."

"They?"

"Our enemies. But I want to be your friend. Tell me everything about yourself. Where do you come from?"

"Oh, around."

"Do you have a family?"

"That depends."

"Don't be so reticent. I want to help you."

"Right, prof."

"Do you have a sweetheart?"

"Could be."

"What are your ambitions, Bernabé? Trust me. I trust you, don't I?"

"That depends."

"It may be that the atmosphere here in the camp is too cold. Would you prefer to continue this conversation elsewhere?"

"It's all the same to me."

"We could go to a movie together, would you like that?"

"Maybe."

"Remember one thing. I can help you humiliate those who humiliate you."

"I like that fine."

"I have books in my home. No, not just books on theory, I have less arid books, all kinds of books for young men."

"Swell."

"Are you coming then, you doll?"

"Let's shake on it, Señor Ureñita."

LICENCIADO MARIANO

They took him to meet him after he bit Ureña's hand, they said the Chief fell out of his chair laughing and wanted to meet Bernabé. He received him in a leather-and-oak office with matched sets of red leather-bound books and statues and paintings of erupting volcanoes. He told him to call him Licenciado, the Honorable Mariano Carreón, it sounded a little pretentious to call him Chief the way they did in the camp, didn't he agree? Yes, Chief, Bernabé said, and thought to himself that the Licenciado looked exactly like the janitor at his school, a janitor who wore spectacles, and had a head like an olive with carefully combed hair and lenses thick as bottle glass and a mousy little mustache. He told him he liked how he'd reacted to that obnoxious Ureña, he was an old pinko who was working for them now because the other leaders in the movement said a varnishing of theory was important. He hadn't thought so and now he was going to see. He summoned Ureña and the theorist entered with bowed head, his hand bandaged where Bernabé had sunk his teeth. The Chief ordered him to take a book from the shelf, any book at all, the one he liked most, and to read it aloud. Yes, sir, at your pleasure, sir, said Ureña, and read with a trembling voice *I could not love within each man a tree/ with its remaindered autumns on its back,* do you understand any of that, Bernabé? No, said Bernabé, keep reading, Ureñita, as you wish, sir, *till in the last of hovels, lacking all light and fire,/bread, stone and silence, I paced at last alone,/ dying of my own death,* keep going, Ureñita, don't swoon, I want the boy to understand what the fuck this culture thing is all about, *Stone within stone, and man, where was he?/ Air within air, and man, where was he?/ Time within time . . .* Ureña coughed, oh, I'm so sorry, *Were you also the shattered fragment/ of indecision . . . ?* That's enough Ureñita, did you understand anything, boy? Bernabé shook his head.

The Chief ordered Ureña to place the book in a huge blown-glass ashtray from Tlaquepaque as thick as his spectacles, put it right there and set fire to it, right now, double time, Licenciado Carreón said with a dry severe laugh, and while the pages blazed he said I didn't have to read any of that stuff to get where I am, who needs it, it would have got in my way, Ureñita, so why would this kid need it? He said the boy had been right to bite him, and if you ask me why I have this library, I'll tell you that it's to remember every minute that there are many books still to be burned. Look here, son, he said to Bernabé staring at him with all the intensity he was capable of behind his eight layers of congealed glass, any dumb shit can put a bullet through the most intelligent head in the world, don't forget that. He told him he was all right, that he liked him, that he reminded him of himself when he was young, that he perked up his spirits and oh, how he wished, he said as he invited him to accompany him in a Galaxy black as a hearse with all the windows darkened so you could look out without being seen, someone years ago had taken an interest in him, someone like himself, they stole the election from General Almazán, synarchism would have taken care of people like them, as they were doing now, don't you worry, if you had had us your life and your parents' lives would have been different. Better. But you have us now, Bernabé my friend. He told the chauffeur to come back about five and told Bernabé to come eat with him, they went into one of the restaurants in the Zona Rosa that a furious Bernabé had seen only from the outside one Sunday, all the majordomos and waiters bowed to them like acolytes during Mass, Señor Licenciado, your private table is ready, this way, what can we do for you, señor, anything at all, I'm putting the Señor Licenciado in your hands, Jesús Florencio. Bernabé realized that the Chief liked talking about his life, how he'd come from the very asshole of the city and with persistence and without books but with an idea of the greatness of the nation, yes that, had got where he was. They ate seafood au gratin and drank beer until El Güero came in with a message and the Chief listened and said bring that sonofabitch here and told Bernabé to keep calm and go on eating. A very cool Chief went on recounting anecdotes and when El Güero returned with a well-dressed paper-skinned man, the Chief simply said good afternoon, Señor Secretary, El Güerito is going to tell you what you need to know. The Chief went on circumspectly eating his lobster thermidor as El Güero seized the Secretary by his tie and mouthed a string of curses, he'd better learn how to treat Licenciado Carreón, he shouldn't get independent and go see the president on his own, everything went through Licenciado Carreón first, didn't the Secretary owe him his job, see? The Chief simply ignored El Güero and the Secretary, he looked instead at Bernabé, and in his eyes at that moment Bernabé read what he was supposed to read, what the Chief intended him to read, you can be like me, you can treat the big shots this way and have no fear, Bernabé. The Chief ordered the remains of the lobster removed and the waiter Jesús Florencio bowed with alacrity when he saw the Secretary but when he saw Licenciado Carreón's face he decided not to speak to the Secretary but instead busied himself with removing the dishes. As they couldn't look at anyone else, Bernabé and Jesús Florencio exchanged glances. Bernabé liked the waiter. He felt as if this was someone he could talk to because they shared a secret. Though he had to ass-kiss the same as anyone, he earned his living and his life was his own. He found out all this because they decided to meet, Jesús Florencio took a liking to Bernabé and warned him, watch out, if you want to come to work as a waiter I'll help you, politics has its ups and downs and the Secretary's not going to forget that you saw him humiliated by the Licenciado and the

Licenciado's not going to forget that you saw him humiliate someone the day they humiliate him.

"But congratulations just the same. I think you've
bought yourself a winning ticket, buddy."

"You think so?"

"Just don't forget me." Jesús Florencio smiled.

PEDREGAL

Bernabé felt that this was really a place with a name.
The Chief took him to his house in Pedregal and said,
Make yourself at home, as if I've adopted you, go
wherever you want and get to know the boys in the
kitchen and in administration. He wandered in and out of
the house, which started at the service area on the ground
level but then instead of rising descended along scarlet-
colored cement ramps through a kind of crater toward
the bedrooms and finally to the open rooms surrounding
a swimming pool sunk into the very center of the house
and illuminated from below by underwater lights and
from above by a roof of celestial-blue lead tiles that
capped the mansion. Licenciado Carreón's wife was a
small fat woman with tight black curls and religious
medals jangling beneath her double chin, on her breasts,
and on her wrists, who when she saw him asked if he was
a terrorist or a bodyguard, if he'd come to kidnap them or
protect them—they all look alike, the brown scum. The
señora was highly amused by her own joke. You could
hear her coming a long way off, like El Güero and his
transistor and the Burro and his braying. Bernabé heard
her often the first two or three days he wandered around
the house feeling like a fool, expecting the Chief to call
him and give him some job to do, fingering the porcelain
knickknacks, the glass display cabinets and large vases and
at every turn bumping into a señora who smiled as end-
lessly as his father, Andrés Aparicio. One afternoon he

heard music, sentimental boleros playing during the siesta hour and he felt languorous and handsome as he had when he looked at himself in the hotel mirrors in Acapulco, he was drawn by the soft sad music but when he reached the second floor he lost his way and walked through one of the bathrooms into a dressing room with dozens of kimonos and rubber-soled beach sandals and a half-open door. He saw a bed as large as the one in the Acapulco hotel covered with tiger skins and on the headboard he saw a shelf with votive candles and religious images, and beneath that a tape deck like the one El Güero had in his secondhand Thunderbird and lying on the skins Señora Carreón stark naked except for her religious medals, especially one in the shape of a seashell with a superimposed gold image of the Virgin of Guadalupe that the señora held over her sex while Chief Mariano tried to lift it with his tongue and the señora laughed a high coquettish schoolgirl laugh and said, Oh no my Lord, no my King, respect your little virgin, and he naked on all fours his balls purple with cold trying to reach the medal in the shape of a seashell, oh my King, plump beauty, oh my saintly little bitch, my perfumed whore, my mother-of-pearl ringleted goddess, let your own little Pope bless your Guadalupe, oh my love, and all the time the bolero on the tape, *I know I shall never kiss your lips, your lips of burning crimson, I know I shall never sip from your wild and passionate fountain* . . . Later the boys in the office and the kitchen told him, you can see the Chief's taken a liking to you, friend, don't do anything to blow it because he'll protect you against whatever comes. Get out of the brigade if you can, that's dangerous work, you'll see. On the other hand here in the kitchen and the office we've got the world by the tail. El Güero walked through the office to answer the telephone and invited Bernabé to go for a ride in the Jaguar that belonged to the Carreóns' daughter, she was in a Canadian finishing school with the

nuns and the car had to be driven from time to time to
keep it in good shape. He said the boys in the office were
right, the Chief sees something in you to adopt you this
way. Don't muff the chance, Bernabé. If you get to be one
of his personal guard you're set up for life, said El Güero,
driving the girl's Jaguar the way a jockey exercises a horse
for a race, I give you my word, you'll be set up. The deal
is to learn every little thing that's going on and then whatever shit they try to pull you've got a stranglehold on
them, you can take any shit they try to pull, unless they
shut you up forever. But if you play your cards right, just
look, you've got it all, money, girls, cars, you even eat the
same food they eat. But the Chief had to study, Bernabé
replied, he had to get his degree before he made it big. El
Güero hooted at that and said the Chief hadn't gone past
grade school, they'd stuck on the Licenciado because
that's what you call anyone important in Mexico even
though he wouldn't recognize a law book if it fell on him,
don't be a jerk, Bernabé. All you need to know is that
every day a millionaire is born who someday is going to
want you to protect his life, his kids, his cash, his ass. And
you know why, Bernabé? Because every day a thousand
bastards like you are born ready to tear the guts out of the
rich man born the same day. One against a thousand,
Bernabé. Don't tell me it isn't easy to choose. If we don't
get away from where we were born we go right down the
goddamn tubes. We have to get on the side of the ones
who're born to screw us, as sure as seven and seven make
heaven, right? The Chief called Bernabé to the bar beside
the pool and told him to come with him, he wanted him to
see the tinted photograph of his daughter Mirabella,
wasn't she pretty? You bet she was and that's because she
was made with love and feeling and passion and if you
don't have those there's nothing, right, Bernabé? He said
in Bernabé he saw himself when he didn't have a centavo
or a roof over his head, but with the whole world to con-

quer. He envied him that, he said, his eyeglasses fogged with steam, because the first thing you know you have everything and you begin to hate yourself, you hate yourself because you can't stand the boredom and the exhaustion that comes of having reached the top, you see? On the one hand you're afraid of falling back where you came from but on the other hand you miss the struggle to reach the top. He asked him, wouldn't he like to marry a girl like Mirabella someday, didn't he have a sweetheart? and Bernabé compared the photograph of the girl surrounded by rose-colored clouds with Martincita, who was plain born for misfortune, but he didn't know what to say to Licenciado Mariano, because either way whether he said yes he did or no he didn't, it was an insult and besides the Chief wasn't listening to Bernabé, he was listening to himself thinking he was listening to Bernabé.

"The pain you go through, you have the right to make others suffer, my boy. That's the honest truth, I swear by all that's holy."

THE BRIGADE

They're planning to mount on Puente de Alvarado and march down Rosales toward the statue of Carlos IV. We're going to be in the gray trucks farther north at the corner of Héroes and Mina, and to the south at Ponciano Arriaga and Basilio Badillo, so we can cut them off from any direction. All of you are to wear your white armbands and white cotton neck bands and have vinegar-soaked handkerchiefs ready to protect yourselves against the tear gas when the police arrive. When the demonstration is a block and a half from the Carlos IV statue you who're on Héroes come down Rosales and attack from the rear. Shout, Viva Che Guevara! over and over, yell so loud that no one can doubt where your sentiments lie. Yell *Fascists* at the demonstrators. I repeat, *Fash-ists*. Get that straight,

you must create total confusion, real pandemonium, and
then lay into them, don't hold anything back, use your
clubs and brass knuckles and yell anything you want, let
yourselves go, boys, have a ball, those coming from the
south will be yelling Viva Mao! but you send them flying,
they won't give you any trouble, the whole thing's a
breeze, let 'er rip, you're members of the Hawk Brigade
and the moment's come to prove yourselves in the field,
my boys, in the street, on the hard pavement, against
posts and steel shutters, break as many windows as you
can, that stirs up a lot of resentment against the students,
but the main thing is that when you overtake them you go
at it heart and soul, have no mercy for the bastards, kick
and punch and knee and you, just you two, ice picks for
you and see what happens and if you put out the eye of
some Red bastard so what, it will be a lesson to them and
we'll protect you here, you know that, get that in your
thick heads, you bastards, we'll protect you here, so do
God's will and do it well and the street is yours, you,
where were you born? and you, where are you from? Azcapotzalco? Balbuena? Xochimilco? Canal del Norte? At-
lampa? the Tránsito district? Mártires de Tacubaya? Pan-
teones? Well today, my Hawks, you get your own back,
just think about that, today the street where you've been
fucked good is yours and you'll have your chance to fuck
them back and go scot-free, it's like the conquest of Mexico, the man who wins wins, today you're going out in the
street, my Hawks, and get your revenge for every sonofabitch who made you feel like a dog, for the abuse you've
taken all your miserable lives, for every insult you couldn't
return, for all the meals you didn't eat and all the women
you didn't screw, you're going out to get even against the
landlord who raised your rent and the shyster who ran
you out of your rooms and the sawbones who wouldn't
operate on your mother unless he had his five thousand
in advance, you're going to beat up on the sons of the

men who've exploited you, right? the students are spoiled young shits who one day will be landlords and pen-pushers and quacks like their papas but you're going to get even, you're going to give blow for blow, my Hawk Brigade, you know that, so go quietly in the gray trucks, then stalk like wild animals, then the fun, lash out, have the time of your lives, think about your little sister had against her will, your poor old mother on her knees washing and scrubbing, your father screwed all his life, his hands misshapen from grubbing in shit, today's the day to get your revenge, Hawks, today won't come again, don't miss it, don't worry, the police will recognize you by your white neck bands and armbands, they'll act like they're attacking you, play along with them, they'll pretend to shove a few of you in the Black Maria, but it's all a fake to put off the press because it's all-important that tomorrow's papers report a clash among leftist students, subversive disturbance in the heart of the city, the Communist conspiracy rears its ugly head, off with its head! save the republic from anarchy, and you, my hawks, just remember that others may be repressed but not you, no way, I promise you, and now, can't you hear the running feet on the pavement? the street is yours, conquer the street, step hard, go out into the smoke, don't be afraid of the smoke, the city is lost in smoke. No escape from it.

A NEW BERNABÉ

His mother, Doña Amparo, didn't want to come because she was ashamed, his Uncles Rosendo and Romano told him, she didn't want to admit that a son of hers was in the clink; Richi now had a more or less permanent job with the Acapulco dance band, and from time to time he sent a hundred pesos to Bernabé's mother; she was dying of shame and didn't know this new Bernabé and Romano said that after all her husband, Andrés Aparicio, had kicked a man to death. Yes, she replied, but he never ended up behind bars, that's the difference, Bernabé is the first jailbird in the family. As far as you know, woman. But the uncles looked at Bernabé differently too, hardly recognizing him; he wasn't any longer the dumb little kid who'd sat on the roof tiles while they shot rabbits and toads on the plain where the greasewood grew. Bernabé had killed a man, he went at him with an ice pick during the fracas on Puente de Alvarado, he buried the pick deep in his chest and he felt how the wounded boy's guts were mightier than the cold iron of his weapon but in spite of it all the ice pick vanquished the viscera, the viscera sucked in the ice pick the way a lover sucks a beloved. The boy stopped laughing and braying and lay staring at the arches of neon light through stiff eyelashes. El Güero came to the prison to tell Bernabé not to worry, they had to put on an act, he understood, after a few days they'd let him go, meanwhile they were working things out and giving the appearance of law and order. But El Güero didn't recognize this new Bernabé either and for the first time he stammered and his eyes even filled with tears, if you had to stab someone, Bernabé, why did it have to be one of us? You should have been more careful. You knew the Burro, poor old Burro, he was a stupid fart but not a bad guy underneath, why, Bernabé? On the other hand the waiter Jesús Florencio came as a friend and told him that when he got out he should work in the restaurant, he could arrange everything with the owner, and he wanted to tell him why. Licenciado Mariano Carreón had got drunk in the restaurant the day of the row in the city, he was very excited and spilled the beans to his friends about how there was this one kid that reminded him of a lot of things, first what Don Mariano himself had been like as a boy and then of a man he'd known twenty years ago in a co-op in the state of Guerrero, a crazy agricultural student who wouldn't give in, who brought what he called justice to the state and wanted to impose it without so much as a fuck-you. Licenciado Mariano told how he'd organized the resistance against this agronomist Aparicio, playing on the unity of the village families, rich and poor, against a meddlesome outsider. It's so easy to exploit provincial ways for your own good. You have to keep the local bosses strong because where there's no law the boss will enforce order and without order you can't have property and wealth and how else can a man get rich fast, he asked his friends. That agronomist had the fanaticism of a saint, a crusading zeal that got under Licenciado Carreón's skin. For the next ten years he tried to corrupt him, offering him one thing after another, promotions, houses, money, voyages and virgins, protection. No dice. Aparicio the agronomist became an obsession with him and since he couldn't buy him he tried to ruin him, to make problems for him, to prevent his promotions, even evict him from the tenement on Guatemala Street and force him into the lost cities in Mexico City's poverty belt. Licenciado Mariano's obsession was so total that he bought all the land in the area where Andrés Aparicio and his family and other squatter families had gone to live, so no one could run them off, no, he said, let them stay here, the old people will die, no one can live on honor alone and dignity doesn't come with marrow-bone broth, it's good to have a breeding ground for angry kids so I can set them on the right track when they grow up, a nest for my Hawks. He told how every day he savored the fact that the agronomist who wouldn't be corrupted lived with his wife and son and bastard brothers-in-law on land that belonged to Licenciado Mariano, and because he allowed it. But the richest part of the joke was to tell the agronomist. So the Licenciado sent one of his musclemen to tell your father, Bernabé, you've been living on the Chief's bounty, you dirty beggar, ten years of charity, you think you're so pure, and your father, who never stopped smiling so he wouldn't look old, attacked Licenciado Carreón's bodyguard and kicked him to death and then disappeared forever because all he had left was the dignity of death, he didn't want to be buried in jail like you, even for a few days, Bernabé. It's better for you to know, said Jesús Florencio, you see what they offer you isn't as great as they make out. One day you'll run into a man, a real man, who'll knock your protection into a cocked hat. It's not much of a life to live under someone's protection, telling yourself, without the Chief I'm not worth a shit. Bernabé fell asleep on his cot, protecting even the crown of his head with the thin wool cover, talking in his sleep to the fucking Chief, you didn't dare look my father in the face, you had to send a hired killer after him and he killed your killer, you asshole. But then he had a dream in which he was tumbling in silence, dying, tumbling like a shattered fragment of indecision, what? what man? He dreamed, unable to separate his dream from a vague but driving desire that everything that exists be for all the earth, for everyone, water, air, gardens, stone, time.

"And man, where was he?"

THE CHIEF

He came out of jail hating him for everything, what he'd done to his father, what he'd done to him. El Güero picked him up at the exit of the Black Palace and he climbed into the red Thunderbird, *so give your heart in sweet surrender,* hey baby, where there's music and fun there's your Güerito. He told Bernabé that the Chief would be waiting in his house in Pedregal anytime the kid wanted to stop by and see him. The Chief was sorry Bernabé had been locked up ten days in Lecumberri. But a lot worse had happened to the Chief. Bernabé hadn't known, he hadn't read the newspapers or anything. Well, a real storm broke loose against the Chief, they said he

was an agent provocateur and they threatened to send
him as governor to Yucatán, which was roughly like being
a ditchdigger on the moon, but he says he'll get even with
his political enemies and he needs you. He said you were
the best man in the brigade. You may have stiffed poor
old Burro but the Chief says he understands that you're
hotheaded and it's okay with him. Bernabé started sobbing like a baby, it all seemed so lousy, and El Güero
didn't know what to do except stop the cassette music out
of respect and Bernabé asked him to drop him on the
road to Azcapotzalco near the Spanish Panteon but El
Güero was worried about him and followed in the car as
Bernabé walked along the dusty sidewalks where flower
vendors were fashioning huge funeral wreaths of garde-
nias and stonecutters were chiseling tombstones, names,
dates, the beginning and end of every man and woman,
and where had they been, Bernabé kept asking himself,
remembering the book burned by orders of Licenciado
Carreón. El Güero decided to be patient and was waiting
for him when an hour later he walked through the
wrought-iron cemetery gate, that's the second time you've
come through an iron gate today, kid, he joked, better
watch your step. Bernabé, still hating the Chief, entered
the house in Pedregal, but the minute he saw that near-
sighted janitor's face he felt sorry for the man clinging to
an oversized tumbler of whiskey as though it were a life
belt. It made him sad to remember him on all fours stark
naked his balls freezing trying to win his wife's cruel teasing game. Hell, didn't Mirabella have the right, after all,
to go to finishing school rather than live in a tin-and-card-
board shack in some lost city? He walked into the house in
Pedregal, he saw the Chief cut down to size and felt sorry
for him, but now felt sure of himself, nothing bad could
happen to him here, no one would abandon him here, the
Chief wouldn't make him bust his ass cleaning windshields
because the Chief had no intention of taking justice to the

state of Guerrero, he wasn't about to die of hunger just to feel pure as the Host, the Chief wasn't a fuckup like his Chief, his Chief Mariano Carreón his Chief Andrés Aparicio, oh Father, do not forsake me. The Licenciado told El Güero to serve the kid his whiskey, he'd been brave and never mind, politics is nothing more than a lot of patience, it's like religion that way, and before you knew it the moment would arrive to get even with the men who were plotting against him and trying to exile him to Yucatán. He wanted Bernabé, who'd been with him in the hour of combat, to be with him in the hour of revenge. They'd change the name of the brigade, it had become too notorious, one day it would reappear bleached clean, bleached by the sun of revenge against the crypto-Communists who'd infiltrated the government, only six years, thank God for the one-term presidency, then those Reds would be out in the street and they'd see, they'd swing back in like a pendulum because they knew how to wait a long long long time like the stone idols in the museum, right? there's no one can stop us. He said to Bernabé, his arm around his neck, that there was no destiny that couldn't be overturned by contempt and he told El Güero that he didn't want to see any of them, not him, not the kid Bernabé, not any of the young toughs in the house while his daughter Mirabella was there, she'd be returning the next day from Canada. They went to the training camp and El Güero gave Bernabé a pistol so he could defend himself and told him not to worry, the Chief was right, there was no way to stop them once they got rolling, *look at that rock, how it keeps rolling,* shit, said El Güero with a shrewd and malicious expression Bernabé hadn't seen before, they could even slip out of the Chief's hands if they wanted, didn't he know everything there was to know? how to set things up, how to go to a barrio and round up the young kids, begin with slingshots if they had to, then chains, then ice picks like the one you killed the Burro with, Bernabé. It was so easy it was a laugh, all you had to do was create a kind of unseen but shared terror, we're terrified of always living under someone's protection, they're terrified of living without it. Choose, kid. But Bernabé didn't answer, he'd stopped listening. He was remembering his visit to the cemetery that morning, the Sundays he'd spent making love with Martincita in the crypt of a wealthy family, remembering a ragged old man urinating behind a cypress, bald, smiling like an idiot, smiling ceaselessly, who with his fly open walked away beneath that Azcapotzalco noonday sun hot as a great yellow chili pepper. Bernabé felt a surge of shame. But don't let it return. A vague memory, a kind of unknowing would be enough for this new Bernabé. He went to see his mother when he had a new suit and a Mustang, second-hand but all his, and he told her that next year he'd have a sunny clean house for her in a respectable neighborhood. She tried to talk to him as she had when he was a boy, My little sweetheart, you're such a good boy, my little doll, you're not a ruffian like the others, she tried to say what she'd once said about his father, *I never dreamed you were dead,* but to Bernabé his mother's words now were neither tender nor demanding, they merely meant the opposite of what they said. On the other hand, he was grateful that she gave him his father's most handsome suspenders, the red ones with the gilded clasps that had been the pride of Andrés Aparicio.